TAMING NICK

SHANDI BOYES

Edited by
MOUNTAINS WANTED PUBLISHING

Illustrated by
SSB DESIGNS

Written by
Shandi Boyes

© Shandi Boyes 2019

ALSO BY SHANDI BOYES

Perception Series - New Adult Rock Star Romance

Saving Noah

Fighting Jacob

Taming Nick

Redeeming Slater

Wrapped up with Rise Up

Enigma Series - Steamy Contemporary Romance

Enigma of Life - (Isaac)

Unraveling an Enigma - (Isaac)

Enigma: The Mystery Unmasked - (Isaac)

Enigma: The Final Chapter - (Isaac)

Beneath the Secrets - (Hugo - Part 1)

Beneath the Sheets - (Hugo Conclusion)

Spy Thy Neighbor (Hunter - standalone)

The Opposite Effect - (Brax & Clara)

I Married a Mob Boss - (Rico - Nikolai's Brother)

Second Shot (Hawke's Story)

The Way We Are (Ryan Pt 1)

The Way We Were (Ryan Pt 2)

Sugar and Spice (Cormack)

Bound Series - Steamy Romance & BDSM

Chains (Marcus and Cleo)

Links (Marcus and Cleo)

Bound (Marcus and Cleo)

Restrained (Marcus and Cleo)

Psycho (Dexter)

Russian Mob Chronicles

Nikolai: A Mafia Prince Romance

Nikolai: Taking Back What's Mine

Nikolai: What's Left of Me

Nikolai: Mine to Protect

Asher: My Russian Revenge

Infinite Time Trilogy

Lady In Waiting (Regan)

Man in Queue (Regan)

Couple on Hold (Regan)

Standalones

Just Playin' (Presley and Willow)

COMING SOON:

Skitzo

Colby

DEDICATION

To my one and only, my inspiration, and my rock.
My husband, Chris.

I love you!

Shandi xx

CHAPTER ONE

NICK

W hen my hand glides over the generous curves of a woman's body, goosebumps prickle her skin, and a deep moan rumbles through my ears. The calluses on my fingertips from years of guitar playing make her skin seem even smoother.

Her voice quivers, shaking in anticipation of her next orgasm. "Oh god yes, right there."

I adjust the tilt of her leg, setting it higher on my shoulder before continuing to pummel her with the rhythm that had her falling into orgasmic bliss only minutes ago. She better hurry if she wants a second taste, because my balls are constricting, preparing for imminent release.

"Oh god, oh god."

I'm tempted to tell her God can't help her right now, but I stay quiet. I'm not here to make her fall in love with my impressive bedroom skills. I'm here to get my rocks off.

Just as her screams reach an ear-piercing level, a door shoots open so fast, it nearly comes off the hinges. "What the fuck?!"

I freeze, and my dick softens.

Slater—my bandmate/arch nemesis—is standing in the doorway.

His fists are clenched at his side, his nostrils flaring. I dart out of his bed, standing before him in nothing but a condom. When his teeth grind together, filling the room's uncomfortable silence with tension, I shift my eyes around the homey space, seeking the closest viable exit.

My options are limited.

Other than the door Slater is guarding like a bouncer at my brother's nightclubs, there's a window to my right. Considering I'm as naked as the day I was born, it's not the most practical choice.

While swallowing to soothe my burning throat, my eyes dart down to my jeans sprawled on the floor—mere inches from Slater's boot-covered feet. When Slater follows the direction of my gaze, he smirks a shit-eating grin. He knows he has me by the throat.

After returning his eyes to mine, he cocks his brow, wordlessly daring me to make a move for my clothes. When I fail to fall for his trick, his squinted eyes shift to the bed I just left. "Get out!"

Happy to leave, I take a step forward. I barely make it two feet when Slater's narrowed gaze pins me in place. "Not you." His eyes narrow even further when they drift to Nikki, his fiancée. "Her."

She's lying on his bed with her head bouncing between us as if she's watching a tennis match. Unnerved by Slater's furious scowl, she slides off the sticky sheets and tiptoes toward him. Bare feet padding across the carpeted floor is the only audible noise in the room, barely heard over the mad beat of my heart.

Once she's within touching distance of Slater, she peers up at him and bats her eyelashes. *Seriously? Pleading with him while buck naked. Could she be any stupider?*

"I'm sorry, baby, I was just—"

Slater cuts off her pathetic excuse mid-sentence. "Get the fuck out."

After huffing at his rude tone, she bobs down to snag her lace dress off the floor. When she bolts past Slater, he barely moves. A door slamming shut bellows up the stairwell not long later. Its loud bang advises there's only one way I'm getting out of this situation alive: it's time to grovel!

After another swallow, my eyes float from my bare feet to Slater. "Look, man, I was doing you a favor. I told you those rumors—"

"Shut the fuck up, Nick."

Okay, I'll admit it. I fucked Nikki because I was horny, and she was available, but at the end of the day, I was also helping Slater. That girl is as slutty as they come. Slater's just too blinded by her big tits and Hoover lips to notice it. I've seen her numerous times wandering off with guys during our performances at Mavericks. When she returned just before our set finished, her hair was ruffled, and her lips were swollen. It didn't take a genius to work out what "entertainment" she was participating in while Slater entertained our fans.

Although I'm pleading guilty, I try to weasel my way out of a fucked up situation. "I wanted to prove what I was telling you was true."

I've told Slater numerous times what I witnessed. Not once did he listen. When he invited me back to his house for a beer after our performance, I accepted his offer. Usually, I make any excuse to leave once our set is done. My bandmates are simply that—bandmates. I don't consider them friends. We have a kick ass group that will make me millions of dollars one day, but that doesn't mean we need to be butt-buddies.

My pickings after tonight's performance were slim. I was beaten to the pick of the bunch because I was stuck talking to my brother, Isaac. When Slater invited me over, I nearly said no. . . until I spotted Nikki's eyes raking my body. She was chewing on her bottom lip, and her eyes reflected her unbridled desire. That's when I decided to prove to Slater he should listen to me more often.

I'm drawn from my thoughts when Slater snarls, "You proved your point; now I get to prove mine."

"What point?"

My hands grow clammy when he takes another step forward.

The closer he gets to me, the firmer his fists clench. When he stops to stand in front of me, a trail of sweat dribbles down my back, the heat from his eyes too much for me to bear.

"That you don't fuck with me." His voice exposes how badly I fucked up. I've never seen him so pissed.

When he launches for me, I take drastic action. As fast as my quivering legs will take me, I bolt to the only window in the room. With every step I take, I pray it's unlocked.

It is—*thank fuck!*

I yank it up with barely a second to spare before diving over the ledge. Slater curses when he narrowly misses snagging my ankle, my scamper into the freezing cold night coming up trumps.

Fighting to ignore the brutal contact my package made with the windowsill, I scurry away from him. "Think about it; I did you a favor."

On my hands and knees, I crawl to the very edge of the roof. My stomach lurches into my throat when I peer down. Other than leaping into a thorny bush, there's no other way for me to get off this roof. Hearing a rustle from behind, my gaze shoots back. Slater is climbing out the window. He's even angrier now that he's been forced to chase me.

His fury leaves me no choice: I have to jump.

After exhaling a shaky breath, I close my eyes and freefall over the edge, praying the bush below will lessen the impact of my fall.

Fuck!

The shrub cushions my leap, but its thorns are an unpleasant addition to my backside and groin. Certain I've survived death by the skin of my teeth, I peer up at the second floor. Slater is glancing down at me. His arms are folded in front of his tattooed chest, his eyes colored with hate.

Not even five seconds later, he smirks a dangerous grin before pivoting on his heels and diving back through the window. Understanding the determination in his eyes, I yank off my condom, rustle out of the bush, then bolt down his driveway. Sweat slicks my skin as

I sprint to my truck parked a few spots down. Thank fuck I keep a spare key in the unlocked cabin, because my current set is stuffed in my jeans on Slater's bedroom floor.

By the time I make it to my truck, my balls are sitting in my stomach. *It's fucking freezing tonight.* Through chattering teeth, I dive into the cab and fire up the engine. The loud purr of my motor rumbles through the eerily black street.

As I pull out of my parking spot, my gaze lifts to the rearview mirror. My heart rate, which was just settled, kicks back up when I spot Slater barreling out of his house. His face is contorted with anger, and he's clutching a baseball bat. With his street being a dead end, I have no other option but to drive past him.

His strong stance doesn't falter when I floor the gas. He's so hardened with anger, I have to veer onto the wrong side of the road to avoid colliding with him. Even in the dark, I see his arms flex when he swings his bat at my truck. His hit is so powerful, he knocks off my side mirror. Metal crunching against asphalt filters through my ears as I guide my truck down isolated streets.

Slater chases me for over half a mile before he becomes nothing but a blur in my rearview mirror. Relieved, I slump into my seat. It wasn't my most brilliant idea to sleep with Nikki at Slater's house. Next time, I'll consider my options with more diligence. . . *maybe.*

———

By the time I arrive at my dad's house in Petersburg, news of my night's antics are already circulating. "You stupid fuck," is the first thing Noah roars down the phone when I answer it.

I chuckle. "I did him a favor. He should be thanking me."

"For fuck's sake, Nick, you knew what it took for me to get you into the band, and this is how you repay me."

Guilt seeps into my veins. It took a lot for Noah to persuade Slater and Marcus to grant me an audition to become a part of their band Rise Up, and even after witnessing my talent firsthand, they were still hesitant to include me. I can't say I didn't understand their reluctance. They formed the band years before Noah stumbled upon me.

Even if Noah isn't a friend, I'll be forever grateful for that day. . . . .

"What else can you play?"

I've just finished performing the introduction of Metallica's "Enter Sandman." It isn't my best performance, but my talent can't be denied.

When I turn my gaze, I see a dark-haired teen wearing dark jeans and a cotton shirt almost as black as his eyes. "Pretty much anything."

I refocus my attention on my guitar. I really shouldn't say "my guitar." Because I don't have enough money to purchase my own, I borrow one from the school band. That's why I only play in the late afternoon when no one is around.

"Are you in a group?" asks the teen I thought had left since my clipped tone implied I wasn't interested in a conversation.

I don't bother looking up. "Nope."

The sound of stomping bounces off the stark white walls of the music room seconds before a pair of black boots enter my peripheral vision. Steadily, I raise my eyes from the motorcycle boots to an equally rigid face. I eye the unnamed teen with just as much curiosity as he watches me with.

He ends our stare-off by asking, "Would you be interested in joining a group?"

When a chuckle escapes my lips, his eyes darken. He's annoyed by my response. I don't know why? His clothes alone tell me he isn't in a band I'd have any interest in being a part of.

"Nope." My tone is jam-packed with arrogance, hoping my rudeness will give him the hint to leave.

All it does is make him laugh. His deep chuckle rumbles in the silence of the room for several long heart beats. Once it settles, he stares me dead set in the eyes. "Your fucking loss then."

With that, he pivots on his heels and stalks to the door. It's only now do I wonder what opportunity I missed. His confidence didn't falter an inch when I turned down his request, showing he believes in his band's ability to make it big.

Setting down my guitar, I chase after him. "Wait up," I call out when I spot him about to exit the large double doors of my school.

He stops for the briefest second, shrugs, then pushes through the open doors.

"I'm not going to beg," I chant to myself.

Numerous girls' heads turn when he walks past them, but he ignores their bright smiles and fluttering lashes.

"Do you know that guy?" I ask a girl watching the spectacle from my side.

She looks at me, baffled. "Doesn't everyone?"

The brunette standing to her left giggles as her cheeks give off a pink hue.

I roll my eyes. "Obviously not."

"That's because you're a guy," the pretty brunette mumbles, still giggling.

Her eyes take their time raking my body before they lift to my face. My chest swells with smugness when her tongue delves out to lick her suddenly parched lips.

"That I am."

While exchanging numbers with my newfound friend, I discover the guy who interrupted me is Noah Taylor. He's the lead singer of a band called Rise Up. During our brief conversation, she divulges that he's playing at a high school party Friday night. That piques my interest. If I watch him perform, like what I see, I could be persuaded into joining them.

Friday night, I borrow a school guitar before heading to the address the brunette disclosed. When I arrive at the party, Rise Up is in the middle of a set. I'll admit, I'm fucking shocked by what I'm hearing. I thought

Noah would be into heavy metal or indie rock shit, so you can imagine my surprise when I discover his band playing a range of top forty hits.

When they announce they're taking a break, I hustle my way over to Noah. "I changed my mind," I shout to project my voice over the noisy hum of drunken teenagers.

Noah's dark eyes drift from a girl cozying up to his side to me. When he realizes who's accosting him, his glare picks up. Without speaking a word, he resumes his conversation with the girl, snubbing me as if I don't exist.

I don't give in easily. "Do I need to audition? Or...?"

He dismisses me with four words. "You lost your chance."

After he finishes chatting with his female friend, he strolls through a swarm of sweaty bodies writhing on the dance floor. Several people fight for his attention as he struts by—myself included.

"I can play anything you request."

Acting as if I never spoke, he heads to a keg set up in the kitchen. He fills a plastic cup to the rim before making his way to a huge guy leaning against the kitchen counter. My throat becomes scratchy when I take in his friend. He is massive. His arms are the size of my head, and he's wider than I am tall. He looks as if he could snap me like a twig.

After growing some balls, I join their little gathering. Noah acts as if I am a ghost. His eyes float around the room, winking at some girls, smiling at others. Even though he's only in high school, he's treated like a celebrity.

I want to be treated like a celebrity too.

"I can play anything you request."

Smirking, Noah shakes his head before making his way back to the makeshift stage. When the band begins performing minutes later, I realize it's my one and only chance to show them what talent I have. With determination, I bolt back to my car to gather the guitar I borrowed earlier.

Not having time to tune it, I place the strap around my neck, then dart back into the party. When I enter the oversized formal living

room, the band is playing Fall Out Boy's "Sugar, We're Goin' Down."
I hesitate. I've only heard this song a handful of times, much less
played it, but since it's my only chance to impress them, I suck it up.

After a deep exhale to rid the nerves in my stomach, I strum the
strings of my guitar in rhythm with Noah's. Several eyes gawk at me,
utterly confused, but one set of dazzling blue eyes nearly make me
miss a chord. They're light blue and simply stunning. Then her lips. . .
damn! They're soft, pouty, and sexy as sin.

When the pretty blonde's eyes nervously dart away, I chuckle
before continuing my mission. Noticing my approach, the crowd part,
creating a clear path between me and the band. Noah's dark eyes track
me, but not once does he falter on his performance. He's paid to
perform, and that's precisely what he does.

Once I reach the stage, I stand opposite the bassist as if I'm
already part of the band. The crowd eat it up, assuming it's a stunt
choreographed by Rise Up to introduce their newest member.

While strumming my guitar, I seek the band members' response to
my boldness. The drummer's eyes are narrowed into thin slits; the
bassist is grinning while shaking his head, and Noah continues
performing with his gaze fixed on the crowd. It isn't the response I was
hoping for, but it's better than leaving with a black eye. . . . . .

Although annoyed at my stunt, Noah agreed to let me audition
for the band the following day—against the wishes of both Slater, the
drummer and Marcus, the bassist.

They hammered me with every song imaginable, and after a
grueling four hours, they reluctantly accepted me into their group.
That night was over a year ago, but I still feel like an intruder.

This time around, my drama could cause a massive rift in the
band, so I start backpedaling. "I wasn't thinking,"

"No, you weren't. I don't know if I can fix this, Nick. You fucked
up; you might need to look for another band."

Even though Noah can't see me, I shake my head. Rise Up will
be mega successful one day, and I want to be a part of that.

"I'll keep it in my pants. I promise."

Noah breathes harshly down the line. "It might be too late for that now."

Slater's nostrils flare when I enter Marcus's garage on Noah's heels. Noah called an emergency band meeting, hoping to settle the tension I caused three weeks ago. I knew how badly I fucked up when Noah suggested I look for another band. Without shame, I begged him to let me stay. I even went as far as vowing never to sleep with another bandmate's significant other ever again.

He didn't believe me, but it kept our negotiations open.

The deeper I descend into the garage, the tighter my brows furrow. Noah's friend Jacob is standing in the middle of the space Rise Up practices in daily. I've seen him at gigs, but he's never shown up during rehearsals before.

Noticing my confused gaze, Noah explains, "I asked him to come in case I needed to pull you two apart."

"He won't fucking stop me," Slater snarls, his eyes narrowing.

If you could die from a death stare, I'd be dead right now.

Jacob chuckles at Slater's snarl before throwing an arm around his shoulders. "Who said I'm here to stop you? I'm here to watch the beat down."

A lump lodges in my throat. *I really need to start thinking with the head on my shoulders instead of the one between my legs.*

Noah glares at Jacob and Slater, unimpressed. Slater doesn't buckle under his furious stare, but Jacob mumbles a quick apology. Happy his soldiers are falling into line, he continues pulling rank. "Last month, we signed to play at Mavericks every Tuesday night. This is the stepping stone we've been waiting for. From here, we'll continue to grow. Do you really want to give up the opportunity to make it big with our band for shit like this?"

I shake my head. "You know my thoughts on this, Noah; I want to stay in the group." I'll do everything in my power to remain a part of Rise Up because I know it's only a matter of time before we hit it big.

Slater stands from the speaker box he's sitting on to bridge the gap between Noah and me, his steps cocky. "You know the deal I've agreed to."

Noah's uneasy gaze bounces between Slater and me for several seconds before settling on Slater. "One hit." He holds his index finger in the air.

Nodding, Slater rubs his hands together like his greatest wish was just granted. When he steps even closer to me, my suspicious gaze floats between four sets of eyes staring at me. Marcus's reveal his concern; Jacob's are shining with excitement; Noah's are as dark as normal, and Slater's look like a kid entering a candy store.

When Slater gets within touching distance of me, my eyes rocket to Jacob, wordlessly begging him to grab Slater before he does something stupid. He doesn't budge an inch—not one.

Unease clutches my throat when Slater comes to a stop in front of me. Then all I see is blackness.

My head is pounding against my temples; my stomach is swirling, and something is running out of my nose. When a shiver darts down my spine, my brows furrow.

Why am I lying on a cold, dirty concrete floor?

While dragging my hand under my nose, I attempt to sit up. My stomach launches into my throat from my sudden movements, then climbs another two inches when I glance down at my hand. It's covered in bright red blood.

"What happened?" My tone relays my confusion. I'm as baffled as fuck.

A loud, boisterous laugh booms around the garage. It's not coming from any of my bandmates. It's coming from Jacob.

I stop glaring at him when Noah's wide shoulders block him from my view. "Take that as a warning. If you *ever* pull a stunt like that again, you'll not only be out of the band, but I'll let Slater unleash more than one punch."

Giddiness clusters in my head when he yanks me to my feet by tugging on my arm. It feels like I've had too much beer, even though I haven't touched a drop of alcohol in days.

The only one frustrated by my unstable swaying is Marcus. He glares at Slater with his dark brows stitched. "You weren't supposed to knock him out."

Slater shrugs before shifting on his feet to face me. He has a shit-eating grin on his face, and the spark of victory is brightening his eyes.

Before he can voice any of the arrogant thoughts in his head, Noah says, "Let's practice," like my assault is now water under the bridge.

I spend the two hours of rehearsal reading the song sheet through my eye that isn't sealed shut. I can feel Slater's slit gaze on me the entire time, but not once do I peer back at him. I can feel his wrath. I don't need to be subjected to it head-on. His anger is so white-hot, it's burning a hole in the back of my head.

I'm pissed too, but if this punishment helps me remain a member of Rise Up, I'll take it. Does that mean I regret my decision to fuck Nikki? No, not entirely. One day Slater will realize I did him a favor.

Hopefully one day soon.

CHAPTER TWO

JENNI

"Please."

I shift my gaze to anything but my best friend Emily's puppy dog eyes before I get snagged by them. I've always been a sucker for her big brown eyes. "I told you, I'm not interested in dating anyone, let alone someone like Christian!"

Emily secures my fleeting gaze before dropping her lip. "It's not a date."

Her pleading eyes weaken my defenses with every second that ticks by. Within a minute, I'm at their complete mercy. "Fine!" I growl, "I'll come, but you owe me big time, Em!"

She squeals before sprinting my way, wrapping me up in a big hug. We stumble onto my bed with giggles bubbling in our chests. Her eagerness cools the fire brewing in my gut.

"You're the best, Jenni! Thank you so much; it's going to be so much fun!"

Fighting to hide my grimace, I return her embrace, shocked I just agreed to go on a double date with a guy I wholeheartedly despise. . .
. . .

"Wow, you must be new in town because I'm certain I've never had the pleasure of meeting you."

Assuming the handsome blond standing in front of me is speaking to someone else, I peer over my shoulder. My heart rate kicks up a notch when I discover there's no one behind me.

When I return my eyes front and center, blinking and confused, he smiles a dazzling grin that causes butterflies to tap dance in my stomach. As he saunters my way, I peruse his body from his almost bare feet to the top of his glossy blond locks. He's wearing flip flops, black board shorts, and a printed surf tee. His body is a cross between athletic and scrawny, but his boyishly handsome face makes up for his lack of muscles. His hair has a bit of a wave to it, sitting just above his shoulders. His eyes are hazel and hazy, like he's been smoking something he shouldn't have. His smile lights up his face. It also adds to the confidence beaming out of him. I've never been good at guessing ages, but I'd guess he's older than my fifteen years by maybe a year or two.

He props his shoulder on the wall I'm standing next to. "I'm Christian."

"Jenni," I reply, my voice quivering.

His body heats my arm when he tilts toward me until our lips are an inch apart. "Whatcha doing?"

My eyes scan our location, wordlessly answering him. The hallway is well decorated, but there's only one reason people stand here. When Christian fails to get the gist, I say, "Waiting to use the bathroom."

Emily and I are attending our very first senior party. It isn't that we were invited—it was an open invitation, and anyone could attend —but it's still exciting. Phillip Rochester turned eighteen last week, so his extremely wealthy parents threw him an elaborate celebration. Unfortunately, the main beverage of choice is beer, which means Emily and I are left drinking the cask of wine Emily snuck out of her parents' house last month. It tastes nasty, but since it's our first official senior party, we need something to celebrate the occasion.

After guzzling down two glasses in quick succession, my bladder protested. That led to me standing in a long line to use the only bathroom available to guests on this floor.

Noticing my uncomfortable squirm, Christian says, "I can take you to another bathroom."

I nearly decline his offer until I do a quick head count. There are still seven people in front of me, and the person using the washroom has been in there for ages.

Seconds from my bladder bursting, I accept his invitation. "Okay. Thank you."

Smiling a victorious grin, he offers me the crook of his elbow. After accepting his odd gesture, we stroll down the long hallway, gaining many admiring eyes. We've never met before, but Christian is clearly well known.

Nerves tap dance in my stomach when we arrive at a room at the end of an elaborate corridor. Christian removes a gold key from his pocket and places it in the lock. Once it's unlocked, he sweeps open the door and gestures for me to enter. He points to a set of white double doors in the far corner of the room. "It's the door on the right."

I make a beeline for the bathroom with my bladder cheering in delight, grateful it's about to be emptied. After doing my business, I wash my hands in the sink, taking in the expansive bathroom in the process. A Jacuzzi tub sitting in the middle of the room. A double-headed shower is concealed behind a tiled wall, and they not only have a toilet, but also a bidet.

Once I've dried my hands on amazingly soft towels, I pace out of the bathroom. My throat dries when I spot Christian sitting on the edge of a huge bed. "Do you feel better?"

Warmth creeps across my cheeks from his brazen question. Upon spotting my flushed look, he smiles again, loving that he's made me nervous.

I blush even more when he says, "You can come over here, you know."

"Umm. . . I have to get back to my friend. She's waiting for me downstairs."

An awkward stretch of silence crosses between us. I feel a little uncomfortable being in this vast room alone with him. Not because he's freakishly good-looking, but because we've only just met. I don't want people to get the wrong idea.

My breath hitches when Christian strolls my way, his wolfish gaze making my palms sweaty. I'm glad he's comfortable in his own skin, but his cockiness is somewhat overwhelming. Once he stops in front of me, his lust-riddled eyes run down my body.

"I won't force you to do anything you don't want to do." He's standing so close, his breath fans my heated cheeks. "I'll only touch you after you beg me to."

Air traps in my throat when he seals his mouth over mine. His kiss starts slow, but in no time at all, my legs are close to buckling. He knows how to kiss.

A whimper escapes my mouth when he inches back from our embrace. "Are you ready to beg yet?"

When my eyes flutter open, I catch sight of his lewd smirk. He thinks one kiss will have me eating out of his hand.

He's wrong.

I might look like a shy wallflower, but I've learned a few lessons in my short fifteen years. The main one: how to spot a player from a mile out.

"Not even close."

Christian's mouth gapes as his pupils widen. I return the seductive wink he gave me earlier before sauntering out of the room with a newfound spring in my step, not once looking back at the player who just got played.

When I amble past the toilet, I notice there are still six people lined up.

Thank goodness Christian kindly offered up his private bathroom.

Once I glide down the stairs, my eyes float around the room, seeking Emily. There's a band playing Fall Out Boys' hit son "Sugar, We're Goin' Down" on a stage against the far wall of the sitting room, and a mass group of people are dancing in front of them.

I stop to admire them for a few seconds before I spot Emily in the far corner of the room. She isn't looking too good. When I leap off the bottom step, a guy with shaggy blond hair steps into my path, blocking my exit. He has a guitar strap curled around his shoulder and is strumming in sync to the song the band is playing. I stare at him, stunned he's performing in the middle of the living room instead of on the stage. He's obviously part of the band because he's very talented, but why isn't he with them?

My palms grow sweaty when the attractive blond catches me gawking at him. His deep blue eyes are even sexier than his panty-wetting face. He has shaggy locks and a body that could only look better with less clothing.

Grimacing with embarrassment about my flaming cheeks, I divert my ogling eyes away from him. His deep, scrumptious chuckle crumbles the wall I just built around my heart. He's loving my shameful attempt at decorum.

After flashing me a quick smirk, he struts to the stage, never once faltering on his awe-inspiring performance. Once he's out of sight, I bolt to Emily, my legs pumping as fast as my heart.

"Oh my god, have you seen the band? They're as hot as hell!"

"What band?" Her slur reveals she snuck a couple of glasses of wine while I was away. When she attempts to get a better look at the band, she nearly loses her footing.

"Oh shit." Giggling at her unusual drunkenness, I curl my arm around her shoulders. It takes everything I have to keep her upright. "How many glasses did you have?"

"Just a few." She leans in closer. "I bub ya, Jen Jen."

A giggle rumbles out of my lips. She's a very loved up drunk. "I love you too, Em, but it's time for us to go home."

She drops her lower lip. "Not yet, I wanna see the band of hotties."

Somehow she frees herself from my embrace and stumbles toward the stage. Unsure whether to laugh or cry, I take off after her. When I catch up to her, I spin her around and guide her toward the front door. "Not today."

"Party pooper," she squeals with a giggle.

For every unstable step we take, she giggles more. She laughs so hard, she occasionally snorts, which in turn, makes her laugh even louder. And thus begins the vicious cycle of drunk girls giggling.

By the time we make it outside, my cheeks are the color of beetroot, and my nape is dripping with sweat. I've also laughed more the prior ten minutes than I have the past month. As we step onto the paved sidewalk at the front of the raging, out-of-control party, a white car pulls in front of us. The pretty girl sitting in the passenger seat eyes us curiously while rolling down her window. "Do you need a lift?"

"I'm about to call a taxi," I advise her while struggling to keep Emily on her feet and removing my phone.

When her eyes drift from Emily to me, the redhead says, "It could be a while. We really don't mind giving you a ride." Her beautiful green eyes don't show any judgment for Emily's inebriated state. All they reflect is genuine concern.

My eyes stray in the direction we just left while contemplating the stranger's offer. My pulse quickens when I spot Christian standing on the front step. His eyes are rapt on me, and he's smirking a smug grin.

Rolling my eyes at his pompousness, I return my gaze to the pretty redhead. "Okay, if you don't mind?"

With a smile, she jumps out of the car and opens the back passenger door. A beautiful floral scent engulfs me when she helps me get Emily into her back seat. Once we have her buckled in, the car pulls away from the curb. Grinning, I crank my neck back to Christian. He's still watching me, but his grin is nowhere near as smug. Good. I wave at him condescendingly as the stranger's car whizzes down the street.

My attention reverts to the front when the cute redhead offers an introduction. "My name is Nicole, and this is my sister, Petra."

Nicole has gorgeous long, wavy red hair, and her skin is Alaska-

white. The contrast of her hair and face is mesmerizing, but her most alluring feature is her stunning green eyes. They pop right off her face.

"I'm Jenni, and this is my best friend, Emily. It's her first time drinking." I don't want them thinking this is something Emily does often. I've been her friend for more than half my life, and this is the first time she's been drunk.

The rest of our drive is made in silence. It doesn't feel uncomfortable; there's just no time for a conversation since I only live a few blocks from Phillip's house.

When we arrive at my home, Nicole helps me carry Emily up the stairs. We giggle, crash into the walls, and fumble precariously down the hallway. Thankfully, my parents are heavy sleepers.

Once Emily is flopped onto my king-size bed, my eyes drift to Nicole. "Thank you so much for everything you did tonight."

"It was my pleasure." She hands me a business card. "I hope to see you around."

Smiling, she briskly exits my room. I follow her downstairs to bid farewell to her and her sister. Once their taillights are nothing but a blur, I study the business card in my hand. "D.S.D. – Designated Sister Driver – Nicole Reed," I read off the card.

It has a cell number attached to it. Shrugging, I slip it into my pocket then dash back to Emily, grabbing a glass of water and some pain relief tablets on my way.

The next morning, Emily wakes a little worse for the wear, swearing she only had four glasses of wine. She has no recollection of the party or how we arrived home. When I tell her about Nicole, she borrows the business card Nicole gave me to send her a message, thanking her for her help. We then spend the rest of Sunday morning hanging in my room, discussing the thrill of attending our first senior party.

Around three PM, a few hours after Emily has left, my phone receives a text message.

Unknown number: Are you ready to beg yet?

One, how the hell did Christian get my number? Two, I thought I was the one who was supposed to be begging.

Me: Yes, I am. . .

Christian's quick reply reveals his eagerness.

Christian: Name the time and the place, baby.

My fingers fly wildly over my cellphone screen.

Me: Now would be great. . .

Christian: Now? I could organize something.

Satisfied I have him trapped, I go in big.

Me: Okay, great! Did you want me to beg you to leave me alone via text message, or would you like me to call you?

When my phone rings, my sassiness is foiled. My heart beats fitfully when I press my phone to my ear. "Hello."

"I'd much prefer to hear you beg in person," *Christian informs me, his voice a deep, seductive purr.*

I roll my eyes even though my heart is doing a weird flippy thing.

"Come on, baby, beg me."

A giggle erupts from my lips over his audacity.

"I don't know what I want to hear more: you begging or you giggling. I think I like them both the same."

My pulse quickens. I know he's a player, but what girl doesn't like a confidence boost?

"Go out with me," *he pleads, confident my silence has me recon-sidering. It does.*

"On a real date. I promise I won't try anything. . . unless you want me to."

I giggle like the teenage girl I am.

"Please," *he pleas.*

My flipping heart is audible in my voice when I reply, "Okay."

Christian and I talk for nearly an hour before we arrange to go on a date the following weekend. . . . . .

Now today, I've just agreed to go on my fifth date with him. It's not Emily's fault. She didn't realize the favor she was asking because I never told anyone what happened between Christian and me all those months ago.

The next morning, I assist Emily in preparing for her date with Zander. She's so excited about going on a date with the guy she's been lusting over since Phillip's party. She's gone all out. Hair. Make Up. Sexy, yet casual clothes. By the time she finishes prepping, even I have a hard time recognizing her. She looks both glamorous and sexy.

I can't be accused of putting in the same effort. I've gone for the minimalistic look, hoping to be as unattractive to Christian as possible. It's not that I'm worried I'll be under his spell in less than a minute. I just don't want him to think he can fool me twice—even if he can.

Butterflies take flight in my stomach when Emily and I make our way to the movie complex. I spot Christian before he sees me. He and Zander are standing at the entrance of the cinema. Feeling the uneasiness roaring through my veins, Emily's grip on my hand tightens. She maintains her death-like clutch until we stop to stand in front of them.

While Emily and Zander greet each other, Christian's eyes scan my body. My heart rate doubles when his perusal ends at the exact moment his face lights up with a smile. The humorous sparkle in his eyes tells me he knows I dressed plainly on purpose, but he isn't repulsed like I hoped.

When Emily introduces us as if we're strangers, Christian tilts his head to the side and cocks his brow. When I refuse to correct her, he shakes his head before leaning in to press a kiss to my cheek. My stomach gurgles when his greeting leaves the scent of his aftershave in its wake.

Narrowing my eyes, I snarl at him. He did that on purpose. Like all the players in the world, he has a thing about marking his scent on women. Misreading my anger, Emily's beautiful giggle fills the silence plaguing our gathering. "Come on, Jen, that was a grandma kiss."

She can say that because she doesn't know how skillful Christian's lips are.

Hoping to get the show on the road, Zander purchases our tickets. I gag at his selection. He picked a dated movie that's packed with action. Loving my newfound attitude, Emily giggles again. Although our double date isn't off to a great start, I'm glad someone's having fun.

Put-off by Zander's unimpressed sneer, she mumbles, "I'll grab snacks," before dragging me to the snack bar.

Hmm. That was odd. Shouldn't Zander want Emily to be happy?

While we gather food, Emily explains that Brad Pitt will be topless in a majority of the movie Zander selected. Her knowledge gives me a brilliant idea. Beaming with excitement, I snatch up the snacks I want, throw a bunch of notes at the cashier, then hightail it back to Zander and Christian. Although Christian's body is more built than it was when I saw him naked, it's not by much. I'm very much looking forward to making numerous comments about Brad Pitt's incredible physique during the movie with the hope of bruising Christian's arrogant, egotistical attitude.

I doubt it will dent his ego by much, but I'll get great pleasure out of it.

"Oh my, would you look at those pecs?" I bite down on my bottom lip while letting out a moan. "I've never seen a pair so impressive."

When I sneakily peer at Christian, my teeth grit. He's not glancing at the movie screen. His eyes are fixed on me, and he's smiling.

"So muscular," I continue, striving to keep my eyes planted on the movie screen, but miserably failing.

Why isn't my plan working? He should be annoyed—not smiling.

When my eyes stray back to Christian, a rush of excitement bombards my pussy. He is undeniably a player, but he doesn't just have the cockiness necessary for the title; he also has the skills—*very impressive skills*. Our time together was fascinating. I'm just frustrated I got snared by his trap.

I shouldn't be so hard on myself. When Christian lavishes you with his attention, you feel like you're the only girl in the world. . . until you give him what he wants. Then he spits you out like a piece of used gum.

With his ego fed by my silence, Christian tilts toward me. "You're still my favorite."

I gag so loud, the couple in front of us spin around to glare at me. After a silent apology, I twist my torso to Christian. "Out of a long list of many."

Undeterred by my snarky attitude, he slants even closer until his lips brush my ear. "You make me want to break all my rules."

My head cranks to his so quickly, our lips briefly brush. As my brain struggles to make sense of his uncharacteristic reply, my brows furrow. Everything he has said today breaks all his "player" rules.

When he smirks at my shocked expression, I screw up my nose and stick out my tongue. I want to act like I'm the innocent in our exchange, but I can't. Christian was upfront with me the instant we started making out at Bronte's Peak after our fourth "date." He explained he wasn't looking for anything permanent, and that he had rules in place to make sure girls like me understood that, such as the one time we have sex will be the *only* time we'll have sex.

He openly admitted he'd never slept with the same girl twice because he didn't want them to become attached to him. You'd think that would have been my cue to leave, but when he looked into my eyes, any reservations I had vanished. I felt truly cherished.

I was an idiot.

Wanting to ensure I don't make the same mistake twice, I grab a handful of popcorn from my box and throw it in Christian's face. I'm here to support Emily, not to schedule another romp in the bedroom with the school's biggest player.

Later that afternoon, when Zander drops Christian home, Christian lets it slip we've met before. I can see the confusion all over Emily's face when Christian asks if I'm sure I don't want to accept his numerous silent offers for a second "date" with him.

I shake my head. I learned my lesson.

I plan to tell Emily about Christian the instant our double date concludes, but I am forced to wait when she accepts Zander's invitation for a second date that very same day.

Things didn't end as amicably for Zander and Emily as they did for Christian and me. I understood Christian's rules. Emily was never made aware of Zander's.

When Zander dragged Emily's name through the mud, I kept quiet on my fling with Christian. There was never the right time to bring it up, and I had more pressing matters to deal with.

Before I knew it, three years had passed.

I haven't spoken a word to Christian since that day all those years ago. The fact he stood by and watched his best friend destroy mine was all it took for any feelings I had for him to turn into a simmering pit of rage.

Even now, years later, I still cringe when his name is mentioned.

CHAPTER THREE

NICK

Three years later. . .

"You can grab a shower in Isaac's bathroom."

When I show Noah the hidden bathroom Isaac has in his office at his dance club in Ravenshoe, he jerks up his chin. "If Isaac is cool with me using his shower, I have some spare clothes in my truck. . ."

His words trail off when Isaac enters his office. "No worries, Noah, you guys really helped me today, so you're more than welcome to use my shower. I also let Tina know your drinks are on the house."

While Isaac answers his ringing cell phone, Noah leaves to collect his clothes from his truck parked outside. He's been helping my brother and me unload and connect the kegs for tonight since Isaac fired his store-man for stealing. I was hesitant to ask for his help, but with Isaac having connections that could help our band reach the success it's aiming for, I'm willing to do anything to get on his good side.

Our band's dreams somewhat stalled two years ago when Noah's brother Chris overdosed. It took a few months for Noah to turn up to rehearsals, and once he did, he wasn't really present. The only good that came from the experience was the song he wrote.

I've never heard a song darker and more sorrowful as "Hollow." The first time Noah performed it, he ripped my heart straight out of my fucking chest. When he never once faltered during his heart-breaking performance, that's when I knew I'd do anything to remain a member of Rise Up. I've never fucked with a band member's girl since that day.

That doesn't mean I don't offer them my services, but none have accepted my offer.

My brother, Isaac, is five years older than me. He's the owner of an eighteen-plus dance club called the Dungeon. I'm going to be honest, I have no clue where he got the money to open such an impressive-looking club. This place screams wealth with its high vaulted ceilings, shackled dance cages, and mahogany trim. I'm reasonably confident the money he pours into his empire isn't from legal activities, but I can't one hundred percent testify to that.

Isaac has always been a business-oriented kid. He'd buy large cases of donuts at the supermarket and sell them for fifty cents apiece to the kids at school. That was a markup of three hundred percent, pocketing him a nice amount of change each week that he'd reinvest into other quick money-making schemes. What he does in his private life doesn't bother me, as long as it doesn't affect my personal life.

When our parents got divorced, Isaac, who was sixteen at the time, moved with our dad to Ravenshoe while I lived with my mom in Miami. I was only a child at the time and didn't realize that a majority of the problems in my parents' marriage stemmed from my mom needing to be the center of attention.

It took me a few years to work up the courage to ask my mom if I could live with my dad. Once the dust settled, it became apparent it was the best decision I could have ever made. It was not long after moving here that Noah stumbled upon me in the music room at our high school.

I've been trying my hardest the past three years to fix the rift I created in the band, but no matter what I do or say, Slater still hates my guts. I can't say I blame him. I'd never forgive someone if they slept with my girlfriend, but I turn up to practice early, I'm always the last one to leave, and I do shit tasks for my brother in the hope he'll mention our band to his music exec friend. It might not seem like much, but it's all I have to offer.

Isaac's deep timbre interrupts me from my thoughts. "What're your plans for tonight, Nick?"

I shift on my feet to face him. "Noah won't drink much if he's driving, so I'll probably just have a few beers with him before finding myself a lady."

His dark gray eyes lift from his wooden desk to me. His brow is bowed, his jaw ticking.

I chuckle. "I'll be sure to take my *escapades* elsewhere this time around."

The last time I spent the night here, I got jumped by Isaac's bouncers in the alleyway because I refused to stop committing a "lewd act" with a lady who enjoyed the thrill of fucking in public. The bouncers didn't realize I was the owner's little brother, and although they were his staff, Isaac didn't take kindly to their rough-handling.

Come to think of it, I haven't seen either of them since that day.

Isaac rifles through paperwork in front of him. "The offer for an apartment still stands."

Many times the past three months, he's offered to rent me an apartment so I'll be closer to Mavericks. The band secured a regular Friday night gig there a couple of months ago, and Isaac said he didn't want me commuting back to Petersburg each night. I'm hesitant to accept his offer. I don't know why. I think part of it stems from spending my teen years watching my mom live off everyone else's money. I don't want to follow her mooching footsteps.

"Thanks for the offer, but I'm fine living at Dad's," I reply just as Noah moseys back into the office.

When my dad retired, he sold his house in Ravenshoe and moved to Petersburg. It means his house is smaller in size, but he has more land to occupy his time. Petersburg is only twenty minutes from Ravenshoe, and the town is so small, it isn't plagued by rush hour traffic, so Isaac's worry isn't necessary.

As Noah heads to the washroom, I nudge my head to the bustling club. "I'll meet you at the bar."

When Noah nods, I head out. Isaac watches me but keeps quiet. He's not the talkative type.

The night is still young, but the floor space inside the Dungeon is filled with partygoers eager to spend their Saturday night bumping and grinding against other sweaty people. My ideal night—I'm just usually in my truck or companion's bedroom, not at a dance club.

"Hey, Tina." I strut up to the main bartender. Tina is one of the most petite girls I've ever seen. Her brown hair is cut in a pixie design, making her look like a fairy. She has stunning hazel eyes that make my dick twitch when I stare at them too long and a fit body. She's attractive, but not in the way you'd expect. The unique mix of her features and attitude doubles her attractiveness.

"How is The Player tonight?" she questions with a grin.

I give her a flirty wink. "Still waiting for that invite."

Her dainty laugh booms around the bar. I've been hounding her the past six months for a chance to see if her allure matches her intensity in the bedroom. I don't even care that she's a few years older than me because I'm pretty sure she'll be crazy between the sheets. Maybe she could teach me some pointers I haven't already taught myself?

"It must have gotten lost in the mail." Tina's voice drips with sarcasm.

Winking, she hands me a bottle of beer. My lips lift against the rim before I take a mouth-filling gulp of the malted liquid inside. After swallowing half the bottle, I ask, "Can I grab another?"

Tina splays her tiny hands on her even tinier hips.

"Please," I add on quickly, recalling how much she likes manners.

Her lips tug into a smirk as she sets down a second bottle in front of me. My eyes drop to her ass when she struts away to serve other patrons requesting her service. Her hips sway in beat to the music booming around the club. She knows she's sexy, and she works it to her advantage.

I jump out of my skin when Noah magically appears at my side. "You weren't kidding about this place getting packed."

Pretending I didn't just jump two feet in the air, I hand him a beer then mosey to a booth located near the bar. I don't want to stumble too far to get a refill. Although, I'm sure if I added a "please" to my request, Tina would deliver my beer.

Over the next thirty minutes, the club becomes more crowded. People dance provocatively under the strobing lights, moving in sync to the music blaring out of the speakers hanging from the ceiling. There's no doubt in my mind, dancing is a form of sexual activity. It's nearly as close to the real thing, except you keep your clothes on.

Although these days, some of the girls' outfits can't really be classed as clothing.

When I hear a remix of Nelly Furtado's classic song "Man Eater" blasting from the speakers, I jump out of the booth I'm sitting in. "I need to get myself a man-eater!" I waggle my brows at a shocked Noah. "You coming?"

Noah shakes his head, mortified I'd even suggest he join me on the dance floor. He has no idea what he's missing out on. The ratio of girls to men on any dance floor sits at around four to one. Four beautiful women per one horny male. Those are ratios I like.

The instant I hit the dance floor, the statistics stack up. Several beautiful women move toward me at once. There's a dampness in the air from the mass of bodies in one space, but it's invigorating. The musky smell reminds me of the scent in a bedroom after hot, raunchy sex.

When the DJ notices me, he drops his chin in greeting before skipping to the next song on his playlist: a dance mix of Justin Timberlake's "Sexy Back."

He knows as well as I do how many women love dancing to this song. They want to feel sexy, and I'm more than happy to help them feel that way.

If you hate being manhandled, I suggest you stay off the dance floor. I've been grabbed, poked, and felt up multiple times the last two songs. I find it amusing that women don't hesitate to grab a feel of my dick without permission, but if I dared to touch their breasts without asking, all hell would break loose.

I guess it's fortunate I don't mind the touchy-feely girls.

By the time the current song fades into a new one, I've found myself two beautiful dance partners. One is plastered to my front, her hips swinging in beat to the music, whereas the other is splayed on my back. She's so close, her erect nipples scratch my back with every grind she does.

When the brunette attached to my crotch bends down to grind her ass on the zipper in my jeans, a flurry of red catches my eye. There's a heart-stopping blonde in a tight mini-dress approaching the dance floor from my right. She has her arm curled around a petite brunette who's cuddled up to an equally attractive redhead. I don't like rating women until I've done an in-depth evaluation of their faces in non-strobing lights, but I can happily testify that this blonde is a knockout. Her heart-shaped face, oval eyes, and dick-twitching body make her an easy eleven out of ten. Her friends aren't bad either.

Excitement overwhelms me. I've hit the fucking trifecta. Three beautiful girls all at once. A blonde, a brunette, and a redhead. You can't get better than this!

The blonde is already holding my interests, but when she twirls and I catch a glimpse of her lace panties, her fate is sealed. I'm more than interested in getting to know her and her panties a little better. When she giggles at something her friends say, I can't help the smirk that forms on my face. Her smile knocks her attractiveness out of the park. She's more than pretty. She's out of this fucking world beautiful!

My dick twitches when the trio begins dancing in the middle of the floor. Its spasms shift to my jaw when a handful of men ditch their dance partners to move closer to the them—not that the girls notice. They have no clue how much attention they're gaining. A dozen men are stalking them like lions eyeing their dinner, but they're utterly oblivious they're seconds from being devoured.

Too busy calculating my next move, I forgot I have company until a pair of lips attach to mine and a tongue lashes them. Usually, I'd appreciate the brunette's forwardness, but the erection I'm sporting isn't from her grinding her tailbone on my crotch. It's compliments of the sexy blonde and her naughty lace panties.

Inching back from my dance partner's embrace, I peer past her slumped shoulders to seek the trio mere seconds from being attacked by a pack of hungry lions. My heart rate kicks into overdrive when I notice the blonde is the only one remaining on the dance floor. Her friends have up and vanished.

Perfect, I chant to myself when a brilliant idea formulates in my head.

I drop my eyes to a pair of lust-filled green eyes. "Did you want a drink?"

The pretty brunette's tongue delves out to lick her parched lips before she nods.

"Great! Grab me a beer while you're there?"

I spin her toward the bar then give her a nudge in the direction I want her to go. I'm being an insensitive jerk, but I need to get her away from me, and I need to do it quick. A handful of men have also noticed the blonde has been left unattended. I don't have seconds to spare. If I want to make a move, I have to make it now, and considering she has my heart racing like no woman ever has, it isn't an option; it's a requirement.

My dance partner's eyes narrow, and she huffs, but she still follows my command. The instant her black pumps step off the dance floor, I rush for the blonde. I reach her with barely a second to spare, barging numerous contenders out of my way in the process.

"There you are, baby cakes, I've been looking for you everywhere."

Not giving her the chance to protest, I plant a long, steaming peck onto her red-painted lips.

Fuck me—is this heaven?

CHAPTER FOUR

JENNI

Have you ever had the feeling you're being watched? Now imagine it times five. That's what I'm experiencing right now. The instant Emily and Nicole left to get a drink, the feeling of a lamb being sent to slaughter overwhelmed me.

While my eyes float over the dance floor, I continue dancing to Marshmello's hit song "Friends." My heart rate increases when I spot several pairs of male eyes gawking at me. Don't get me wrong, I like attention just like any other girl, but it's unnerving when eyes of all ages and sizes are staring at you like you're their last meal.

Just as I'm about to wander off in search of Emily and Nicole, my exit is blocked by a black shirt-covered chest. "There you are, baby cakes; I've been looking for you everywhere," declares a voice from above. Even with music blaring from the speakers, his deep timbre rumbles through the club.

Before I can advise him he has the wrong person, a set of warm lips seal over mine. I freeze, equally shocked and excited. I'm being kissed by a stranger, but my first thought isn't to pull away. *What the hell is wrong with me?*

When the mysterious stranger withdraws from our embrace, I'm quickly mesmerized by a pair of dark blue eyes. While standing frozen in the middle of the dance floor, I drink in his handsome face. His shaggy blond hair hangs loosely on the top of his head; his blue eyes are surrounded by thick lashes, and his lips are full—and for the quick second they were pressed against mine, they tasted delicious.

I watch him in reverence when his narrowed eyes dart around the bustling space. When I follow his gaze, I notice the handful of the men who were closing in on me are backing away. He didn't speak a word, yet his slit gaze was enough to send them packing.

Happy the men have gotten the hint, the stranger wraps his arms around my waist. My skin grows clammy when he tugs me into his fit, athletic body. When he swings his hips in rhythm to the music, my jaw drops. I'm stunned at how well he dances. *He must do this regularly.*

Suddenly clued in to what he's doing, I whisper, "Thank you."

I'm more than grateful he saved me from a pack of hungry wolves. I felt seconds away from being massacred before he entered the picture.

His breath flutters against my ear when he replies, "You're welcome."

A shiver courses through my body, his sexy voice too splendid for my body not to react. Noticing my childish reaction, he chuckles, but that's as far as his conversation goes.

In silence, he spins me around the dance floor Emily, Nicole, and I only arrived at a few minutes ago. For the past two months, we've frequented the dance clubs in our hometown of Erkinsvale. Emily and Nicole have had access to their sisters' ID for months, but since I'm an only child, we couldn't hit these types of clubs until I was legally old enough. I did consider getting a fake ID, but when your parents are well-known lawyers, there aren't many people willing to accept money for an illegal service.

Our trio has an agreement that we are to deny any offers to buy us drinks, and we only dance with each other when we visit establishments like this. This guy didn't request permission to dance, so technically I'm not breaking the rules. Furthermore, he did save me from being slaughtered, so it's only fair I dance with him for a song or two to show my appreciation, isn't it?

As we dance, the stranger's hands drift over my body. He takes in my curves, but not once does his groping go over a PG rating—*unfortunately*.

As if he heard my private thoughts, he spins me around to grind his crotch against my backside. Images of my favorite classic movie *Dirty Dancing* flash before my eyes. This guy—who still remains nameless—has all the moves like Patrick Swayze did in that movie.

"Nobody puts Baby in the corner," I murmur to myself, my mood picking up.

When my gaze lifts to check on the location of Emily and Nicole, I'm shocked to discover Emily dancing with a man in gray trousers and a white business shirt. She hasn't stopped talking about a guy she met months ago called Noah. I thought part of her reasoning for the mini makeover we did today was to impress him, so I'm somewhat surprised she's dancing with a man who appears several years older than her.

Guilt for breaking our girl-code lessens when Emily seduces the good-looking businessman. Her flirty dance moves free me to enjoy the sensuality you can only experience when dancing with someone as equally captivated by music as you. I lean in deeper to my dance partner, making sure my backside is firmly planted on his crotch, before bringing out my best moves.

Within minutes, the heat on the dance floor becomes stifling. Sweat from my drenched hair rolls down my neck unchecked as my body temp triples. I'm about to wipe away the mess on my neck when the rigid bumps of a tongue lap it up.

Oh my, did he just lick me?

My pussy pulses with desire when the stranger's first lick is quickly followed by another. And another. And another. From the erection digging into my ass, I can easily perceive I'm not the only one aroused by his wickedly sensual moves.

I don't know how many licks occur before I spot a concerned Emily pacing my way. The man she was dancing with is nowhere in sight, and she looks genuinely upset.

When I twirl to face my dance partner, his closed eyes flutter open. "I'll be back," I inform him, praying he knows this is only an intermission in our exchange, not the end of it.

I wait for him to nod before closing the distance between Emily and me.

"I'm not feeling very well, so I'm going to take a taxi home and jump into bed," I overhear Emily telling Nicole.

Knowing Emily wouldn't leave without a good reason, I say, "We'll come with you."

I hate that I'm leaving just as things are getting exciting, but Emily means more to me than a nameless sexy-as-hell guy. Besides, another one of our rules is that no one leaves alone. If one goes home, we all go home.

"No, Jen, I'm not ruining your night just because I have a little headache. Please don't worry about me; I've already called a cab."

Something about Emily's voice is off. She's not known for fibbing, but I have a feeling there's something more going on with her than she's letting on.

When my gaze strays back to the dance floor, I see the cute blond I was dancing with standing frozen, waiting for my return. His eagerness makes me torn. I don't know whether to force the truth from Emily now or let it wait until morning.

Emily makes the decision for me. "Go on, babe, have fun. I'll call you tomorrow, and you can give me all the details."

Stealing my chance to protest, she wraps me up in a firm hug.

"Are you sure?" My words are brimming with concern. I know how stubborn Emily is. If she sets her mind to something, she won't let anything deter her, so even if I begged and pleaded for her to stay, she wouldn't, but this still feels wrong.

"I'm sure. Now go."

Confident I'm reading her wrong, I give her another big hug before returning to my dance partner. I'm sure tomorrow she'll tell me what's wrong. Until then, I get to enjoy dancing with a much younger and more attractive version of Patrick Swayze.

"Is everything alright?" the blond asks upon my return.

I halfheartedly shrug. "Yeah, my friend isn't feeling well, so she's going home."

He glances past my shoulder to Emily and Nicole before returning his eyes to mine. "Did you want me to give you a ride home?"

I try to mask my disappointment that he wants to take me home. My attempts are fruitless. I'm beyond disappointed.

Spotting my sullen expression, he smiles. "Not right now, I meant I can take you home later."

"Oh." A huge grin adorns my face. I love dancing in general, but when you dance with a guy who has moves like his, it's an entirely new experience. "Thanks for the offer, but I brought my car. Maybe next time?"

I cringe. I just insinuated there'd be a second date, with this not even being a date.

He assesses my face for the hundredth time the past twenty minutes before slowly breathing out, "Maybe."

As mortified by his response as I was mine, he spins me on my heels, plasters himself to my back, then swings his hips. Nerves take flight in my stomach when one of his hands spreads across my stomach. His firm hold secures me to his body, while his other hand explores mine. When his rough fingertips glide past my budded nipple, a breathless moan parts my lips. Our dancing becomes more provocative with every minute that ticks by, stepping over our previous PG rating.

My heart beats in an unnatural rhythm when I gaze up at him. His dark blue eyes are glancing down at me, full to the brim with lust. After returning my eyes front and center, I snap them shut. The darkness enhances the sexual sparks firing between us.

Not even two seconds later, my fantasy bubble is burst by an annoying cough. When I pop open my eyes, they're met with the sneer of a beautiful brunette. I peer at her, stunned by her fury.

Recognizing I'm clueless about what has made her angry, she shifts her narrowed eyes to my dance partner. Utterly oblivious to her deadly rays, he continues grinding his erection against my ass.

She cocks out her right hip, her nostrils flaring. "Seriously?"

I nudge him in the ribs, stopping his grind mid-pump. When he stiffens, I crank my neck back. Anger boils my blood when I see the guilt marring his face.

I've just been played—*again!*

Stepping out of his embrace, I stand next to the furiously angry woman, signaling to her I was unaware he was on a date. Women need to stand united against the players of the world.

When my dance partner's gaze bounces between the pretty brunette and me, and he has the gall to smile, I snap. "Do you mind?" I gesture my head to the bottle of beer my new friend is clasping.

A smirk curls on her lips. "Not at all."

After accepting the frosted bottle, I saunter to the arrogant jerk with my hips swinging provocatively. He stops watching their healthy roll when I balance on my tippy toes so I can pour the beer over his head. He doesn't move out of the flow of the freezing cold liquid. He just stands there smirking, while his face and shirt accept the brunt of his punishment.

Once the bottle is empty, I spin on my heels and briskly walk away. I didn't consider how much trouble I could get in when I put my plan into action. I was angry, so I ran with the first notion that crossed my mind.

It was a silly thing for me to do.

The first person I see during my frantic flee is Nicole. Her wide eyes reveal my theatrics weren't done on the down low. "Time to go."

I loop my arm around her elbow then dart for the club's exit, dumping evidence of my crime into the trash on the way by. Just as we're about to exit the main club area, our path is blocked by a t-shirt-covered chest. My pulse quickens when my eyes drink in the enormous-looking man whose shoulders are as wide as my height.

I cringe when I notice he has "Bouncer" written in white across his black shirt.

"I'll clean it up," I inform him, confident his angry sneer is because he witnessed my incident with the unnamed blond.

When the bouncer's head—which is roughly the size of a watermelon—drops down to me, Nicole nearly faints. Her skin pales even more than usual, causing me to giggle. I didn't think she could get any whiter.

The more Nicole pleads with me to stop laughing, the harder I giggle. I'm not meaning to be a pain, but the fact she can go any paler than she is has laughter erupting from my throat without warning.

Nicole squeezes my hand. "Jenni."

"I'm sorry." I battle to simmer down my giggles, but when she stomps down her foot like she's about to have a tantrum, my giggles start up all over again. Tears stream down my face, and my stomach cramps. I'm laughing like an absolute lunatic.

My giggles cease when a snort escapes my nostril cavity. Mortified I snorted in public—*again*—I clamp my hand over my mouth and nose.

Now I'm not the only one struggling to hold back my giggles. Nicole's O-formed mouth lifts into an uneasy smile. Her eyes stray to anyone but me as her body fights to keep her laughter on the down low. The only person not amused is the bouncer. His stern face remains firm, never once losing its hostile expression.

After bumping Nicole with my hip, I clear my face of any amusement, then raise my eyes to the bouncer. "I'm sorry." I award him the best puppy dog eyes I can conjure while praying he didn't think we were giggling about his massively large head.

"Apology accepted."

Acceptance of my apology didn't come from the bouncer. He's standing in front of me; the voice came from my side.

When I turn my teary face toward the voice, I spot the guy I was dancing with earlier. He's drying his beer-stained clothes with a small white tea towel, and he has a smug grin on his face, like he has the entire world at his feet.

If the bouncer's whitening gills are anything to go by, he does.

CHAPTER FIVE

NICK

"Oh no. Now she's in trouble."

Catching my confused gaze, Tina tosses me a tea towel before nudging her head to the nearest exit, pointing out the girl I was just dancing with. She and her redhead friend are being blocked from leaving by Travis.

Oh shit.

Travis is the number one bouncer at the Dungeon. He's a huge son of a bitch who doesn't have a funny bone in his entire body. His thick arms are crossed in front of his chest, revealing he is unimpressed by the mess the blonde left on the dance floor.

"Go and save her, Nick."

My gaze flicks back to Tina, who grins at me before adding a nod to her suggestion. I don't usually jump to anyone's defense, but I am partly responsible for the mess, so I shouldn't let the blonde endure all of Travis's wrath.

I want to say tonight is the first time I've been reprimanded for having multiple partners in one night. Regrettably, it isn't. But it's the first time I've had a bottle of beer poured over my head. I knew the blonde wouldn't be a shy wallflower, but I had no idea when she got angry she turned into a firecracker. Even though the beer was fucking freezing, I couldn't stop the smirk that morphed onto my face from her audacity. Imagine taking her feistiness and unleashing it in the bedroom. Just the thought makes my dick twitch, and it has me thinking recklessly.

Tina cackles when I reluctantly stroll toward Travis. Travis and I don't get along. It might have something to do with me sleeping with his baby sister then *accidentally* losing her number. Then, when he gave it to me, it somehow got deleted from my phone—*numerous times.*

It's lucky my brother owns this club, or Travis would have wrung my scrawny neck by now.

As I approach their gathering, mopping up some of the beer my shaggy hair is drenched in with a scratchy tea towel, I realize I have it all wrong. The blonde doesn't need me to jump in and save her. She's laughing, not the least bit concerned about Travis's angry glare. Her beautiful giggles only stop when a loud snort bellows out of her. When she slaps her hand over her mouth, mortified, it's the fight of my life not to break into boisterous laughter. I never knew such a vicious roar could come out of such a teeny mouse.

Hearing my quiet snickers, Travis's dark eyes snap to mine. His stern gaze stuffs my laughter into the back of my throat. I thought Noah's friend Jacob was huge, but he's a midget compared to Travis.

While running her hands down the front of her red dress, the blonde settles her composure. When she's satisfied she has everything under control, she lifts and locks her eyes with Travis's. "I'm sorry." She amazes me that she can go from a giggling maniac to prim and proper in a matter of seconds.

Seeing this as my way in, I say, "Apology accepted."

I use the tea towel to dry my polo shirt that's clinging to my chest while stepping closer to her. When she cranks her neck my way, her eyes thin even more. It's all a ploy. She's discreet, but even if a bus was lodged between us, there's no way in hell I could miss her scan of my now skin-tight shirt and ripped designer jeans.

When her focus returns to my face, a cocky grin etches onto my mouth. Her eyes are sparked with lust. Realizing she's been busted ogling me, her neck turns pink as her eyes rocket back to Travis. "I'm sorry about the mess."

Her light blue eyes plead with Travis to accept her apology. He's not as eager to accept her apology as I was. "Tell that to the boss." He grabs ahold of her forearm and drags her toward Isaac's office. When her panicked eyes stray to mine, wordlessly requesting my assistance, I shrug, acting coy.

I tried to help; you weren't interested.

As if she can read my silent thoughts, her eyes narrow even more. Yep! She's definitely a firecracker—ready to explode at any moment.

Against my better judgment, I shout, "She's with me, Travis."

The redhead standing frozen at my side releases a deep exhalation of air when Travis's brisk strides halt a few feet away from us. "She's with you?"

His tone relays he thinks I'm full of shit, but it doesn't stop me from saying, "Yep!"

I stare into the relieved eyes of the pretty blonde, ensuring she knows how I want my restitution paid, only prying away my eyes when Travis asks, "What's her name, then?"

Oh, fuck.

I've pulled this type of prank on Travis before, but it was with girls doing a runner before paying their bar tab. Those times, I was smart enough to ask Tina their names before rushing in to save them.

"Penny." I think that's the name the blonde's friend is whispering to me. "Her name is Penny." I shout to project my voice over the thumping music.

With a sly grin, Travis glances down at Penny before holding his other hand out palm side up. "ID."

Penny's mouth forms an O while her hand digs into the little black purse under her arm. When she hands Travis what I assume is her driver's license, her concerned eyes stray to mine.

"Jenni Murphy," Travis reads off the license.

Fuck—I was close.

"Yep, that's what I said."

"You said 'Penny.'" Travis's voice is an angry roar.

"Nah, I said 'Jenni.' You just can't hear properly over the music blaring out of the speakers . You must be going deaf. I said 'Jenni.'"

I struggle not to laugh. It would be a lot easier to hold in my chuckles if Jenni wasn't smirking at me. She has a beautiful smile, but her smug grin reveals her naughty side I'd give my left nut to explore further.

Travis's furious gaze strays to the blonde now known as Jenni. "Are you with him?"

Looking up at him, she nods. My heart stops beating when Travis's gaze flicks between Jenni and me for several heart-clutching seconds. I don't know what he sees, but he loosens his grip on her arm not even five seconds later.

Jenni continues our deception by racing my way. My heart begins beating again when I spot her cheeky smile. After throwing her arm around my waist, we dart through the club's double exit doors with her friend shadowing closely behind.

"Oh my god, Jenni, don't you ever do that to me again!" her friend squeals when we hit the sidewalk.

Giggling, Jenni pulls away from me. "I'm sorry, Nicole."

"Why are you laughing?" Panic is relayed in Nicole's low tone. "You nearly had a meeting with a mob boss."

My eyes bug. Isaac may be a little sneaky with his business deal-ings, but calling him a mob boss is a bit of an exaggeration. Somewhat agreeing with my silent thoughts, Jenni rolls her eyes before pacing toward a dark blue BMW parked at the back of Isaac's club.

"You should be the one worried." Jenni's tone is more playful than snarky. "You were *illegally* in his club."

I choke on my spit. Isaac would shit bricks if he knew he had underage girls in his club.

Nicole makes a *pfft* noise with her mouth. "Three months isn't that far away."

Like every girl I've ever known, their conversation veers in another direction without warning. "Did you see the guy Emily was dancing with? Oh my, he was smoking hot."

My nose screws up when Jenni fans her flushed cheeks. While biting down on her lip, Nicole nods. Blinkers light up the dark night sky when Jenni pushes the unlock button on the keys in her hand. When her empty hand wraps around the door handle of a slick new BMW, I cough, signaling I'm still in their presence.

Their attention snaps to me in an instant. In silence, their eyes roam over my body before they drift back to my face. Then they burst out laughing.

Ouch! That's a slap my ego never anticipated.

As their laughter dies down, Jenni removes the tears tracking down her face before connecting her eyes with Nicole. "Give me a minute?"

Nodding, Nicole curls into the passenger seat. Jenni waits for her to latch her belt before shifting on her feet to face me. "I'm sorry about the beer." Her tone is a mix of sympathetic and amused. "And the clothes." The humor in her voice simmers when she notices my ruined shirt and jeans.

I hate the regret in her eyes. "It's okay; I've heard beer is fantastic for split ends." The blush creeping across her neck nearly knocks me on my ass. "You can make it up by going out with me."

She holds my gaze for several terrifying seconds before shaking her head. "I don't date players."

"Oh, come on, I just saved you from a huge beast." I don't know whether it's my shouted words that stop her from entering her car or my honesty. Whatever it is, I'm grateful. "What about if we go out as friends? We could go to the movies? Or grab a bite to eat?"

I'm not a "dating" type of guy, but I'll say anything if it increases my odds of discovering if it's just her neck that blushes when she comes or her whole body.

It feels like a thousand years pass as she takes her time absorbing my face. When her gaze lowers to my body, I stand taller. I'm definitely not as built as my bandmates, but I wouldn't be considered scrawny either.

I swear she can read my thoughts when she murmurs, "I don't sleep with friends."

Smiling, I nod. *We'll see how long your defensive wall stays up.*

"Pick me up next Friday."

She paces toward me with her hand held out palm side up. It falls to her side when I reply, "I can't do Friday."

I shouldn't love her angry face, but I do. "My band has a gig every Friday night, but I can do Saturday?"

As her plump lips curl into an uneasy grin, she raises her hand to its original position. "Phone," she informs my shocked expression.

I yank my cell out of my pocket, unlock the screen, then hand it to her. When she goes into my contacts to add her number, I pray for her not to scroll through the names displayed. Nearly every number in my phone belongs to a girl.

My prayers are left unanswered when she asks, "Should I put my last name or where we met?" I pretend I'm confused by her statement when she adds on, "So you know which Jenni I am? There's already three Jenni's in your phone."

"I'll know which one is yours," I reply, my tone cocky.

I'm planning to add a note the instant she leaves. *Jenni, the firecracker with the knockout smile* will be her display name.

I snatch my phone out of her hand before she can delete her number, then give her a frisky wink. "See you Saturday."

CHAPTER SIX

JENNI

I s there such a thing as a taste for players? If so, I must have it. Why am I attracted to guys who happily admit they're players? You'd think I would have learned my lesson with Christian. But no, instead of ignoring my stupid neurosis, I'm lying in my bed striving to work out how I agreed to go on a date with a guy who's still nameless.

During my trip home from the Dungeon, it dawned on me that I hadn't asked him his name. I don't even have his contact details, for crying out loud. I guess it's lucky we're only going out as "friends."

Leaning over, I grab my phone off the bedside table and send another message to Emily. It's my fifth the past ten minutes. When Nicole and I arrived home last night, we realized neither of us had received a text from Emily to say she made it home safely. Worried out of our minds, Nicole called Emily on repeat. After several long, painstaking minutes, we discovered she was out with Noah—the guy she's been lusting over the past few months.

I knew there was more going on with her last night than she let on. I just don't know why she needed to be sneaky. She could have told us she was leaving the club with Noah, and Nicole and I would have been fine with it. She's an adult who is capable of making her own informed decisions. We wouldn't have babied her—much.

Not long later, my phone dings with a message. Peering down at the screen, I see it's from Emily.

Em: *Going on a date with Noah. I'll call you with all the juicy details tonight. My phone is nearly dead. Love you xx*

I smile, glad she's having fun. She hasn't dated anyone since her disastrous date with Zander years ago. Could you imagine giving your virginity to a guy, then having it broadcast to the entire school?

Emily was called every name under the sun during the three months we had left of school before summer break. One time, I even found her name and cell phone number scribbled on a door in the girls' bathrooms. As much as Christian was a player, he never disrespected me the way Zander did Emily. His rules didn't just protect him; they protected everyone around him as well.

When the alarm on my phone hollers, I reply to Emily's text, throw off my comforter, scamper out of bed, then gallop down the stairs.

"Good morning, Princess," my dad greets me when I hop off the bottom step.

Warmth blooms across my chest. My dad is the number one man in my life. He reminds all the kids in the neighborhood of Father Christmas. His hair is silver, and he has a wiry beard that covers his jawline. He doesn't like to admit it, but his rounded belly also adds to his Santa appeal.

"Good morning, Daddy."

While greeting my dad with a hug, my mom saunters into the kitchen. My mom is often described as having a Barbie doll appearance. She has long blonde hair that sits halfway down her back; she's four inches taller than my five-feet-four-inch height, and she's also eighteen years younger than my dad.

It doesn't take a genius to work out I was born only six months after my parents married, and only eleven months after they met. I'm the very definition of a shotgun wedding baby.

My dad has often told me the story of how they met. He was a partner at the law firm where my mom did her internship. My father had spent eighteen years of his life working his way up the ladder at a very lucrative law agency in Hopeton. He said my mom was a shy twenty-year-old stenographer who made his heart flutter every time she entered the room.

He asked her out numerous times over a period of three months. Every single time she said no. One late Friday afternoon, after my dad had just won a very impressive case, he decided to try his luck one more time.

That time, my mom said yes.

Once their courtship started, my dad helped my mom apply to college. Even with being pregnant and then raising a small child, my mom graduated with distinction and was accepted to attend law school. She's now a partner at the same law firm my dad gained his partnership at over nineteen years ago.

They have what I'd describe as an odd relationship. They communicate every day, but when you watch them interact, they appear more like long-time friends than husband and wife.

My parents aren't lacking money. Our house sits on over an acre of manicured lawns in the middle of town. We have seven bedrooms —actually, it may be eight. I can't remember because I've never used any room but my own. I'm an only child, so it's a little strange we live in such a large house. Even when Emily and Nicole stay over, we all sleep in my room.

Needing a stiff shot of caffeine, I make my way to the coffee machine in the corner of the kitchen.

"Let Maria get that for you." My mom's tone is as snappy as her hands as she shoos me away from the three thousand dollar machine. "It's her job to make you breakfast."

I roll my eyes. Maria is our housemaid. She's the sweetest little old lady I've ever met. She was my dad's nanny when he was a child and became his housemaid before my mom was in the picture. I've always seen her as a grandmother, whereas my mom only sees her as a maid.

"It's fine, Mom; it's just a cup of coffee."

When my dad snickers at my response, my mom's eyes narrow into thin slits. My dad coughs to clear his throat before he pretends to read the newspaper resting next to his empty plate.

Many times the past two years, my mom has requested that my dad hire a new housemaid. Maria is well past retirement age, but neither dad nor I want anyone else. If Maria is happy living with us, Dad and I are more than happy to pretend she's doing the tasks required to fulfill her employment, even when she isn't.

When Mom leaves for the day, Dad and I do the washing and vacuuming, then pretend Maria completed them. My dad only works part-time now that he has also hit retirement age. He prefers spending his days on the golf course instead of in the courtroom.

Once I've finished breakfast with my dad, I throw a load of clothes into the washing machine then make my way back to my room. Just as I enter my room, my phone pings, indicating I've received a text message.

Unknown Number: *Is it Saturday yet?*

My lips tug high as my palms slick with sweat. After saving his number under an appropriate alias, I sit on my king-sized bed to reply to his message.

Me: *Not yet.*

My palms grow clammier when his reply arrives a few seconds later.

Blue-Eyed-Hottie: *Bummer.... do you have any plans today?*

Usually my Sundays are spent with Emily, but she's a little preoccupied today.

Me: *No.*

Blue-Eyed-Hottie: *Do you want to go out today?*

I stare at my phone, pondering what to do. I don't want another player in my life, but I hardly slept a wink last night because I kept daydreaming about his captivating blue eyes and ruggedly handsome features.

Me: *As friends?*

Blue-Eyed-Hottie: *If that's what it will take for you to go out with me, then yes, friends!*

I can't help the smile that forms on my face.

Me: *Okay.*

Blue-Eyed-Hottie: *What's your address?*

My eyes scan my ridiculously oversized room. I don't usually invite strangers to my home. It isn't that I'm a snob; I just hate the thought of being treated differently if they assume I'm rich.

I'm not rich; my parents are.

Me: *Can I meet you in town?*

Blue-Eyed-Hottie: *Alright. Where?*

I rack my brain, struggling to think of somewhere that would be considered a "friendly" location. I'm stumped.

Me: *I'll let you pick . . .*

His reply makes my stomach swirl with unease.

Blue-Eyed-Hottie: *Bronte's Peak.*

Me: *So much for us being friends. . .*

This reply isn't as fast as his former ones.

Blue-Eyed-Hottie: *Oh, so you have been there before? It's daylight. Your virtue can't be tarnished in the middle of the day.*

I giggle loudly. Every teenager knows Bronte's Peak. . . unless they've been living under a gigantic rock.

Me: *Alright, I'll meet you there, but I'm parking in front of the diner.*

Blue-Eyed-Hottie: *Ha, alright. I'll meet you at the diner in an hour?*

My eyes rocket to the clock on my bedside table. I should be able to get ready and to Ravenshoe in an hour—barely!

Me: *Okay, see you in an hour.*
Blue-Eyed-Hottie: *I look forward to it.*

I spend the next thirty minutes getting ready before rushing downstairs. "Bye, Dad, I'll be back this afternoon!" I push out while sprinting to the blue BMW my dad gave me on my eighteenth birthday two months ago.

I arrive at the café ten minutes later than we arranged. As my car glides down the dusty parking lot, I spot the mysterious blond. He's leaning against the front window of the café with his knee bent up. His dark blue jeans, tight shirt, and fitted jacket reveal he has a nice runner's build. He's not overly bulky with muscles, but he's not skinny either. He has a perfect body that makes my pulse race.

When he notices me pulling into a parking spot a few places up from him, he smiles before pushing off the wall. He's confident in his own skin, even a little bit cocky as he struts to my car.

I pop open my car door. "Sorry I'm late."

Because he's wearing aviator sunglasses, I can't see his captivating blue eyes. *Dammit!*

"That's okay, I only just got here myself."

When his head angles to the side as if his eyes are absorbing my body, I roll my shoulders and stand straighter. Since he didn't give me much notice, I threw on the first outfit I stumbled upon in my closet. If I'd known he was going to eyeball me like a freak, I would have put in more effort.

Once his perusal is over, he nudges his head to the cafe. "Are you hungry?"

I'm not because I just finished eating breakfast when he messaged me, but with the awkwardness of first dates already lingering, I'll eat again just to force my hands to do something other than fidgeting with my floral skirt like they are now.

"Yep! I'm hungry." I conceal my apprehension with a friendly tone.

What is it about this guy that makes me act like a blushing idiot? *He's just a guy, Jenni. A player you poured freezing cold beer over just last night.*

When images of last night replay in my head, I can't stop the smile that forms on my mouth. The surprise on his face over my audacity also settles the butterflies fluttering in my stomach.

Noticing my smile, a crass grin etches on the handsome stranger's face. I'm tempted to ask why he is smiling, but the curl of his hand over mine stops me. Remaining quiet, he guides me through the entrance of the café. Because it's too early for the lunch crowd, we're promptly seated at one of the window booths that has spectacular views of Bronte's Peak.

"It's so beautiful," I whisper with my eyes arrested on the dazzling blue ocean.

"It sure is."

When I turn to face him, my pulse quickens. He isn't looking at the scenery. His beautifully tormented eyes are staring straight at me. They reveal his hunger, making heat rush to my cheeks. He watches me with hooded eyes, throwing down the blinders I erect specifically for men like him. The prospect of him breaking through my walls makes nervous goosebumps spread across my skin. I won't mention what it does to the lower regions of my body. A gaze shouldn't be a turn on—his is.

Our intense stare off is interrupted by the waitress handing me a menu. Grateful for a break from the intensity of his stare, I use the menu to hide my flaming cheeks. This guy's sexiness is off the Richter scale. Just sitting across from him for five minutes already has me wanting to break my rules on not dating players.

The stranger's deep chuckle vibrates the menu when he notices I'm using it to hide. "Don't go hiding." He pulls the menu away from my flaming face. "I've been wondering if you blush anywhere other than your neck when you're flustered."

My cheeks go from a slight pink hue to flaming-with-embarrass-ment red. I inwardly sigh when the waitress saves the day for the second time by asking if we're ready to order. My companion chuckles at my eager nod before placing an order for a burger, fries, and a milkshake. When I request a cup of coffee, his confused gaze strays to me.

"I only had breakfast an hour ago," I admit.

Shaking his head, he grins a smile that makes my heart flip.

Incapable of waiting a second longer, I blurt out, "What's your name?"

The waitress' brows meet. She doesn't know us, yet even she can feel the sexual attraction bristling between the mysterious stranger and me, making it even more awkward that I don't know his name.

CHAPTER SEVEN

NICK

When the waitress skedaddles away to prepare our order, I stare at Jenni, striving to work out what is it about her that made me lose sleep last night. She's incredibly beautiful, but it feels like there's more at stake here than my wish to strip her naked and see how flushed I can really make her.

I arrived at the café twenty minutes before the time we agreed to meet.

Twenty. Whole. Goddamn. Motherfucking. Minutes.

I was getting so anxious she wasn't going to show, when I spotted her little blue car pulling into the parking lot, I sighed like a girl. You'd think her knee-length skirt, dusty pink shirt, and matching cashmere cardigan would have lessened my desire to have her beneath me, but nope. If anything, it made it worse.

At first glance, you'd swear she was on her way to mass. . . until you spotted the killer high white stiletto boots she's wearing. The chunky heel makes her taller while adding a bit of sexiness to her seemingly innocent ensemble.

My dick twitches when my focus shifts from her body to her face. The strobing lights at the club made me misread the true color of her hair. It's more a strawberry blonde than platinum; her eyes are a lighter shade of blue than mine, and the pink hue I saw on her neck last night extends to her cheeks when she's flustered.

It isn't just her beauty I'm taking note of, though. The attraction bristling between us is so obvious, I'm tempted to pull her pouty lips to mine by the back of her head. I would if the waitress didn't foil my brilliant idea by returning to fill Jenni's cup with coffee. I was surprised when she only ordered a cup of coffee, but also grateful. I may have died from malnutrition if she hadn't agreed to a late breakfast.

When the waitress finishes filling Jenni's mug, Jenni mumbles a "thanks" before her wide eyes float to mine. Spotting my smirk, she shoots daggers at me, unimpressed.

"I'm glad *you're* enjoying yourself. The waitress thinks I'm a tart." Her smile weakens her scorn. She's not angry. She's more amused than anything.

After adding cream and sugar to her coffee, she lifts her mug to her mouth. Her lips purse when she blows on the scorching hot liquid. The sexy curve of her mouth has my dick stiffening so quickly it's almost painful.

When she peers at me over the rim of her mug, her brows furrow. "You okay?"

Smiling to hide my grimace, I nod. I'm not a fan of lying, but I don't think she would appreciate me telling her she makes my dick rock hard when we're on a "friends only" date.

Hoping to smooth the deep groove between her brows, I disclose, "My name is Nick."

She eyes me curiously for several long seconds before shrugging.

"What?" I'm confused by her response. I thought she'd smile upon discovering my name, not shrug it off.

Her lips curl into a smirk. "It's nothing. I just pictured you as more of a Jacques, Pierre, or Christian." When I gag at her hideous choice of names, her smirk transforms into her knockout smile. "They're names more suitable for players; Nick just seems too. . .

nice." Her voice gains an edge of wittiness at the end of her sentence.

"Clearly, you've never met a *true* player." I give her a cocky wink. "You won't call them anything but Nick once I'm done with you."

She laughs. "I know more about players than you're giving me credit for, *Nick.*" She says my name with a chuckle.

I'm about to demand names and numbers, but our waitress returns to our table with my food, saving me from making a fool out of myself for the third time in twenty-four hours. Thank fuck. I'm a lover not a fighter. I also don't hunt down past dates of girls I hardly know.

But, I guess, I've never been on a real date either. . .

Over the next thirty minutes, Jenni and I sit in complete silence. It isn't awkward. It's more interesting than anything. She watches me consume my burger while occasionally stealing fries from my plate.

The silence gives me time to learn her little traits. Like how she always double dips her fries in ketchup before popping them into her mouth. How she chews slowly as if she's relishing every bite. That she blinks just before she swallows, and that her pupils dilate every time she busts me staring at her.

I like her last trait the most.

Once I've paid our bill, we leave the cafe via the door we entered only an hour ago.

"Thanks for the coffee." Jenni paces toward her car. "It was. . . *nice.*"

Grinning, I follow after her as my brain works hard to come up with a way I can convince her to stay a little longer. The hour we've spent together wasn't nearly long enough. I didn't get the chance to charm her with my intelligence, much less woo her out of her panties with my wit.

"Did you want to go for a walk on the beach?" I fight not to roll my eyes at my corniness. I don't do romance and flowers, but using the world's worst pickup line is supposedly ay-oh-fucking-kay.

There's only one thing I've ever done at that beach. It wasn't walking on it.

When Jenni spins around to face me, I switch the expression on my face to a more gentlemanly one. She sees straight through my act. "Thanks, but I really should get going." She purses her lips. "I'm not in the mood for sand in my pants."

Even knowing she's teasing me doesn't stop my dick from hardening. "Maybe next time." My tone is confident there will be a next time because I'm not taking no for an answer.

I need to rethink my plans when Jenni replies, "Maybe?" After hopping into her car, her eyes lift to mine. "Bye."

Her smug grin enlarges with every inch she reverses away from me. She thinks she won. I've yet to reach the same conclusion. After seeing how much she blushes and the fact she doesn't fall for my tricks, I'm one hundred percent confident I need to see inside her panties.

I just need to up my game first—because I think this player just met his match.

Tina chuckles when I enter the Dungeon. "That was quick."

"If given the chance, I'll be more than happy to show you *exactly* how long I last," I reply, strolling toward Isaac's office.

Tina's laughter dies down when I close the office door. Sensing my presence, Isaac's dark gray eyes lift from the barrage of paperwork he's perusing. He drinks in my attire, his brows stitching when his eyes land on the jacket I only pull out for special occasions.

"You went on an actual date?" His voice is as high as his brow.

"Yep!" I chuckle. "And I even ate real food." I'm not a dating type of guy. . . unless certain parts of the female anatomy are on the menu.

I slump into a black leather chair opposite Isaac's large wooden desk before connecting my eyes with his. "Whatcha looking at?"

His sullied expression grows. "Just some personal stuff."

He gathers the paperwork into a pile. Once he has them nicely stacked, he leans back in his chair, sending the squeak of worn leather into my ears. My interests pique when he locks his eyes with mine. I've never seen them filled with as much hope as they have right now.

"How much do you know about the girl Noah was talking about yesterday?" His tone is more serious than the one he was using moments ago.

I adjust my position in his uncomfortable chair before answering, "I don't know her at all."

My reply is honest. Noah mentioned an Emily when we assisted Jacob in pulling his famous panty-dropping prank months ago, but other than yesterday, he's never mentioned her to me before. I asked him to help us out in the hope of getting our band's name mentioned to Isaac's music executive friend, but instead of talking up the band, he used the time to talk about some chick he only met a handful of times.

My knee bobs up and down when Isaac asks, "Can you see what you can find out about her for me?"

I prop my ankle onto my knee to hide its bounce. My brother has an annoying habit of studying my every move, and I don't want to add fuel to his annoying neurosis.

Wanting to keep the focus off me, I ask, "What's your interest in her?"

He didn't seem interested when Noah went on and on and on about Emily yesterday, so my curiosity is piqued as to why he wants information now.

"Just see what you can find out, then I'll give your band a mention to Cormack." His words are practically growled, but they have both my heart and ego paying attention.

"Seriously?" I've been doing shit chores for him for months

hoping he'd mention our band to his music executive friend, so if I have to snoop on Noah's love life for that to happen, I'm willing to do that.

When Isaac nods, I say, "I'll see what I can find out."

Smirking, he opens his drawer, gathers out a handful of photos then hands them to me. The first photo is a pretty brunette in a fluorescent yellow dress. She's standing on the edge of a dance floor, her face etched with concern as she stares at something in the distance. The image is grainy, as if it were printed off the security cameras Isaac has installed around his nightclubs.

"Is this her?"

Isaac smirks before dipping his chin in confirmation. I can understand Noah's fascination. She's stunningly beautiful—if you're into brunettes.

When I flick to the next photo, a line of sweat dots my forehead. The same girl is pictured wedged between Jenni and Nicole. She has her arms wrapped around their waists as they saunter down the entrance of the Dungeon nightclub.

Oh shit.

If the girl Noah is interested in is friends with Jenni, that not only means she could ruin my plan to get into Jenni's panties; she could also stop our band from making it big.

Fuck!

CHAPTER EIGHT

NICK

"Do you need a lift? Or do you often stand on the corner?" I fill my tone with cheekiness to hide my excitement. I drove to Erkinsvale hoping to see Jenni, and to my surprise, the first person I stumble upon is her. She's standing on the corner of a busy intersection, waiting to cross.

Ever since our date weeks ago, I haven't been able to get her out of my fucking head. I reached out to her a few times to schedule a second date, but all my calls were forwarded to her voicemail, so my ego decided to spend its Monday afternoon driving to her Hicksville town. I had no clue what I planned to do when I got here. I just wanted a chance to talk to her. I knew it would only be a matter of time before Emily warned her to stay away from me, but I don't give up easily. When I want something, I don't stop until I get it.

I want Jenni.

I want her underneath me.

I want her in my bed.

And I want her screaming my name when she comes.

I'm torn from my wicked thoughts when Jenni's light blue eyes stray my way. Air escapes her nostrils when she discovers who's accosting her. With a snarl, she pivots on her heels and briskly strolls down the sidewalk.

Not willing to let her flee without hearing me out, I yank my truck down the side street. Numerous motorists honk their horns, angered that I ran a red light. I didn't have much choice. With how fast Jenni is fleeing, I needed to act quickly so I didn't lose her from my sight.

Once I'm illegally parked in a handicapped space, I undo my seatbelt, throw open my door, then bolt across the bustling main street of Erkinsvale. For its low population, there are a lot of people milling around.

I use my body to stop Jenni's quick strides down the street. "Just give me five minutes."

When she tries to sidestep me, I block her path again. Her angry eyes lift to glare into mine.

Such a firecracker.

"I don't date players." Her voice is sterner than her little stature should be able to pull off.

"I know that, but I thought we had fun the other weekend?"

Incapable of harnessing my desires for a second longer, I rake my eyes down her body. This girl is a chameleon. She adapts her outfits to her surroundings. Today she's wearing a pair of ripped jeans, white Van shoes, and a one-shoulder, loose-flowing crochet shirt with a tight white cami underneath. She's full on casual, yet she's still as hot as hell.

Noticing my prolonged gawk, Jenni's brow arches high into her hairline. I smile at her. I was perving, so there's no use lying. She has a nice body I can't help but look at. Sue me.

"Your band has a song dedicated to how much of a player you are."

It takes a shit ton of effort not to throw my fist into the air. I fucking love that song. Noah was stirring shit when he wrote it, but it's one of those songs that once you hear it, you can't forget it. I was ecstatic when the band added it to our playlist a few months ago. Our fans love it, and before Noah hooked up with Emily, he benefited from it just as much as I did.

Unhappy with my lack of remorse, Jenni rolls her eyes as her lips curve into a ghost-like grin. It isn't her knockout smile, but I'll take any she's willing to give.

"You're unbelievable." She skirts past me then marches down the street.

I throw my hands in the air. "I'm more than happy to show you how *truly* unbelievable I am."

Several locals stop what they're doing to gawk at me. They're not the only attention I'm gaining, though. Jenni has pivoted to face me. She's still walking, just pacing backward. "Better luck next time."

Stealing my chance to reply, she darts across the street and curls into her blue BMW. Now she's wearing her knockout smile.

Jenni - 2

Me - a big fat 0.

A dismal score won't stop me. She can pretend all she likes that she doesn't want me, but I know that's part of the game. Anytime you tell someone they can't have something, they want it even more. It's physics—or some shit like that.

Once Jenni's car is no longer in my vision, I hotfoot it back to my truck. My teeth grit when I find a parking attendant in the process of giving me a ticket. "I was gone for like two minutes."

I snatch the ticket off my windshield before pivoting to face the balding, middle-aged douchebag. He's not the least bit concerned by my anger. He seems pleased. Shrugging, he mumbles something under his breath about my brother not owning this town before climbing into his dated sedan and taking off in the direction Jenni just went.

After scrunching up my ticket, I throw it on the floor of my truck, hop into the driver's seat, then reverse out of the parking lot. Getting inside Jenni's panties will be worth a one hundred and eighty dollar fine. She might even be worth double that.

Halfway back to Ravenshoe, my cell phone rings. You can imagine my surprise when I peer down at the screen and see Slater is calling me. I'm as stunned as fuck.

Shrugging off my confusion, I hit the call button then press my phone to my ear. "Hey, I'm heading to rehearsal now."

My confusion doubles when I notice the time on the clock in my car radio. I still have an hour before I need to be at practice, so why is he calling me?

Some of my confusion eases when Slater snarls, "Practice has been canceled, fuckface," but it does little to subdue my worry. The only time the band has canceled a rehearsal the past three years was when Noah's brother committed suicide. That can mean only one thing: something is going down.

"Is everything alright?" I ask, talking through cotton-mouth.

Slater exhales deeply. "Not that you'd care, but Jacob is in some deep shit. He went and beat some guy nearly to death with his bare hands. Noah is getting him a lawyer, but it doesn't look good for Jakeyboy."

Not giving me a chance to reply, he disconnects the call.

I don't know what's more shocking: the fact Slater called me, or that Jacob has been arrested. Jacob is huge bitch, but he's a teddy bear. I didn't think he had an angry bone in his body.

"What are you doing here on a Monday afternoon?" Isaac orders a nip of whiskey from Tina before filling the vacant stool next to me.

I take a swig out of my beer before answering, "Rehearsal got canceled."

With a crystal glass in her hand, Tina sashays our way. Her hips have an extra swing to them, and she's fluttering her eyelashes at a completely oblivious Isaac. A chuckle rumbles in my chest when she slams down the glass of whiskey on the bar top with force, annoyed by Isaac's lack of attention.

Isaac stops undoing his cufflinks to glare at her. I can tell he's not impressed Tina stained his expensive suit with smelly, brown liquid, but Tina hasn't reached the same conclusion as me. Grateful she's finally caught his eye, she smiles broadly before she bats her lashes again.

The obvious smacks into her hard and fast when Isaac says, "Leave the bottle." His tone is firm, ensuring she knows there's no possibility of her title changing from employee to bed companion anytime soon. Sighing, Tina makes her way to patrons requesting her service.

Once she is out of earshot, I whisper to Isaac, "Put her out of her misery." When his confused eyes stray to mine, I nudge my head to Tina.

A smug grin crosses Isaac's face. "I already have; that's why she wants more."

I chuckle before I can stop myself. I'm not surprised he uses his "player" skills on his staff; I learned most of my best tricks from him.

When Tina hears me laughing, I swear I can see steam billowing out of her ears. I stop watching her anger stretch from her stomach to her face when Isaac asks, "Why was rehearsal canceled?"

I wait for him to swallow his nip of whiskey before replying, "Noah's friend Jacob got arrested for battery."

Nodding, Isaac pours another generous serving of whiskey.

With alcohol heating my veins, I'm more chatty than usual. "Slater said Jacob nearly beat a guy to death with his bare hands." My voice relays my surprise. I'm still stunned.

Isaac freezes with his glass halfway to his lips. He's staring into space, his mind ticking a million miles an hour. I can see how fast it's working in his eyes.

He crashes back to earth by downing his second nip just as eagerly as the first. After placing his empty glass on the counter, his dilated eyes drift to me. "Do you know this guy Jacob?"

My nose screws up. "Not really. He's more a friend of Noah's. He's a huge bastard, though, nearly the size of Travis."

Isaac racks his knuckles on the bar top. "Tina, I'm heading out. If I'm not back by close, make sure Hugo places the day's takings into the safe."

He squeezes my shoulder. "Don't forget to pay your tab before you leave."

I roll my eyes. "Yeah, sure, no worries." My voice is lined with sarcasm.

Isaac laughs while strolling out of the nightclub. I've never seen him so eager to leave before. Usually, he's the last man standing.

CHAPTER NINE

JENNI

When I enter the parking lot at Bronte's Peak, I spot Emily standing next to a red truck. I pull into the empty space at the very end of the lot before jumping out of my car. My steps are eager, beyond excited to meet the guy she's been gushing about nonstop the past two months. Emily and Noah planned a BBQ so their friends could meet one another. At the start, I was hesitant. Nick is Noah's bandmate, so the possibility of him attending the BBQ is high.

I nearly backed out, but one glance into Emily's puppy dog eyes made me cave within seconds. That and the fact I can't get Nick out of my head. I know he's a player, but no one can accuse the chase of being boring.

When I reach Emily, she clasps my hand in hers. "Jenni, this is my boyfriend, Noah." Her voice is extra sugary since it's fueled with excitement. "Noah, this is my best friend, Jenni."

"Hi, Noah. It's nice to finally meet you."

When I accept his offer of a handshake, he smiles a full-toothed grin. "It's nice putting a name to a face. Emily talks about you all the time."

My knees go a little weak when a set of perfectly placed dimples pop into his cheeks. Emily's description of him was spot on. He's dark and mysterious, but smoking hot. Upon spotting my flaming cheeks, Emily giggles. Jealousy will never be a concern of ours. We respect each other too much to step over any line that would affect our friendship.

When Noah suggests we head down to the beach, I sling my arms around Emily's neck. "Photos don't do him justice. *My god.*"

She nods. "I know. It's like his sexiness burns up the film or something."

When we reach the stairwell that will take us down to the blue water beach below, we interlock our elbows. Our climb down the hundreds of wooden stairs of Bronte's Peak is filled with conversation. Emily tells me everything she and Noah have done the past two months, while I update her on my less than stellar social life.

After trekking across white sandy dunes, Noah introduces me to two of his band members, Slater and Marcus. Slater looks slightly out of place on a beach wearing a pair of jeans, a gray Harley Davidson shirt, and black motorcycle boots. His blond dreadlocks sit just above his shoulders, and his strong jawline has a small amount of stubble covering it. He's attractive, but in a bad boy, *your momma might faint* way.

Marcus has ravishing dark skin and the most mesmerizing green eyes you could imagine. He looks more suitably dressed for a day at the beach in a pair of long black board shorts and a white t-shirt. He has a face that makes your heart beat faster and your head a little woozy.

"And this is Nick."

Slater's brows shoot up from Noah's awkward introduction. If Slater and Marcus weren't already suspicious of our prior meetings, they are now.

"Hi, Nick." The fluttering of my heart can't be concealed by my short greeting. There's no denying the sexual attraction between

Nick and me. I just refuse to be another name on his long list of conquests.

Nick's chin dips in greeting before he scans my body. Today I'm wearing a pair of denim shorts and a midriff top. I tried to convince myself it was perfect beachwear, but in reality, I just wanted to see if I could spark a reaction out of Nick. From the way his eyes bugged when they zoomed in on my practically bare thighs, I'd say my plan has worked.

Over the next two hours, we sit around the campfire Noah lit. Slater keeps me in stitches by telling me stories about Marcus and Noah in their teen years. I've only known Slater for two hours, but it feels like I've known him for a lifetime. That's how well we clicked. And Marcus. . . my god. He's the very definition of a sweetheart. He's well spoken, polite, and always acts like a gentleman.

Nick, on the other hand, all he has done the past two hours is glare at me. He's not happy about the instant bond I've created with Slater and has no qualms ensuring everyone else is aware of it as well. I've tried to settle the tension. Any time I catch his gaze, I offer him a small smile. Very rarely does he smile back.

Frustrated, I make my way to the cooler to grab a drink. It's not hot; I just need something to take the edge off Nick's heated gaze. I've just snagged a can of Coke when the hairs on the back of my neck stand to attention. My lungs struggle for air when a body warms my back. I should spin around to see who is approaching me, but I don't. I know who it is. The electricity that zapped between us the past two hours is still in abundance, assuring me it's Nick.

His hot breath fans my earlobe when he asks, "Do you want to go for a walk?"

I'm prepared to shake my head, but when my eyes flick up to his, my defenses crumble. Ignoring his calls and messages were easy, but having him standing directly in front of me makes it impossible to deny my attraction to him.

When I nod, he caresses my hand in his then guides us to the water's edge. The sun is setting, illuminating Bronte's Peak in shades of orange. I stop marveling at the beautiful views when Nick asks, "Why aren't you returning any of my calls?"

I sit cross-legged on the sand. "I already told you: I don't date players."

"So you don't talk to Emily on the phone?"

When he sits down next to me, his thigh rubs my kneecap. I don't care what anyone says, I swear a spark ignited inside me when our skin touched. I shift my eyes from the ocean to him. His eyes are as murky as the waters of Bronte's Peak when it's plunged into darkness. He's either genuinely frustrated by my limited contact the past month or a mighty fine actor. I have a feeling it may be a bit of both.

"I talk to Emily on the phone—every day, actually."

He licks his dry lips. "Then why can't you talk to me? I want to be your friend." If I missed the sexual innuendo in his tone, I sure as hell can't miss his avid scan of my body.

"I don't sleep with friends." My hammering heart minces up my words.

My breathing shallows when he locks his heavy-hooded gaze with me and murmurs, "There are things we can do that won't require sleeping."

Goosebumps skate across my skin when he unexpectedly presses a kiss under my left earlobe. He's barely touching me, but every inch of my skin burns up. When he plants another kiss two inches lower than his first, I slant my head, giving him unrestricted access to my neck.

"Don't deny it; I know you feel it too." The deep rumble of his voice vibrates my reservations straight out of my body. I feel its shudder all the way to my pussy.

"Why fight something you know you'll never beat? Just surrender. It'll be a lot more fun this way."

When he pulls away, a shameful moan escapes my mouth. He smirks, knowing he has me trapped in a lust haze. With a cocky wink that reveals this is just the beginning, he stands, pivots, then strolls back toward the campfire. I watch him interrupt Emily and Noah in the middle of a make-out session. After he bids them farewell, he climbs the stairwell that leads to the parking lot.

Once he disappears from my view, my eyes drift back to the ocean. I'm utterly confused by what just happened. I don't know why. You'll never make sense of a player. They're unexplainable.

I've just brushed half the sand off my backside when a deep voice from behind cautions, "Don't give him what he wants."

When I spin around, I'm met with the concerned face of Slater. His brows are scrunched together so tightly, a large V has burrowed into his forehead, and his thick arms are crossed in front of his chest. Nothing but honesty shines in his eyes when he says, "The instant you give him what he wants, he'll be gone."

"I know," I reply sullenly. I know exactly what he's saying, but it doesn't make my attraction to Nick any less intense. I haven't experienced anything this crazy in a very long time—if ever.

After giving me a wary smile, Slater paces over and wraps his arm around my shoulders. In silence, we make our way back to the firepit. While the sun rapidly sets, Noah and the guys from the band pack away the equipment we've been using. Bronte's Peak only has natural light, so it won't be long before the beach plunges into darkness.

Like my mood could get any worse, the stairs of Bronte's Peak test how low it can go. The beach is gorgeous, but the stairs you climb to access it are a mood killer. By the time I make it up to the top, my legs feel like jelly, and my body is covered in a dense layer of sweat.

"It was a pleasure meeting you." Marcus slings his arms around my shoulders to give me a quick, friendly hug.

Since I'm juggling a cooler and a picnic blanket, I return his farewell with a one-armed hug. "The pleasure was all mine."

After promising Emily and Noah he'll make sure I get to my car safely, Slater and I stroll down the nearly isolated parking lot.

"They're so cute together." I wave goodbye to Emily and Noah driving out of the lot in a rusty truck before shifting on my feet to face Slater. He has his fingers lodged down his throat as he makes gagging noises. I giggle at his playfulness. We were strangers only hours ago, but I already know he isn't a fan of public PDAs.

Slater stops at the side of a black Harley Davidson. "This is me; where are you parked?"

I'm not surprised he rides a motorcycle. His whole persona screams biker.

"I'm over there." I point to my BMW parked two spots down from a large black truck.

"Okay, hold up. I'll walk you to your car."

He dumps some containers into the saddlebags on his bike before twisting to face me. The caution on his face makes me smile. He's panicked that he's giving me mixed signals. He shouldn't be. He's a cutie, and any girl would be lucky to have him, but there are no sparks firing between us whatsoever. Slater knows it. I know it. Hell, the entire world most likely knows it. . . except perhaps Nick.

"I can manage," I assure Slater, stopping him mid-stride.

Certain a smile can't relay my thanks for a wonderful afternoon, I lean in to give him a friendly hug. He returns my gesture, just more awkwardly than mine.

When I walk to my car, my pupils widen. Nick is stepping out of the black truck parked two spots up from my car, his chest thrusting up and down as his narrowed gaze shoots daggers at Slater. He's clearly pissed.

After several terrifying seconds, he nudges his head to his truck, wordlessly demanding I get in. I shouldn't love the arrogance beaming out of him, but I do. My palms are slicking with sweat just from the dominance he's exuding while his senses are clutched by jealousy.

Noticing my wavering constraint, Slater warns, "Think about it."

Nick's already narrowed eyes slit even more. He's giving Slater clear signals to back away. . . so does my head when I read the sticker on the back of his truck.

My other ride screams my name.

When my eyes missile to Nick, he winks. His cockiness seals his fate. You can't change a player, and I don't date players—nor do I have sex with them.

Cranking my neck to Slater, I mouth a silent goodbye before hotfooting it to my car. Dirt kicks up under my feet from my mad dash. I'm so eager to leave, I'm practically running. When my eyes unwillingly float to Nick, a victorious grin stretches across his face. He thinks he won. I haven't reached the same conclusion.

His foolishness is unveiled in the most brilliant way when I jack-knife to the left. His mouth gapes as his brows furrow. When I reach my car, I throw open the door, toss my picnic blanket and cooler inside, then curl into the driver's seat. I muster a fake smile before reversing out of my spot like I'm outrunning a tornado.

A dust cloud rises in my wake when I leave Nick and Slater standing across from each other in an intense standoff.

CHAPTER TEN

NICK

When Jenni's car rockets out of the parking lot like a mad woman, leaving nothing but a cloud of dust, Slater's chuckle pummels my chest. "You just had your shit handed to you on a silver platter."

Smirking like the smug fuck he is, he kicks over his motorcycle, then takes off in the direction Jenni went. I stand still, frozen and confused as fuck. I could have sworn Jenni was ready to give me what I wanted. It's been an afternoon of mixed messages, but I thought our plans tonight were sealed after our exchange on the beach.

I spotted Jenni the instant she glided down the stairs of Bronte's Peak nearly three hours ago. Her teeny tiny shorts and midriff top had my dick paying careful attention to every move she made. That's not surprising considering her outfit didn't leave much to the imagination. Nearly ninety percent of her skin was on display, and I wasn't the only one taking notice.

I've lost count on the number of times I clenched my fists today. Slater's corny ass jokes were rewarded with Jenni's knockout smile, but anytime I gained her attention, all I got was a smirk.

That pissed me the fuck off.

I only turned up to the BBQ today because Noah said Emily was bringing her friends. I generally avoid these types of get-togethers like the plague. I spend enough time with my bandmates practicing five days a week and performing at Mavs every Friday night that I don't need to spend my Sundays with them as well.

When Jenni headed to the cooler for a drink, I realized that would be my only opportunity to speak to her without her posse of male fans listening in. I couldn't have my bandmates discovering my plan, because the instant they know I'm interested in Jenni, they'll warn her to stay away from me.

When I asked Jenni if she wanted to go for a walk, her light blue eyes weren't the only set fixated on me. Slater was eyeballing our exchange from the side, but thankfully, Marcus stopped him from interfering.

My jaw tensed when Jenni gave me the same excuse she's given me the past two times I've asked her out. *She doesn't date players.* I don't want to date her; I want her underneath me. That's why I went in all gung-ho. I knew the instant I got my hands on her, her defensive wall would crumble.

I was right.

One innocent peck on her neck, and she was melting under my embrace. If we weren't being spied on by Slater, I reckon I could have taken her on the very beach we were sitting on. Unfortunately, no amount of spark could stop me from feeling Slater's furious wrath burning a hole in the back of my head.

Confident I had a night with Jenni in the bag, I jumped up from the sand and made my way to Emily and Noah. I nodded at Slater on the way past, ensuring he was aware I knew he was watching.

I waited in my truck for over thirty minutes before Jenni showed up. When I noticed she was with Slater, I figured it was best for me to stay in my truck until he left. It was only when Jenni wrapped her arms around his neck did I feel the need to mark my territory.

I glared at Slater, warning him to back the fuck off. Jenni may not be mine, but she sure as fuck isn't going to be his either. When Jenni's lusty eyes took in the sticker on the back of my truck, I gave her a flirty wink. I had every intention of making her scream my name the instant she got her ass in my truck. But for some unknown fucking reason, she left me hanging.

Although my ego is still feeling the sting of her rejection, it will only take a couple of minutes to recover. Then. . . then nothing will stop me.

I just need to get her alone.

My plan would be a lot simpler if Noah and Emily did anything without our bandmates. Every time I turn up to one of their lame ass BBQs the past three months, Slater and Marcus are there.

Marcus is okay, but Slater. . . he's a fucking thorn in my backside. He keeps himself so firmly attached to Jenni, he must watch her pee to ensure I don't get her alone. He never lets her out of his sight—not once. He's worse than a fucking leech.

Do you remember when you were a kid and you desperately wanted the latest toy or gadget? You did everything in your power to get it. Well, that's the best way I can explain my wish to bed Jenni. I want it; I need it, and I'll do anything to get it.

This is why I've decided drastic action needs to be taken.

"I'd like a haircut, please, and I want her to do it." I point to Jenni, who is in the back of the salon sweeping up hair from the floor.

The lady manning the counter at Aunt Dee's Hairdressing Salon cranks her neck to Jenni before returning her eyes to me. "She's only an apprentice."

"That's fine," I reply a little too quickly.

My plan was to act cool, not desperate, but that flew out the window the instant I saw Jenni. Even doing something as simple as sweeping hair into a dustbin is a riveting visual.

My heart leaps out of my chest when the lady behind the counter screeches, "Jen, you have a customer!"

Her nasally voice shreds my eardrums and apparently kickstarts Jenni's heart. She leaps up from her crouched position before skipping to the front of the salon. Her broad grin vanishes when she spots me standing behind the counter, and her brisk pace slows. After crossing her arms in front of her chest, she raises her brow. She doesn't speak. She doesn't need to. The angry sneer crinkling her forehead speaks volumes. She's pissed.

Just when I think she's going to toss me to the curb, she nudges her head to the black salon chair she's standing next to. The lady manning the counter stalks me when I span the checkered floor separating us. She's loving the tension. Me. . . not so much.

The closer I get to Jenni, the more her eyes slit. "I just want a trim," I inform her, talking through the brick lodged in my throat.

Not speaking a word, she grabs my shoulders and yanks me into the chair. While spinning the chair to face the mirror, she places a black apron over my torso. She fastens the straps so tight, she cuts off my circulation. Wheezing, I yank the material away from my neck so I can breathe unaided. With a smug grin, she snatches a water bottle off the cart. She drenches my hair and face before dragging a comb through my blond curls. She doesn't stop for knots; she just rips straight through them.

Once my hair sits flat on my head, she moves the scissors in real close to my scalp. I freak the fuck out.

Maybe this wasn't such a good idea.

I stare at her in the mirror, praying to god she doesn't hack my hair to pieces. I'm a confident son of a bitch, but I'm nothing without my hair. I'm not tall, and I don't have a shit-load of muscles, so when my cock is excluded from the equation, my hair is the best thing about me.

Jenni's chest thrusts up and down with every inhalation. She appears truly torn. The crazy beat of my heart slows when she lowers her scissors to the tips of my hair. I suck in my first breath in nearly a minute when she trims the smallest snippet of hair from the ends.

"You're lucky I like your hair." Her growl reveals my worry was warranted. I was minutes away from being scalped.

Over the next twenty minutes, I watch her trim my hair. The silence unveils even more of her traits, such as, how every time she snips the scissors, she bites her bottom lip, and that her nose screws up more times than her brows furrow. I occasionally catch her gaze in the mirror, but the instant she sees me watching, her eyes dart away.

"There you go, all done." She flicks off my apron, sending fragments of hair into the air. "Unless you want me to shave you?"

Her mood is more playful than it was when I arrived, but not enough for me to feel comfortable with her having a blade near my throat. "Thanks for the offer, but I'm good."

I shadow her to the counter located at the front of the salon. She rings up a sale on the cash register before locking her eyes with mine. "That'll be eighty dollars."

I choke on my spit. "What?"

My wide eyes dart to the prices displayed next to the cash register. It states a men's trim is only eighteen dollars.

My eyes stray back to Jenni when she explains, "Those are regular prices; you got special treatment today."

She holds out her hand, wordlessly requesting I pay up. Smirking at her cheek, I hand her my credit card. The lady who was serving at the counter when I entered watches our exchange with a hint of amusement on her face. She's enjoying her daily dose of daytime soap opera drama so much, I'm surprised she hasn't gotten herself some popcorn.

Jenni hands me my credit card and receipt. "Thank you so much; be sure to book another appointment in six to eight weeks—or never, whatever suits you better."

I slide my card back in my wallet. "What time is your break today?"

"I don't have a break." I don't need to see her eyes to know they're narrowed. I heard their squint in her snappy tone.

Never one to back away when challenged, I swing my gaze to the lady lurking behind us, spying on our exchange without apology. "Can you see them?" Shock crosses the lady's face; I'd guess her to be in her mid-fifties. "The sparks, can you see the sparks firing between us?"

The hairdresser tries to hide her smile, but the corners of her lips turn upwards, exposing her deceit. With a broad grin, she briskly nods.

My eyes drift back to Jenni. "See, even she can see it."

"Aunt Dee, you're supposed to be on my side." Jenni slaps the smiling lady's arm.

Her aunt's smile enlarges. "I'm sorry, honey, but there are so many sparks flying between you two, I'm getting worried I'm about to combust."

CHAPTER ELEVEN

JENNI

What a traitor!

I can't believe my Aunt Dee is on Nick's side. We share the same blood—where are her family values?

Incapable of ignoring Nick's cocky expression for a second longer, I huff before storming back to the pile of hair I was clearing away before he arrived. He and Aunt Dee can continue their conversation without me!

After the hair is taken care of, I enter the storeroom to remove the towels from the dryer. With my Aunt's salon being the most popular in our town, I have enough laundry to keep my thoughts occupied for the next several hours—way longer than it will take to get *him* out of my mind.

By the time I've finished folding and restacking the entire linen cabinet, I'm overdue for my break. My heart rate has returned to a normal level, but my mind is still hazy. I'm not sure what Nick's plan was today, but I'm reasonably sure he won't do it again. He was scared out of his mind when I pushed my scissors to his scalp. Rightfully so, it was a close call.

I pop my head into the main section of the salon. "I'm going on my break, Aunt Dee."

After collecting my satchel, I pace toward the back door. I've been working at my aunt's salon the past year as an apprentice. Hairdressing isn't really my thing, but it's the only place my dad would agree to let me work. He didn't want me working at all, believing my time was best used on my studies, but my mom thought it would be a good life lesson. To my surprise, I agree with my mom. I've learned a lot about business from Aunt Dee, and her clients are great sounding boards when annoying men won't get the hint that you're not interested in them.

I throw my satchel strap over my shoulder as I exit the back door of the salon. When I lift my gaze, my heart jumps. Nick is leaning against the wall in the alleyway. He has his knee cocked and a cunning grin stretched across his face.

Cursing, I spin around with the hope of stopping the salon door from closing, because once it's shut, it's shut. You can't open it. A string of obscenities runs through my head when a click breaks through my pulse shrilling in my ears. I was too slow. The door is locked firmly in place.

"Damn it!"

Snubbing my sweaty palms, I make a beeline for the sidewalk. My head is hanging low, my heart rate high. Just before I step onto the cracked concrete path, a pair of polished black shoes interrupts my vision. I swallow the lump in my throat before raising my eyes. Stupid move. Now my skin is even clammier. Nick is smiling. Not a half-assed, *I'm cocky* smirk. A full-on, genuine smile.

"Your Aunt told me to wait here for you."

I snap my eyes to the glass window of the salon. My Aunt Dee and salon regular, Shirley, are standing near the window, eyeballing my exchange. When I snarl at them, they flurry away, pretending they weren't spying on me.

My eyes return to Nick when he pleads, "Give me an hour; if you don't want to see me again after that, I'll leave you alone."

"One hour, then you'll leave me alone?" When he nods, I huff, "Fine!"

Undeterred by my snark, Nick grasps my hand in his, then guides us onto the street. When my gaze turns back to the salon, Aunt Dee and Shirley are once again standing at the window with their hands held over their hearts. I roll my eyes at the two sappy romantics before preparing for battle. I only have to survive an hour, then I'll be scot-free. Nick will leave me alone.

Don't ask me why, but disappointment was the first feeling that bombarded me during my unspoken thought. Nick is annoying as hell, but what girl doesn't like being chased?

The smell of grease smacks me in the face when we enter one of the numerous cafes lining the main street of Erkinsvale. This time, when the waitress takes our order, I request an overloaded burger, fries, and a coke. I'm famished since I haven't eaten a thing since breakfast.

"I'll have the same as her," Nick informs the waitress before handing back our menus.

When the waitress leaves to prep our order, Nick scoots closer to my side of the booth. "Hungry today?"

My lips purse. "Not really, I just figured since you were paying, I may as well order the most expensive thing on the menu."

I'm partly lying; I'm starving, but I also did order the most expensive thing I could find.

When Nick laughs, he gains the attention of several patrons in the café—both male and female—and my pussy tingles. Not just because everyone is staring at us, but because Nick's hearty chuckles are vibrating my core, shattering not just the walls I built around my heart specifically to keep him out, but my morals as well.

Once his laughter simmers, he snickers, "At this rate, I'll be broke by the end of the day." He scoots in until our thighs touch. "But I'm sure you'll be worth it."

The most amazing thing happens over the next hour. Nick and I sit in the café like regular friends do. We eat and talk, and not once does he overstep any of the boundaries I place between us.

At first, it feels a little odd, but as our conversation progresses, it reminds me of the chats Emily and I have every time we see each other. He asks about school and what my plans are now that I've graduated. He tells me how his band has been in contact with a music executive, and that they're scheduled to meet him at his head office later this month.

I'm ecstatic for both Nick and his bandmates. Slater has become a close friend of mine, so I'm well aware this is what the band has been aiming for the past three years.

I enjoy my time with Nick so much, I'm reluctant to go back to work. I haven't experienced this side of him before. He's always been overly cocky, and his sexual hunger beams out of him, but today, he made an effort to get to know me instead of what color my panties are.

It feels so natural being around him, we walk back to the salon hand in hand. His palms are as clammy as mine, his pulse just as strong, but the electricity zapping between us makes the less than stellar conditions worthwhile.

Once we reach the entrance, Nick shifts on his feet to face me. Butterflies take off in my stomach when his eyes leisurely assess my face. It seems as if he's taking in each detail, like he may soon lose the opportunity. When he lifts his hand to rub my earlobe, an unexpected moan spills from my lips. It shifts to a growl when he lowers his mouth to give me a heartfelt kiss.

The gentle movements of his mouth and the wicked curls of his tongue have my knees buckling in no time at all. I've never been kissed like this before. It's an all-encompassing embrace that warns of danger while also advising the reward will far exceed the threat. Just like him, it's both dangerous and worthwhile.

When Nick inches back from our embrace, my sluggish eyes open. The excitement tingling low in my core doubles when I notice his eyes are as hooded as mine and his lips just as swollen. There's just one difference: his brows are furled in anger instead of being arched with excitement.

The reason for his sour expression comes to light when he murmurs, "My hour is up."

Ensuring he maintains his side of our deal, he spins on his heels and bolts to his truck parked across the street. The smell of burning rubber lingers in my nostrils when he leaves me standing on the sidewalk utterly dumbfounded.

How can you kiss someone like that and leave? Did he not feel what I felt?

Only once his truck is nothing but a blur do I enter my aunt's salon.

"Oh my goodness, Jenni, when you said he was a player, you failed to mention he is gorgeous!" my Aunt Dee squeals, gaining the attention of customers waiting to be served.

I don't know whether to laugh or cry when Shirley says, "That boy can play me like a fiddle anytime he likes."

Gagging, I stride past the two perverted middle-aged women. I place my satchel in my locker in the back of the salon. When I catch my heated cheeks in the shiny metal, I head to the washroom to splash some water on my face, hoping it will settle the redness.

Nothing works. Just spending the last hour with Nick revealed there's no chance in hell my head will ever overrule my heart when it comes to him, then our kiss sealed my fate.

I'm a goner.

CHAPTER TWELVE

NICK

One fucking kiss. That's all it took. The instant my lips touched hers, I knew I was gone. I want her now more than ever. But I can't have her. I don't do hearts, flowers, and romance. I don't do relationships.

And I don't fuck the same girl more than once.

Today was the first time I've had an actual conversation with a girl. Normally, I do small talk, a few good one-liners to woo them out of their panties, but I don't talk like I just did with Jenni. We actually talked. She told me things she was doing in her life, and I found myself so interested in what she was saying that I wanted to listen.

I even told her about the band getting a meeting with some executives from Destiny Records. She looked genuinely pleased for me. Even happy. She's different than the other girls I've bedded. Maybe that's because I haven't had sex with her yet?

I hadn't meant to kiss her when I was leaving. I just couldn't help myself. I can't deny the attraction between us. It's not that I have feelings for her. . . Well, I don't think I do?

I don't know what the fuck I'm thinking.

I know what I do need, though. I need someone to make me forget her. I need someone underneath me, and I need it now.

My gaze flicks to the clock in my dashboard. I grimace when I spot the time. Two PM is too early to be hitting the club scene. The prime specimens don't arrive until well after eleven. Don't get me wrong, you'll find someone suitable at any time of the day, but I've learned over the years, you only get the clingers during daylight hours, the ones who are a little more desperate.

Oh, fuck it; I'm desperate. Desperate to get a pretty blonde firecracker out of my fucking head.

When I pull into the Dungeon, I notice the parking lot is only half-full. Usually, it's bumper to bumper with cars. Ignoring the niggle in my gut cautioning me to slow down, I throw open my door, climb out of my truck, then stride through the large double doors of my brother's club.

I make a beeline for the bar, hoping a nip or two of whiskey will lessen my need to hump the leg of the first girl I see. It might even weaken the knot my stomach has held since I left Jenni standing dumbfounded on the sidewalk.

"Oh no, someone doesn't look happy." Tina glances at me with pity while placing a beer down in front of me.

I plop onto the barstool opposite her. "Can I get a whiskey?"

Her brows shoot up into her hairline, but the foul look crossing my face stops her from giving me any sass. Not speaking a word, she snags a bottle of whiskey from the shelf and a shot glass from a rack behind the bar, places them in front of me, then serves a patron on my left.

I've lost count of how many nips of whiskey I've had. It could be three; it could be a hundred. I honestly don't know, but I nearly return to the land of the living when my cellphone unexpectedly rings, scaring the shit out of me.

After settling my manic heart rate, I yank it out of my jeans. When I peer down at the screen, my lips quirk. Noah is calling me. Like a freight train, lucidity forms. I'm late for our gig at Mavericks.

Fuck!

As I stumble off my barstool, my hand delves into my jeans to pull out my car keys. I've just flung them in the air when Tina snatches them out of my hand. "You can't drive anywhere." She shoves them down the front of her shirt, like a bit of cleavage will scare me.

"You really think that will stop me?" My slurred words reveal the level of my intoxication. I'm way past drunk.

After cocking her hip, Tina gives me her best *just try and see how far you get* face.

I'm about to dive for them when a sweet voice at my side says, "I can drive you anywhere you need to go." A young lady with long, light brown hair and hazel eyes stands beside me. Her curvy legs are crossed in front of her body, and she's fidgeting with the hem of her modest cotton dress. "I was just about to leave anyway."

She's pretty, but I wouldn't say she's stunningly beautiful. I shift my eyes to Tina to gauge her response on the brunette's offer. Snubbing the stranger's glare, Tina shakes her head. When my eyes lower to her cleavage, wordlessly requesting my keys back, she shakes her head more firmly.

That tells my drunken brain I'm making the right decision. "A lift will be great."

The brunette's eyes spark with excitement as she claps her hands together. When I wrap my arm around her shoulders, Tina growls, "Nick. . ." Her tone is dangerously low.

I shoot her a cheeky wink before guiding my savior to the parking lot.

During our drive to Mavericks, I find out my savior's name is

Megan. She just turned twenty-something and recently moved to Ravenshoe from some Hicksville town in the middle of Whoop Whoop. I'm not really paying any attention to what she's saying because I'm too busy wondering how badly my ass is going to be chewed out for rocking up to a gig late. Tonight is the first time I've ever shown up late, but I don't see the band accepting that as an excuse.

When we arrive at Mavericks, Megan follows me inside. I stumble onto the stage, mumbling an apology to Noah on my way by. Noah's curious gaze turns to me, but he doesn't speak a word. I could fob off my tardiness, but it would be a woeful waste of time. I'm reasonably sure he can smell the liquor seeping from my pores.

———

The instant our performance is over, I bolt to the men's restroom to expel the copious amount of whiskey I downed too quickly. It takes several long stomach-cramping heaves for my body to rid itself of the alcohol, and by the time I head back to the bar, my bandmates are nowhere to be seen.

"Are you okay?" Megan nearly makes me scream like a girl. I hadn't noticed her standing to the side of me.

I'm not eager to admit I just threw up half a bottle of whiskey. "Yeah, I must have a stomach bug or something."

When I find myself comparing Megan's lackluster hazel eyes to Jenni's dazzling icy blue gaze, I stumble toward the bar. A bottle of whiskey couldn't erase Jenni from my thoughts, so how about I give beer a shot?

The band is granted unlimited free beer every Friday night at Mavericks. I plan to take advantage of the situation.

———

The next morning, I wake up with the worst headache you could imagine. You'd think with how much whiskey I vomited the night before, I'd have no alcohol left in my system. But nope, I still feel drunk.

When I attempt to rub the sleep out of my eyes, I freeze. There's a warm body lying on my chest. With my heart in my throat, I lower my frightful eyes. Light brown hair is fanned across my chest.

Oh, fuck.

I must have been so drunk last night, I forgot to sneak out once my companion fell asleep.

As my blurry gaze bounces around the unfamiliar environment, I struggle to gather my bearings. I appear to be at a cheap motel. The alarm clock shows it's 11:14 AM. No wonder my head is thumping. The last time I peered at the clock it was a little after 4 AM.

"Good morning," is breathed heavily on my chest before a set of lips land on mine.

Shocked, I peel her off me by her shoulders. When she is far enough back, I scan her face, hoping her features will register as familiar.

I'm drawing a blank. I swear I've never seen her before.

"Morning. . . *babe.*"

Over the small talk, I jump out of the double bed, grab my jeans off the floor, then yank them up to cover the cotton boxer shorts I'm wearing.

The nameless brunette watches me in silence as I gather her clothes in haste before handing them to her. "You get dressed, then I'll meet you in the hall." I keep my tone friendly, not liking the tears welling in her eyes.

When she nods, I dart into the corridor where I spend the next several minutes biting out a string of curse words.

I'm still pacing the stained concrete floor when she opens the motel door and heads my way. The closer she gets to me, the more she fiddles with her floral dress. "Did I do something wrong?"

"Umm. . . no. . . not at all. . . I just. . . umm. . . have to go to work."

I catch my eyeroll halfway. This is the exact reason why I leave while they're sleeping—to avoid the awkward next morning conversation.

"Okay." Her lips quiver against mine when she presses a kiss on my straight-lined mouth. Not picking up the signals I'm throwing out, she inches back and says, "See you next week?"

I nod. It's stupid of me to do, but I'll say anything if it gets her out of here a little quicker. In silence, I usher her down the hall of a Motel Six on the outskirts of town.

"Bye." She waves before pacing to a yellow car in the middle of the empty parking lot.

The instant her car exits the lot, I circle my throbbing temples. I'm never drinking whiskey ever again.

After taking a few seconds to settle my sky-high heart rate, my bleary eyes scan the parking lot, seeking my truck. My nose crinkles when I fail to locate it. My confusion doesn't linger for long. I may have the worst hangover I've ever had, but I'm reasonably sure I left it at Isaac's club last night.

Exhaling, I yank my cell phone out of my pocket to call a taxi. When I peer down at the screen, I notice I have a text message from Jenni.

Jenni: *Did you want to go out tonight?*

Fuck yes! After four months of chasing, it's time for me to collect my reward.

I call a cab before returning Jenni's call. Although she only sent me a text, I'd rather talk to her in person.

"Hello." I can't see her, but her breathless greeting has me imagining her smile.

I rock back and forth on my heels to calm my excitement before asking, "One hour not enough?"

Her beautiful giggle sounds down the line.

This is the first time I've made her laugh, but you can be assured it won't be the last.

CHAPTER THIRTEEN

JENNI

My head spent all last night striving to convince my heart Nick wasn't what it wanted. My heart never listened. Not once. I know I'm getting the same deal with Nick I got with Christian, but I no longer care. It's like anything in life, when you're told you can't have it, you want it more than anything.

I want Nick.

I want him so much, he makes it hard for me to breathe when he's in the same room as me. I haven't eaten, slept, or breathed without him entering my thoughts the past four months, so why fight the inevitable? I only have two months left of summer break before I leave for New York to study Fashion Design, so it's time for me to have some fun.

No commitments.

No boyfriends.

No expectations.

Just fun!

Before I can chicken out, I send Nick a message asking him out tonight. I'm shocked when my phone rings not even five minutes later.

I laugh when he asks, "One hour not enough?"

I don't think any time period will be sufficient to get my fill of him, but I'm willing to take whatever I can get.

"Where do you want to go?" His tone is friendly, but I hear the sexual undertone it naturally holds.

With fond memories still highlighting my dreams the past four months, I suggest, "The Dungeon?"

"Okay."

A grin curls on my lips. I can't see him, but I can picture him rubbing his hands together. I'm sure he's loving the fact that I've finally caved.

"Can you pick me up?"

When he remains quiet, I begin to wonder if our call has been disconnected. Yanking down my phone, I check his number is still displayed on the screen. It is.

"Nick, are you there?" I ask down the line, suddenly fretful our call only dropped on his end.

He coughs. "Yeah, sorry, I'm here. Bad line or something. I can pick you up, if you want? What's your address?"

After exchanging details, we agree for him to pick me up at nine PM. My first thought upon disconnecting our call is to share my excitement with Emily and Nicole, but that notion doesn't hang around for long. Emily has been so preoccupied with Noah the past few months, I rarely see her as it is, but anytime we do get together, she gives me a very stern warning to stay away from Nick.

I understand her concern, but sometimes a girl's gotta do what a girl's gotta do. I tried to ignore Nick. I never returned a single text message or phone call the past four months, but yesterday proved there's a side to him no one has ever seen.

I liked who he was yesterday. He was kind and sweet and made my heart do a stupid flippy thing. That's why I'm going out with him. I want to give him a chance to prove the man he was on our mini-date yesterday wasn't a one-time thing.

If that is the case, maybe we'll create more than just sparks on the dance floor tonight.

I spend my day with my dad and Maria, watching movies and eating popcorn. When it reaches seven PM, I head to my room to get ready for my date with Nick. I don't need to primp and pamper myself for tonight. My Aunt Dee made sure every surface of my body was waxed and polished before I left her salon yesterday afternoon. She could see what took me a night of no sleep to figure out, so she made sure my body was prepared for when my brain jumped on board.

My heart beats double time when I spot Nick's headlights pulling into my driveway promptly at nine. With butterflies tap dancing in my stomach, I dart down the stairwell. I mumble a goodbye to my dad before curling my hand around the handle of our front door.

I freeze when my dad grumbles, "Wait a minute."

My nervous eyes shift to my dad's office. He's in the process of absorbing my super short, skin-tight red dress, and sky-high stiletto heels. A vein in his neck works overtime before his worried gaze lifts to my face. I eye him with suspicion when he stands from his chair and walks around his desk. "Are you going to introduce me?"

The doorbell rings, breaking the thick stench of awkwardness. "Please, Daddy," I beg. I don't want him to embarrass me in front of Nick.

"A real man has no problems meeting his date's father," Dad responds while finalizing the last steps between us.

"It isn't a date; he's just a friend."

My dad crosses his arms in front of his rounded stomach, his stance advising I'm not allowed to leave without a proper introduction.

"Fine!"

With a huff, I crack open the front door. Nick is already halfway back to his truck. Upon hearing the door creak open, his puzzled gaze drifts back to the house. Excitement slicks my skin when his eyes leisurely scan my party-ready dress.

His seductive grin is wiped right off his face when my dad steps into view. He heads for Nick with his hand held out in greeting and his lips set in a hard line. "Michael Murphy, Jenni's dad." He shakes Nick's hand so firmly, Nick's body shudders.

"Nick, uh, Nicholas Holt."

I try not to giggle at the rattle of Nick's vocal cords. It's ridiculous that my dad has made him nervous, but it's also endearing. When his freaked-out eyes turn to me, I can't help the smile that crosses my face. Inwardly giggling, I save a petrified Nick from my dad's grasp, then hightail it to his truck, just as grateful to skip the dreaded meet-the-parents routine as he is.

"Thank you, Daddy," I whisper from Nick's truck before slipping into the passenger seat. "Don't wait up."

Nick remains quiet for the first five miles of our trip to Raven-shoe. I don't mind. It gives me plenty of time to study his profile. He's a very handsome man with defined cheekbones, a strong, prominent jawline, alluring eyes, and a luscious thick mane of hair.

But unfortunately, even with him being ravishingly handsome, I can't miss the freaked-out expression on his face. He has swallowed several times in a row the last five minutes, and he keeps rubbing his hands down his jean-covered thighs, no doubt to remove sweat.

Certain I know what has him rattled, I say, "I'm sorry about my dad."

Air blasts out of his nose. "He doesn't own a gun, does he?"

I quirk my lips. "I don't think so."

His eyes widen as his throat works hard to swallow.

"Does he need one?" My voice is laced with cheekiness.

He scans my body. When his eyes return to my face, he smiles a heart-stopping grin. "Yeah, he does."

My heart does a weird flippy thing when he grabs my wrist to drag me over to his side of the bench seat. I remain cradled under his arm until we pull into the Dungeon parking lot forty minutes later. The place is so bustling, the line to enter stretches halfway around the block.

A grin curls on my lips when Nick runs around his truck to help me down. My killer high heels and super tight dress make it nearly impossible for me to step down, but an average man wouldn't think to help. My heart thrashes against my ribs when his assistance has my body gliding along his. His build is stronger than it looks. I don't miss the hard bumps in his stomach, much less the impressive muscle below his belt.

Remaining quiet, Nick guides us straight to the club's entrance, not bothering to stand in the line with the rest of the patrons. He ignores the annoyed gasps of the partygoers queued outside as he makes a beeline for the bouncer I had a run-in with months ago.

"Travis," Nick greets him, strolling past him.

Travis's lips straighten when his narrowed gaze zooms in on Nick's hand clasped around mine. We weave through a mass of sweaty bodies dancing in the packed club until we reach a large mahogany bar on the far wall. The smell of sweat and alcohol lingering in the air is intoxicating.

Nick releases my hand so he can gesture to a female bartender serving rowdy patrons halfway down the bar. Even though it's still early, the Dungeon is jam-packed with clientele. Upon spotting Nick's request for assistance, the petite bartender makes her way to us, ignoring the two dozen or more patrons vying for her attention.

Goosebumps break across my arms when Nick whispers into my ear, "What did you want to drink?"

"I'm not twenty-one," I inform him quietly, not wanting anyone to overhear me.

He chuckles. "I know that; neither am I for another few months, but age doesn't count here." He runs the back of his hand down my inflamed cheeks before asking again, "What would you like to drink?"

My teeth scrap my bottom lip. "Wine?" I half-answer, half-question, truly unsure if that's okay.

My attention diverts from his captivating blue eyes when a sultry voice says, "It's a little early for The Player to be arriving, isn't it?"

The petite bartender waggles her brows when Nick responds, "It's never too early to play."

I roll my eyes, sickened by their flirty banter. Hearing my disgust, the bartender's gaze rockets to me. The longer she scans my face, the tighter her brows become. "Beer girl?" she questions through a giggle.

Nick snickers while shaking his head. "Tina, this is Jenni; Jenni, Tina."

"Nice to meet you," I say with a smile, even though I'm feeling anything but friendly.

Snubbing the tension teeming between us, Nick asks Tina, "Can we grab a glass of wine and a beer, please?"

Tina stares at Nick for several heart-clenching seconds. I'm certain she's going to card him, so you can imagine my surprise when she stalks away to collect his order as requested without demanding our IDs.

My lungs have just returned to their normal breathing pattern when she places our drinks in front of us. Nick dips his chin in thanks before gathering our drinks and directing me to a booth on the left-hand side of the bar.

Incapable of ignoring the niggle in my gut, I ask "Did you two. . . umm—"

"No," Nick interrupts. He gestures for me to enter the booth before him. I'm halfway in when he adds on, "Not from a lack of trying, though."

My heart slithers into my gut. With my back molars grinding together, I attempt to scoot out of the booth.

My anger reaches boiling point when Nick blocks my exit with his well-formed body. "I was joking."

I take several deep breaths before lifting my eyes from his chest to his face. The contemptuous gleam in his eyes reveals he's lying. My nostrils flare as my eyes narrow even more.

"Okay. I wasn't joking. But I haven't tried anything for months." He stares straight into my eyes, ensuring I can see the truth in his murky blue gaze. Even knowing what he is saying is true, my jealousy doesn't lessen in the slightest. He still wanted to sleep with Tina—*he probably still does.*

With a sigh, I plop into the booth before scooting as far away from him as possible. He's not afraid of my anger. If anything, he finds it entertaining, like it's a challenge.

After placing our drinks on the tabletop, he slides across the black leather until he's sitting so close to me, our thighs touch. "Now you're trapped." He tips my head back so he can press a kiss under my left earlobe like he did at Bronte's Peak all those months ago. "You can't run, and you can't hide." He presses three kisses along my jaw. "Because I'll *always* find you."

A moan rumbles through my parched lips when he drags his lips down my neck to nibble on my sensitive skin. His pace is teasingly slow, but oh so perfect. By the time he pulls back, any jealousy hampering my mood becomes a distant memory.

No commitments, no boyfriends, no expectations, just fun, I remind myself.

When he smiles his panty-combusting grin, I pull his torturous lips back to mine by the back of his shaggy blond hair. This kiss is the one I've been fantasizing about the past four months. It goes above and beyond my greatest expectations, making me realize I've just made a second fatal mistake.

I'm once again putty in the hands of a player.

CHAPTER FOURTEEN

NICK

Jenni tastes even better than I expected, but now that I've had a taste of her, I want so much more—and I want it now. A smile slides across her face when I reacquaint our lips. I try to kiss her like her daddy is watching, hoping it will dampen the electricity firing between us. It does no such thing. The sparks are already lit—there's no shutting this down.

Instead, I surrender to the madness. I kiss her how I've fantasized kissing her since the day we met. I kiss her until her toes curl and our breaths are shared. I kiss her until the music dulls to a hum and my pants are tight at the front. Then I kiss her some more.

The more our make-out session intensifies, the more I wish to take it somewhere private. Usually, public displays of affection don't bother me, but I'm not willing to share an inch of Jenni's body with any perverted man in this club tonight.

When I pull away from our embrace, Jenni whimpers, making my dick even harder. It's digging into my zipper, the metal's painful bite not dampening its eagerness in the slightest.

After peering into her lust-filled eyes, I ask, "Do you want to get out of here?"

She bites on her bottom lip while contemplating. Her lips are swollen from our kisses, her eyes sparkling. I mentally fist pump when she nods a few seconds later. Clutching her hand in mine, I sprint for the parking lot. We barely make it halfway across the dance floor before her high heels hinder my swift getaway.

She squeals when I scoop her into my arms to throw her over my shoulder. While her giggles vibrate my back, I hotfoot it to the closest exit. It isn't that I'm desperate; I just want to get her naked before she changes her mind.

I place her in the passenger seat of my truck before darting around to the other side. After jumping into the driver's seat, I fire up my engine, then reality dawns: I have no fucking clue where I'm going. Generally, I'd head to my companion's house, but I don't think Jenni's dad would appreciate that. We could fool around in my truck, but I'd rather find a location that isn't so dark and dingy. I've been dying for this day for months, so I don't want anything to take away from it.

When I sneak a glance at Jenni, taking in her thrusting chest as she battles to secure a full breath, I break the very first rule in my player handbook.

Because it's nearly 11 PM, I'm not surprised to find my house plunged into darkness. My dad is an early riser, which typically means he's fast asleep by no later than nine. After pulling into my usual parking space, I round my truck to help Jenni down. Instead of setting her on her feet like earlier, I keep her body flush with mine. We make it halfway to my house before I'm forced to reacquaint our lips. It's been over twenty minutes since our kiss, so my mouth is missing her taste.

Fuck—she tastes good—as sweet as her beautiful face but as wicked as the sexy dress she's wearing. She grins at my eagerness before returning my kiss with just as much intensity. Let me tell you, this girl knows how to kiss. We breathe as one while our tongues dance an erotic tango. It's a fire-sparking kiss that has my dick attempting to break the zipper in my jeans.

Our fumble down the hallway is clumsy. We're too busy kissing, groping, and fondling each other to watch where we're going. It's playful but not loud enough I'm worried about waking my father. He's a heavy sleeper—thank god.

When we enter my room, I set Jenni on her feet before spinning around to close my door. My heart beeps in my throat when I notice my dad's bedroom light flicking on. Our sneaky tiptoe down the hallway must not have been as quiet as I thought.

Struggling not to laugh, I shift on my feet to face Jenni. I have my index finger pushed against my lips, but she doesn't see my wordless code to be quiet. She's too busy absorbing my moderate-sized room to speak. Although my dad's house is tiny compared to my mom's, the bedrooms are a decent size. I have my own bathroom, and the kitchen is large enough to cook a meal suitable for two—three would be a stretch. It's modest, but homey.

Jenni's avid perusal of my room stops at my bookshelf. A selection of photo frames have caught her eye—one more than the others. After picking up a photo, she pivots to face me. "That's the guy Emily was dancing with months ago, isn't it?"

I nod. "Yeah, that's my brother, Isaac."

When a beautiful pink hue creeps across her neck, my thoughts shift far away from my brother. While my eyes dance over her face, I remove the frame from her grasp and place it back on the shelf. The air crackles with sexual chemistry when I stare into her hooded gaze. "Do you want to do this?"

Her eyes are telling me yes, but I want to make sure she understands my intentions tonight. I know she isn't drunk; she only had a sip of her wine, but I still want her complete approval for what I'm about to do.

She licks her lips before whispering, "Yes."

When my fingers weave through her hair, she makes a low,

moaning noise. It vibrates on my chest as we fall onto my bed, my hand reaching out to catch her halfway. The hem of her skirt bunches up high on her milky white thighs when I brace my knee between her legs to take in the entire picture. She's so beautiful. Her hair looks lighter against the darkness of my bedding, and her lips are plump and begging to be kissed, but it's the need in her eyes I'm paying the most attention to.

"Are you sure?" I double-check.

With a nod, she pulls my lips to hers by the back of my head. "Yes," she whispers over my mouth before kissing me like she's starved of my taste. When I trail my lips down her neck, her mouth parts to suck in much-needed breaths. The flush on her neck reflects the heat roaring through her body; she's heated with anticipation.

As my lips drop to her erratically panting chest, I squeeze my dick, begging for it to calm down. I'm dying to be inside her, but I also want to take my time with her. I've been dreaming about this for months, and with the reality of her beneath me far exceeding my wildest dreams, I'm not going to rush this for anything or anyone.

I smooth out the wrinkle between her brows with my tongue. I trace it down the tiny ridges in her stomach before shifting it to the pasty, smooth skin on her thighs. My dick feels like a rock sitting behind my zipper when goosebumps follow the trek my tongue just took. I've not yet touched a section of her skin covered by clothes, and she's still heating up for me. She's hot and raring to go.

As I inch her skirt to her midsection and lower her panties down her thighs, I sneak a glance at her face. Her cheeks are flushed, matching the color of her lipstick, and her eyes are brimming with lust and fixed on me. When she rocks her hips upward, I smirk. I fucking love her eagerness, and I can't wait to see what she looks like when she comes, but it doesn't increase my speed in the slightest.

I play with her for a few minutes, teasing her to the point the wetness between her legs can't be denied. Then, when she's on the verge of begging, I do something I've being dying to do for months. I utterly devour her.

Her back arches off the bed as a throaty moan rips from her throat. Her thighs clamp around my head, shocked by my mouth's sudden attachment to her pussy but also loving it.

Hell.

Heaven.

Bliss.

It all pumps through me when I consume her with hungry, well-timed licks, playful bites, and sucks strong enough she can't stop whispering my name, but weak enough she won't fall through a lust cloud until I want her to.

She weaves her fingers through my hair when I suck her clit into my mouth. She's done waiting. She wants to come, and she wants to come now. I could hold her off a little longer, but since I'm dying to taste her arousal as much as she's dying to come, I increase the pressure of my sucks before slipping two fingers inside her.

"Nick. . ." This call nearly has me coming undone. Fuck me, I've never heard a noise so perfect.

I kiss her pussy until her lips part and her eyes shut. It's a rough, sloppy embrace that has my dick aching to sink inside her. I stop driving my fingers into her when the walls of her pussy clamp around me, and my name is purred from her throat in a long, shuddering moan.

I don't think things can get any more perfect. . . until Jenni's orgasm unleashes a tiger. Once she finishes shuddering, she crawls across the sticky sheets to free my cock from my jeans, then wraps her lips around my throbbing crown I close my eyes when the image of her red-painted lips inching down my stiff shaft becomes too much. She knows how to give head, so she's seconds from making me look like a fool. I could come in her mouth right now. I would, if I were only here to get my rocks off. Tonight isn't just about me. I want her to be as sexually satiated as I am.

After popping my eyes open, I gather Jenni's hair to the side, then use it as leverage to slow her greedy pace. The image is better than anything I've been picturing the past four months. She peers up at me with wide, lusty eyes, like I'm her savior instead of the man who will most likely tear her apart.

If I were a man, I'd stop this exchange in an instant. It's a pity I lost my morals somewhere between her scent tickling my senses and her taste igniting the fire in my gut. There's only one way our exchange will end: by Jenni stopping it.

I really fucking hope that doesn't happen.

Needing to get in on the action, I adjust the spread of my knees before leaning Jenni back to fondle with her pussy from behind. She's so goddamn wet, my fingers slip in without any resistance as my thumb braces the puckered hole in her rear. While she sucks me like she's seconds from extricating my brain from my knob, I finger fuck her as if my fingers are my cock. It's a fast pace, but we're certainty not fucking.

Our connection is unreal though. I've never been with a woman where we instantly mesh like this. Usually, it's pretty fucking awkward moving from third base to the home plate. I'm not feeling that tonight. Sleeping with Jenni feels natural, like we've been fooling around for months. I guess in a way we have been. We just kept our hands to ourselves during the foreplay hot enough to be felt states over. Jenni often popped into my head while pleasing myself in the shower. I can't recall one dream that hasn't featured her in some way the past four months. They were deliciously wicked, but real life is ten times better.

When her pussy shows signs of another orgasm, I withdraw my fingers from her slick canal. I want my cock inside her when she comes so I can feel her squeezes. A squeak pops from Jenni's lips when I inch back to grab a condom out of my bedside drawer. She's disappointed, but it doesn't linger for long. Nothing but excitement features on her face when I tear open the package before rolling it down my cock.

After licking her wetness from my fingers, I cup her thighs then raise my eyes to hers. "Wrap them around me. I want to take you deep."

I bite out a healthy number of obscenities when the curl of her legs coincides with the wetness of her pussy bracing against my cock. Even wearing a raincoat, nothing can take away from the heat pumping out of her.

"You sure?"

She nods, almost making me come undone from the eagerness in her eyes. I press on the brakes, giving myself a few minutes to calm down before slamming home.

Christ.

Fucking.

Heaven.

Did I just die?

CHAPTER FIFTEEN

NICK

O ver the next two hours, I sample every delicious inch of Jenni. My deliberate and purposeful dedication to her body gives away even more of her quirks. Like how she squirms when I kiss her behind her kneecap, that her skin is as soft as it looks, and when she moans, it vibrates from deep within her chest.

I could happily spend several more hours exploring her, but her hazy eyes expose her exhaustion. She's moments from collapsing.

After placing a trail of kisses on her sweat-slicked collarbone, up her flushed neck, then on her kiss-swollen lips, I crank my elbow to glance down at her satisfied face.

"Wow." Her eyes remain locked on my ceiling as her chest rises and falls in a steady rhythm. "That was. . . I don't have any words. It was just—"

"Perfect?" I fill in.

Nodding, her sparkling eyes drift to mine. The heated flush extending from her nape to her knees deepens when her eyes rake my naked torso. She takes in the beads of sweat dotted across my hairless pecs before dropping them a few more inches. When they stop on my naked package, her mouth forms a perfect O.

"Unless you want me inside of you again, I suggest you stop looking at my cock."

I meant my comment in jest, but it doesn't stop her eyes from rocketing back to mine. Her pupils widen as her breathing turns labored.

Maybe she isn't as exhausted as I thought?

After bouncing her eyes between mine for several electrifying seconds, she snaps them back to my once again erect dick. "I thought you didn't sleep with the same girl twice." She slaps her hand over her mouth, mortified. "I was supposed to say that in my head."

When she buries her flaming face into my chest, all playfulness stops, and a new friskiness fills the air. Her needy breaths fan my overheated skin as the smell of her arousal intensifies. She smells fucking delicious.

When her longing eyes drift to my face, any reservations I had about sleeping with the same girl twice vanish. I've already broken one rule tonight by bringing her here, so what's another?

By the time we finish round two, I'm literally fucked. I've never worked so goddamn hard in my life. Beyond exhausted, I snag the comforter from the bottom of my bed, lift it to cover both Jenni and me, then roll onto my hip so I can spoon her.

My heart bangs my ribs when I take in how perfectly our bodies align. Her curvy ass is nestling my dick; her back is heating my chest, and the little curve in her nape is the perfect resting place for my lips. It's as if she were made for me.

The warmth of her body snuggled against mine and the exhaustion from our activities see me quickly falling into a blissful, uninterrupted sleep.

The next morning, I wake up feeling fresh. This is the first time I've woken without a hangover in nearly three years. My nostrils flare when they detect Jenni's floral perfume lingering in the air. Our rigorous activities infused her scent deep within my skin.

Smirking like a cat staring at an empty fish bowl, I stretch out my arm, eager to mix more of her scent with mine. My eyes snap open when my hunt comes up empty. Excluding me, my bed is void of a living thing.

I scan my room, seeking any evidence Jenni is still here. Her purse, shoes, and dress have been collected from my floor, and her phone is no longer on my bedside table.

A smile etches onto my mouth when reality dawns: *this player just got played.*

After yanking my cell phone off my bedside table, I send Jenni a text.

Me: *Great ditch and run. You must have been taught by a pro?*

My laugh echoes around my room when she replies:

Jenni: *Only the best. . .*

Still smiling, I jump out of bed and throw on a pair of boxer shorts. When I walk into the kitchen, I spot my dad standing near the coffee pot, waiting for it to finish its latest brew.

"Morning." My voice relays my excitement. Last night was so *out of this fucking world* good, my mood can't help but reflect my happiness. I grab an empty mug and place it next to my dad's. His gaze lifts from the coffee pot to me. After screwing up his nose, he returns his focus to the brown goop dribbling out of the machine.

"What's wrong with you?"

He watches me put two slices of bread into the toaster before grumbling, "I thought I taught my boys better than that."

"Better than what?"

I spin around to face him head on. He doesn't speak, but he doesn't need to. His lowered lids reveal everything.

"Please don't tell me you thought I was saving myself for marriage?" I ask with a laugh. "That ship sailed a long time ago."

My chuckles are cut in half when my dad snaps, "Don't get smart with me, Nicholas."

Oh shit. He only calls me Nicholas when I'm in trouble.

While I rack my brain about what I could have done, Dad fills our mugs with coffee. After adding sugar and milk to mine, he hands my mug to me. I nearly drop it when he mumbles, "Next time, be man enough to drive the girl you kept up half the night home." After a final snarl, he leaves the kitchen.

I stare at the doorway for several long minutes, utterly baffled. It's only once a hefty dose of caffeine hits my senses does the fog in my mind lift. I brought Jenni here in my truck, meaning she didn't have access to her car.

Fuck.

A taxi to Erkinsvale must have cost her a small fortune.

Lucky I made the expense worthwhile.

I'm halfway through breakfast when my eyes catch sight of the time on the kitchen clock. Without a second thought, I guzzle down my recently refilled coffee. It scorches my throat, but I've got places to visit and people to see. I don't have time to dawdle.

I hadn't planned on going to Emily and Noah's gathering today, but after the events of last night, nothing could keep me away.

When I pull into Jacob's driveway, I spot Jenni's BMW parked next to Slater's motorbike. I slot my truck behind her car, ensuring she can't leave before me. The first thing my gaze zooms in on when I enter the sprawling backyard is Jenni. Her back is facing me as she talks to Emily. Noah and Slater are manning the open-fire BBQ, and Jacob is chatting to Marcus near an unlit fire pit.

I barely take two feet toward Jenni when Slater detects my approach. Smirking like the smug fuck he is, he quickly spans the distance between Jenni and himself.

It's too late for that now.

When Slater reaches Jenni, her head cranks my way. The pulse in her neck twangs when she scans my body. I can tell the exact moment she's finished her avid assessment because a shade of pink creeps across her cheeks.

I wink at her before making my way to Noah. "Do you need a hand?"

Noah's brows scrunch when he realizes who the offer is coming from. "Oh, hey, Nick. I didn't think you could make it?" He sounds surprised but pleased. His shock is understandable. I've attended more band functions the past four months than I have the past four years. "I'm nearly done here, but you can take these to the table."

When he nudges his head to a plate of charcoal-grilled beef patties, I grimace. Noah has many talents, but BBQing isn't one of them. The patties are so hard, you could throw them against the wall, and they wouldn't crumble.

Just as I reach the outdoor table we regularly dine at, Jenni takes a seat across from me. Forever a cock-blocker, Slater rushes over to slip into the empty space next to her. He sits so close to her, their thighs touch.

Fighting to leash my unusual anger, my eyes drift to Jenni. With a slanted head, I cock my brow, wordlessly questioning if she's planning to tell Slater his protective big brother job is no longer required. My back molars smash together when she shakes her head, but before I can announce my annoyance, we're joined by the remaining members of my band and a handful of their friends.

For the next hour, we sit at the wooden table eating Noah's burnt burgers while talking all things band-related. Most of the conversa-tions are held by Noah, Marcus, Emily and Nicole. I'm too busy studying every move Jenni makes to participate in anything intel-lectual.

Any time Jenni catches my gaze, she smiles before her cheeks get a rush of heat behind them. Then, not long later, I get kicked in the shins by Slater's boot. My shins will be black by the end of today because I can't help but stare. I know what Jenni tastes like. I know what she sounds like when she comes. And I also know the harder Slater fights to keep her away from me, the faster she'll run toward me.

I'm reasonably sure Jacob is the only one noticing the exchanges occurring between Slater, Jenni, and me. Every time Slater kicks me, he bursts out laughing, startling everyone with his big chuckles.

When the girls begin gathering the dishes, a brilliant idea pops into my head. Slater avoids domestic chores like they're the plague. I don't think he's ever stepped inside a kitchen, meaning this is the perfect opportunity for me to get some alone time with Jenni.

Emily appears baffled when I offer to dry the dishes upon entering the kitchen. She eyes me with suspicion while handing me a tea towel. In silence, Nicole and Emily wash the dishes while Jenni and I dry. I purposely slow down my drying technique, praying they'll leave the kitchen long before Jenni and I are done with our share of the chores.

My ruse is working. . . until Jacob enters the scene.

When Emily and Nicole exit, he snags a fresh bottle of beer out of the fridge before leaning his back on the counter. His gaze flicks between Jenni and me, his watch noticeable.

Spotting my soured expression, Jenni giggles. I glare at her, lost on what she thinks is funny. Not deterred by my glare, she smiles even brighter.

Once she finishes drying the last dish, she throws her tea towel into the laundry attached to the kitchen, then makes her way outside. The smile she gives me on her way out nearly knocks me on my ass.

Confident she's out of earshot, my eyes stray to Jacob. "Thanks for the cock block, Jake."

A massive grin stretches across his face. "No worries." With a shoulder bump, he shadows me out of the kitchen, happy his ruse worked.

Mine failed, but I'll give it another go in a couple of hours.

CHAPTER SIXTEEN

JENNI

I've barely made it three steps out of the kitchen when Slater once again glues himself to my side. His sudden attachment exposes that Nick must be close on my tail. As I did nearly an hour ago, I glance over my shoulder to drink him in. He's wearing his favorite designer jeans and a dark polo shirt, but I'm not seeing him with the same set of eyes I usually do.

Only mere hours ago, I saw him naked. The visual—*My. God.* I thought he was handsome with his clothes on. The view is ten times hotter when he's stripped bare. He has a fit, athletic body that had no trouble keeping up with our rigorous activities last night.

Spotting my flamed cheeks, Nick awards me a knee-weakening smirk before he makes his way to Noah. Slater laughs, pleased his plan to keep us apart is working.

His chuckles halt when I elbow him in the ribs. "Stop being mean."

He makes a face like he vomited in his mouth. "I'm not being mean; I'm saving you from catching something."

I don't have the heart to tell him I'm beyond saving. Last night set the bar way out of his reach. I can't see anyone slowing this freight train down.

Well, not anyone who isn't named Nicholas Holt.

I'm confused as to why Nick is here today. If you look up "player" in the dictionary, I'm reasonably sure a picture of Nick would be displayed. I gave him what he wanted, so why is he is still chasing me?

I bolted out of his house this morning because I wasn't waiting around for him to give me my marching orders. I would have never in a million years guessed he'd continue the cat and mouse game we've been playing the past few months.

Don't get me wrong; I'm not complaining. I'm just shocked.

Not as much as I was when my endeavor to sneak out of his house unannounced was foiled by his father. . .

I sneakily tiptoe out of Nick's bedroom a little after 10 AM. My body is aching, but the relief I feel when I hit the front patio unnoticed makes up for the stealthy steps I uses to exit his house undetected.

I think I'm in the clear. . . until my gallop down the front three stairs has me stumbling upon an unknown spectator.

"Good morning," greets a deep voice behind me.

I freeze in place, my pulse skyrocketing to match my panic, before I pivot to face the voice. Although my eyes are blurry from a lack of sleep, they have no trouble assessing an older yet still handsome gentleman sitting on a swinging chair at the side of the wooden porch.

"Good morning," my voice shudders, mortified I've been busted doing the walk of shame. My hair is a mess; my dress is crumpled, and I'm carrying my shoes in my hand. The signs don't get more obvious than this.

The blond gentleman stands to his feet and ambles closer to me. "Do you need a lift home?"

I shake my head. "No. It's fine. I'll call a taxi."

His brows furrow as his lips purse. When he scans our location, I follow his gaze, inwardly cursing. I'm in the middle of Timbuktu. There isn't another house as far as the eye can see. When Nick drove us here last night, I didn't pay attention to my surroundings. I was too busy getting my heart rate under control to concentrate on anything else.

I return my eyes to the unnamed gentleman. "Do cabs come out here?"

Smiling a shy grin, he shakes his head.

Crap!

"I'll grab my keys." Not giving me the chance to protest, he reenters his home.

The drive to my house is as awkward as they come. I watch the scenery flicking by the passenger side window, wanting to say something, but unsure what I can say to lessen the discomfort.

By the time his big blue truck pulls into the front gate of my parents' property, over twenty minutes of silence has passed between us.

"Impressive." A notable whistle sounds from his circled lips. He smiles at my grimace. His home is cute and friendly-looking. Mine is a modern-day eyesore.

I awkwardly slide out of his car, my dress so tight, I can't step down. After adjusting my hem to a decent length, I lift my eyes to his. "Thank you for the lift."

He dips his chin before releasing his parking brake and reversing out of the driveway. His twenty-minute trip home doesn't start until he watches me enter the heavy front door of my home.

His caution isn't necessary. The only person I need protecting from is my father, who's standing in the foyer, glaring at me.

"You're lucky you're an adult, young lady," he snarls through clenched teeth before storming into his office.

I stand in the foyer for several long minutes, utterly shocked and hurt. This is the first time I've made my dad upset, and I don't like it.

After running upstairs for a quick shower and a change of clothes, I head back downstairs to confront my dad. I'm an adult, but I also understand he'll always see me as his little girl. . .

Our conversation went a lot better than I was expecting. My dad only issued one death threat against Nick during his hour-long lecture. A lot of what he said was true, and it strengthened my belief that Nick would no longer be in the picture now that our game of chase was over.

Now. . . now I'm not sure what to think. Nick broke several rules Christian disclosed on the "player" lifestyle last night. Is today just another bend of the rules? Or are an entirely new set of rules being brought into play?

I hope it's the latter.

I don't get a chance to talk to Nick all afternoon. Slater hasn't left my side—not even for a second. He's even walking me to my car to ensure he maintains an amicable distance between Nick and me.

When I spot Nick shadowing us, my pulse quickens. He looks determined, like he's had enough of Slater's games, and he's ready to put an end to it.

Disappointment smacks into me when the real reason for his tail comes to light. His truck is parked behind my car. I can't leave without his assistance. Although disappointed, I return his farewell wave before hopping into my car and following his truck out of Jacob's weaving driveway.

I'm scared to within an inch of my life when my exit from Jacob's street is followed by the deep rumble of Slater's motorcycle, the power of his engine rumbling in my chest when he barrels past me.

My heart continues to jump when I peer into my rearview mirror a few minutes later. Nick is following me. I'm certain he turned left at the end of Jacob's street, not right, otherwise why would Slater think the coast was clear?

When I take a right at the next intersection, Nick also turns right. There's no way this is a coincidence. There's a massive street sign for Petersburg pointing to the left. He's following me on purpose.

Noticing he's caught my attention in the rearview mirror, Nick flashes his headlights. I wave my hand in the air, acknowledging I saw his request but that I need to find somewhere safe to pull over first.

I find that spot a few minutes later. I won't lie; butterflies take flight in my stomach when I pull my car onto a small patch of grass on the side of a busy main road. They have nothing on my excitement when Nick's truck parks behind me a few seconds later. He climbs down from his vehicle before strolling toward my driver's side door. Even the way he walks alludes to his cockiness. It's a sexy swagger that suits his job description to a T.

When he reaches my window, I roll it down, expecting him to talk to me. My mouth falls open when he cracks open my door to assist me out. With my hand firmly clasped in his, he guides us to the front of my car, ensuring we're protected from the vehicles roaring past us. Their brutal speed barely swallows the moan rolling up my chest when he cups my cheek to rub my earlobe.

Who knew an earlobe rub could instigate sexual pleasure?

I would have laughed if you told me that last week, but I swear, every time Nick rubs mine, my pussy throbs.

The intensity of its ache grows when he leans down to seal his mouth over mine. His kiss is both ravishing and sensual. Just like last night, he holds nothing back. He kisses me until my breathing is labored and my panties are moist. Then he kisses me some more.

I don't know how long we stay on the side of the road, making out like crazy teens, but by the time he pulls back, my knees are weak, and my chest has swollen to accommodate my enlarged heart. He lazily absorbs my face, assessing every feature in great detail, before he spins on his heels and strides back to his truck. His gaze remains arrested on mine as he fires up his truck and completes an illegal U-turn to head back in the direction of his hometown.

Once his taillights disappear, I hop back into my car and drive home. I'm utterly confused. He's never been much of a talker, but his words aren't the cause of my confusion. His actions are.

My bewilderment intensifies when I get a message from him later that afternoon.

Nick: *Next week?*

I stare at the screen of my phone, seeking the hidden message behind his short text. Is he asking me out on a date? Or is he seeking a booty call?

Realizing there's only one way to settle my confusion, I return his message.

Me: *Where?*

The biggest grin stretches across my face when I read his reply.

Nick: *The Dungeon.*

My smile is so large, my cheeks burn from their sudden incline. If he was only after a booty call, he wouldn't have replied with a public place.

My phone feels my excitement when I punish the screen with my quick typing.

Me: *Okay.*

I grow giddy when his next reply pops up.

Nick: *You and me getting sweaty with our clothes on. I'll pick you up at nine.*

Grabbing my pillow off my bed, I squeal into it, ensuring my dad doesn't hear my excited screams.

Nick arrives promptly at nine PM the following Saturday. Thankfully, this time, my dad stays inside the house. Dancing with Nick the second time is even more exhilarating than the first. I know his skills on the dance floor match the impressive moves he uses beneath the sheets. That alone enhances our sexual connection.

When we arrive at the bar to replenish some of the fluids we've lost dancing, Tina's brows join. A thick cloud of awkwardness plagues our group when her shocked gaze dances between Nick and me for several long seconds. Certain she has the facts straight, she locks her eyes with mine. She doesn't talk, but the concern in her eyes speaks volumes. She's warning me to stay away from Nick, worried I'm walking into our relationship with my eyes closed.

I'm not. I know what I'm getting myself into. Nick has never given any indication that I'm here for the long haul, and I'm fine with that. I'm having fun and enjoying my life before I ship off to my next big adventure.

This isn't a permanent arrangement.

For the next two months, things follow along a similar path with Nick and me. We spend every weekend dancing at the Dungeon before an impromptu romp either in his truck or his bedroom. When we take our fun back to his house, I drive my own car. I'm not adding more embarrassing walks of shame to the measly one I have on my list.

We've also had a handful of "dates." We either go to the café at Bronte's Peak, or we catch a movie. Nick definitely isn't the talkative type, but my heart races every time he holds my hand or kisses me with so much tenderness my knees buckle. I know the more time we spend together, the harder it will be for me to leave for New York, but I can't give up a single moment he's willing to share with me. I cherish every minute I have with him, because deep down inside, I know something will eventually come between us.

I just didn't realize it would be me leaving for college.

I've mentioned my plans to Nick a few times, and for the most part, he didn't seem fazed by it, but he's a lot quieter tonight than usual.

"Only one round?" I give him a flirty wink, ensuring he knows my comment is in jest.

We're parked at Bronte's Peak. The foggy windows expose how we've spent the last fifty minutes. Our make-out session was out of this world, but it's unusual for Nick to only go one round. Usually,

I'm the one who ends things from exhaustion kicking in, so you can imagine my surprise when he tucked his dick away within seconds of coming.

"Keeping up with you on the dance floor must have worn me out," he replies with a chuckle. His laugh isn't his full-hearted one. It's reserved and withdrawn. After yanking up his zipper, he lifts his eyes to me. "What time do you fly out on Friday?"

A stabbing ache hits my chest. "Ten AM."

"Do you need a lift to the airport?"

I shake my head. "No, Emily is dropping me off."

His lips twist as he struggles to hold back a snarl. "Alright."

Not speaking another word, he fires up his truck and begins our trip home. He doesn't talk the entire time, but he does kiss the living hell out of me outside of my front gate. His kiss is so tender, it shatters my heart into a million pieces. It's a goodbye kiss, the one you give someone when you know you're not going to see them for a very long time—if ever again.

When he pulls back, I stare at him, wordlessly begging him to say or do something to show he wants me to stay. If he were to ask me right now to stay, I would. Falling in love was never part of our plan, but that's what makes it so exciting. We've created something unique, something worth exploring. He just needs to ask me to stay.

He won't, though, because I'm not just requesting he bend the rules he lives by; I'm asking him to snap them.

He won't do that for anybody.

Not even the girl who fell in love with him before she slept with him.

CHAPTER SEVENTEEN

NICK

I push my cell close to my ear as I continue strolling toward the entrance of Mavericks. "How's the big city?"

"It's okay, a little daunting," Jenni replies, her voice shuddering.

She left two weeks ago to start college in New York City. We've exchanged a handful of texts during that time, but I was so desperate to hear her voice tonight, I called her instead of replying to the "good luck" text she sent me.

"It will get better. You just need to give it some time." I'm sure it won't take long for her to settle in. She has a personality that draws people to her. That's why Slater took her under his wing so quickly.

"Hopefully." She breathes out her unease before taking on a more carefree tone. "Are you excited about tonight?"

My shoulder notches up. "Yeah, I'm excited. . . and maybe a little nervous."

She giggles. "You'll be fine."

She can say that. She's not the one about to perform for a handful of music execs. Tonight, Isaac's friend is coming to watch our band perform. Because I never gave Isaac the information he wanted on

Emily, he never mentioned my band's name to his friend. It was just lucky I met Cormack in passing one day and mentioned my band to him myself. He didn't seem that interested, so you could imagine my surprise when he showed up to Mavericks a few weeks later. He was so impressed with our performance, he took one of our demo CDs home with him.

During an informal meeting with him last Sunday, he advised he had arranged for some music scouts to come and watch us perform tonight. Hence my nerves.

My nerves take on a whole new meaning when Jenni whispers, "I miss you, Nick." She is so quiet, if I weren't in the deserted lot at the back of Mavericks, I may not have heard what she said.

I'd be lying if I said I didn't miss her too. I miss her every day. I miss her when I walk into the Dungeon and she isn't holding my hand. I miss her when I order a bottle of beer and a glass of wine because I had become accustomed to doing it every weekend for the past two months. I miss the way she smells, and I miss her knockout smile, but I'll never tell her that. Why? Because I've broken so many of my "Player" rules for her, but there's one rule I'll never break – I'll never fall in love.

When I fail to reply to Jenni's declaration, a harsh exhalation of air sounds down the line. "I have to go."

"Wait—"

My demand comes too late; she's already disconnected the call. I redial her number. Our conversation just started, so it can't be over already.

My fists clench when my call gets sent to voicemail. "Fuck!" I curse into the warm night air.

I type a text message into my phone, my fingers shaking with every syllable I stroke.

Me: *I miss you too.*

Admitting I miss her isn't telling her I love her. This doesn't break any rules. It just shows her I like her—*right?*

My pulse thrums in my neck as my index finger hovers over the send button. I'm torn on whether I should hit send or delete. I don't like that she's angry at me, but I don't want her getting the wrong idea.

Fuck—why is this so complicated?

Certain I'm seconds away from shattering my phone from how hard I'm gripping it, I shove it into my pocket, not hitting either of the buttons I was debating.

My hand is only halfway out of my pocket when a female voice scares the living daylights out of me. "Hi, Nick."

I clutch my chest to ensure my heart remains in place before spinning to face the person who snuck up on me unaware. My stomach creeps up my esophagus when she moves far enough out of the shadows I can see who she is. She's the girl from a few months ago. The young brunette with hazel eyes. I still can't recall her name. I think it starts with an M, but don't quote me.

Grinning a full-toothed smile, she throws herself into my arms. The chances of me vomiting double when the smell of bleach engulfs my nostrils. She either dipped herself in the chemicals, or she works with them daily.

After prying her hands off my neck, I pull her far enough away from me to see her face. Her wild eyes dart between mine as she bounces on her heels. She looks like she just won the jackpot. Although she seems harmless, I race for the front doors of Mavericks, more than eager to get far away from her and her skitzo eyes.

"It was nice seeing you again." The band has a couple of groupies who get a little handsy, but the craziness in this lady's eyes freaks me the fuck out.

I freeze with my hand wrapped around the door handle of Mavericks when she asks, "Do you want a boy or a girl?"

My heart plummets into my stomach as my wide eyes turn back to her. Smiling, she bridges the gap between us. "I think we will have a girl."

The way she says "we" makes me cringe.

I swallow down the bile in the back of my throat before replying, "I'm not planning on having kids for *many* years to come."

"Oh, yes you are," she says, nodding. "In around seven months."

What the fuck?

My stomach swirls as regret plagues my usually carefree attitude. Certain I'm being pranked, I scan the parking lot, seeking Slater or Jacob. They have to be here, because there's no way what she's saying is true. I always use protection. If I don't have it, I don't have sex. It's that simple.

Failing to find anyone in the vicinity, I return my eyes to little Ms. Skitzo. "You're joking, right?" I should be ashamed of my trembling words, but I'm not. I'm scared as fuck right now.

Narrowing her eyes, she folds her arms in front of her chest.

When two drunk women exit the door we're standing next to, I wrap my hand around the unknown lady's arm and drag her into the darkness of the parking lot. I don't want anyone overhearing our conversation. "This isn't possible; I never have sex without protection." My tone is sterner since my anger is being unleashed.

This can't be happening. Not now. Not after everything that's happened the past few months.

She bats her eyelashes as if I'd break the rules just for her. *Unfucking-likely.* "You did that night; you said you wanted to have a baby with me."

"That's not possible!" I snap, my voice roaring. I was smashed on the night in question, but there's no way those words would have *ever* left my lips.

When she takes a step closer to me, I take one back. "You're the only guy I've ever slept with, so you're the father."

I scrub my hand down my face as my brain scrambles to think of a way I can get out of this fucked-up situation. Two seconds later, a light bulb switches on. "I can give you money to take care of it."

Excitement lines the brunette's face. . . until reality dawns. I'm not offering to look after her and the baby; I'm proposing she get an abortion.

"I could *never* do that." She clutches a gold cross hanging around her neck as her eyes fill with tears. I feel bad, but I don't know what she expects from me. We got together once—*one fucking time*—this can't be the outcome for an event I don't even remember.

"I can't take care of a kid right now. I'm not financially stable; I don't have a house. I don't have anything I could offer a kid." *I also don't want to be a father, especially not with you.*

"That's okay; I can support all three of us. I have some money my daddy left me, and I could get a job. It'll all work out."

My heart wallops my ribs as everything I've ever wanted slips between my fingers. This is why I have rules, to stop shit like this from happening.

I stop staring into space when Noah's voice filters into the parking lot. His jagged sentence reveals he is completing a sound check. It also reminds me about our important performance tonight. "I have to go. I have to go perform." My words are as dazed and dizzy as my head.

"I can meet you after the show?" she suggests, following me into Mavericks.

In my disoriented state, I nod. It's stupid of me to do, but I've got more important matters to take care of right now. I'm late—*again*—and my bandmates won't be happy about it.

"About time, fuckface," Slater growls when I stumble onto the stage.

I flip him the bird before crouching down to help Noah set up my guitar amp. "Sorry I'm late. I had some shit to sort out." *Shit that's going to turn my life upside fucking down.*

The lady claiming I've fathered her child takes a seat at one of the barstools at the back of Mavericks. Even though I avoid looking at her, I can feel her beady eyes watching my every move. Her eager gaze has my stomach swirling so much, I know there's no way I'll complete our set without barfing.

When Noah jumps off the stage to take a leak, I make my way to the still nameless stranger. Her seedy smirk morphs into a full smile when I stop to stand in front of her. "Can I grab your details and call you tomorrow?"

With the fog in my head lifting, so is my rationality. Our band has been waiting years for this opportunity, and I refuse to let a little slip-up fuck with our chance of making it big.

Smiling a fake, weirdo grin, she nods. After snagging a napkin off the countertop, she scribbles her name and number on it, marks the corner with her bright pink lips, then hands it to me.

"Megan," I read off the napkin. "I'll talk to you tomorrow."

She hops off the barstool, then balances on her tippy toes to press a kiss to my cheek. "I'll see you tomorrow."

With that, she skips out of Mavericks with an extra spring in her step. I return to the stage, but my steps are nowhere near as springy as hers.

Halfway through our set, Noah motions for me to look at the bar. I balk when I witness Emily stumbling. I've never seen her touch a drop of alcohol in the six months she's watched us performed, let alone in private.

When a guy bands his arm around Emily's waist, my heart sinks into my stomach. There's something very wrong with this picture.

Before I can work through my confusion, Noah dives off the stage. He charges for the man dragging a nearly unconscious Emily toward the back alley of Mavericks, his steps as tight as his fists are clenched. Shockingly, I follow after him.

After pulling Emily to a safe distance, Noah begins pummeling the guy's face, while I stand by and watch. I don't have a chance in hell of lugging Noah off him. He's a good four to five inches taller than me, and a couple of pounds heavier.

It's only when I yell that Emily needs him does he stop beating the guy's face in. She's lying on the ground with her flopped head resting on Jacob's thigh.

I get a bit of dirt in my eye when Noah scoots across the wooden floorboards to cradle Emily in his lap. The look in his eyes. . . *god.* Pure devastation. As he begs for Emily to wake up, my thoughts stray to Jenni. I've never been a fighter, but I'm pretty sure I would have responded in the exact manner Noah did if it were her lying unconscious on a dirty bar floor.

The next twenty minutes pass in a blur. Noah goes to the hospital with Emily, while the band issues statements to a detective who is a friend of Noah and Jacob's. Although tonight was our chance to showcase our talents to the music executives who turned up specifically to watch our show, no one cares. At the moment, ensuring Emily is safe is the only thing on our minds.

When I finish giving my statement to Ryan, he gives me permission to leave. My jaw muscle spasms when I walk past the man who roofied Emily. I've never understood why guys drug women to sleep with them. Believe me, there are plenty of women on the prowl every weekend. If you can't find the one you're looking for, you've just got to lower your standards.

As I break through the main doors of Mavericks, I yank my phone out of my pocket. The message I should have sent hours ago sits open on the screen. It adds to the heaviness on my chest while also ensuring I'm doing the right thing.

After hitting send, I dial Jenni's number. She's so devastated when I inform her what happened to Emily, she instantly begins packing. I hear her sobs over the clunking of her suitcase when she drags it down from her closet.

It takes a lot of pleading, but I eventually convince her not to catch the first flight home. Noah has everything under control, and she has classes to prepare for in the morning. She only agrees to my suggestion because I promise to check on Emily with my very own eyes, and even then, it was still one hell of a fight.

Around an hour after Emily is admitted for observation, I spot Cormack knocking on her hospital room door. I signal for Marcus and Slater to look at the door. They smile, feeling the shift in the air just like I do.

With Noah's focus on Emily, we sneak out of the room without him noticing. Our conversation with Cormack doesn't get off to a great start. He's pretty stern while expressing his disappointment about the band running off stage during our performance, but considering the circumstances, he also understood why we did it.

When he says his record company wants to offer us a contract, the excitement is so overwhelming, even Slater slaps me on the back in euphoria. Eager to share our news with Noah, Slater and Marcus shake Cormack's hand before making their way back to Emily's room.

I stop watching Emily's room door swing when Cormack says, "Congratulations, you have a great group, and I think this is the beginning of a very successful collaboration."

With excitement lacing my veins, I accept the hand he's holding out before using it to pull him in for a hug. He's shocked, but not as much as Jenni is when I call her to share our news. It's been one of those nights: wild and crazy, with more emotions than I know what to do with.

After promising to call Jenni the instant Emily wakes, I call Isaac. I don't mean to brag when I tell him our band gained a lucrative record deal without his help, but that's kind of what I do.

"I had no doubt you'd do it, Nick. You'll treasure it even more now that you achieved it by yourself."

I guess what he's saying is true. The fact Rise Up earned this on our own makes it even more worthwhile. During our chat, I inform him about my run-in with Megan. He reprimands me for not using protection, but when I blatantly insist that I *always* use protection, he suggests I look further into

Megan's claims, even more so since we're being signed to a label.

"Some women will do anything for a free ride," he warned.

That's when I decide not to call Megan tomorrow morning.

Instead, I call a lawyer.

CHAPTER EIGHTEEN

JENNI

M y first two months of college have been a confusing time, a jumbled mess of conflicting class schedules and adapting to new surroundings. But, if I'm being honest, most of my bewilderment at the beginning centered around Nick. His lack of contact my first few days in New York was an obvious sign that he was no longer thinking about me. His texts were short and infrequent. So, imagine my shock when he called me out of the blue on the very night Rise Up was scheduled to perform in front of the music executives from Destiny Records. I was stunned but immensely pleased.

I hadn't considered what his reaction would be when I told him I missed him. It was a thing I said in the heat of the moment, but my heart did crack when he didn't respond. Feeling like an idiot, and a little heartbroken, I disconnected the call. I nearly didn't answer when he called to inform me Emily was roofied at Mavericks. If his message hadn't flashed up on the screen seconds before his call, I probably wouldn't have.

When he said Emily had been drugged, I wanted to catch the first flight home. She's been my best friend for over half my life, so I wanted to be there for her.

I don't know how he did it, but Nick convinced me that the best thing I could do for Emily was to stay put. I didn't sleep a wink that night while waiting for updates. Half my stomach was twisted up in knots because of Emily's condition, whereas the other half was filled with excitement. Even with the band missing three-quarters of their performance, they secured a record deal. I wasn't surprised because they're extremely talented, but I was shocked I was the first person Nick shared his news with.

After our call ended, I messaged Slater. Our texts from that night still make me smile.

Me: *Congrats xx*

Slater: *Thanks! How do you already know?*

Me: *I have my sources. . .*

Slater: *Ha, well thanks. I'm fucking stoked.*

Me: *You should be! You deserve it!*

Slater: *I'll see you in a few weeks, city slicker?*

Me: *Can't wait, bye.*

Slater: *Bye.*

Now, after two long months, I'm finally traveling home to spend the long weekend with my family and friends. After his dismal efforts my first two weeks in New York, Nick upped his game the past two months. He maintained regular contact, and not just via text messages. He calls me often, usually once or twice a day, and we've also FaceTimed a bit.

I stop reminiscing when my taxi pulls to the curb at the front of my parents' law firm. My flight home wasn't supposed to arrive until late Friday afternoon, but I managed to get an earlier one. I was a little homesick, and I couldn't wait to see Emily, my parents, and, of course, Nick for a moment longer.

Hoping to surprise my parents, I didn't update them on my change of plans. I'm the one left stunned when I enter their firm to discover Nick striding out of my mom's office. When he spots me, his pupils widen, and his mouth becomes ajar. He stares at me like he can't comprehend how I'm standing in front of him.

As quickly as his shock arrived, it leaves. Heat spreads across my cheeks when he spans the distance between us to plant a kiss on my cheek.

"Hi." I return his gesture while sneakily taking a deep whiff of his alluring scent. "What are you doing here?"

His lips twitch, but not a word spills from his mouth. It's as if he is too shocked by my presence to speak.

He loses the chance when my mom lets out a cough. It bellows off the stark white walls of the reception area before jingling into my ears.

"Hi, Mom." Reluctantly, I pace away from Nick to greet my mom with a hug. It isn't that I haven't missed her—I have—I just hate the way her eyes narrow the longer they bounce between Nick and me.

The confusion on Nick's face jumps to mine when my mom says, "I'll talk to you next week." Her tone is stern and straight to the point.

Nick's eyes stop bouncing between us to briefly nod. His tongue swishes around his mouth as his eyes stray back to me. "I'll see you tomorrow?"

"Yep." Heat creeps across my cheeks as I flash him a flirty smile.

Emily and Noah have planned a BBQ at Bronte's Peak like we did regularly before I left for college. After taking in the way my body blooms around him, Nick waves, spins on his heels, then bolts out of my parents' law firm.

The frosted glass door hasn't even snapped shut when my mom blocks it from my view with her brooding frame. "How do you know Nick?" Her tone hangs as low as her brows.

I drag my teeth over my lower lip. "He's a friend of mine. . ." My reply falls short when I spot my dad in the corner of my eye. "Daddy!"

With a squeal, I throw myself into his arms. The past two months have been the longest period I've gone without seeing my dad. I've seen him every day of my life for the past eighteen and a half years.

I've missed him so much, my chest felt hollow from not seeing his face every day.

"How's my princess?" My dad wraps me up in his famously warm hugs.

I've barely climbed out of my car at Bronte's Peak when Slater pounces on me. His dreads tickle my neck when he engulfs me in a huge hug. My heart warms from his friendly gesture. I've missed out on so many important things the past two months. It's hard having a life both here and in New York. Although Emily attends school at Parkwood, she gets to come home every weekend. I'm not that fortunate. I didn't realize how homesick I was until this weekend.

Slater pulls back from our embrace, then drops his big brown eyes to mine. "How's city life?"

"You know how it is: wild sex parties and orgies every other weekend." My words are jam-packed with wittiness.

Slater laughs a full and boisterous chuckle. "Sounds like my type of place."

In the corner of my eye, I spot Nick eyeballing our exchange. The flare of his nostrils tells me he heard my comment to Slater. He's not happy, but he's not going to react to my attempt at goading him either.

After greeting Marcus, I make my way to Nick. "Hello."

I sling my arms around his shoulders the same way I did with Marcus and Slater. The only difference this time around is Nick holds on to me longer than they did.

There's no surprise that during the rest of the BBQ I never get the chance to talk to Nick. Slater's imposing frame was wedged between us at all times. It's only when everyone packs away our equipment and begins heading home do I discover a way for us to have a little alone time.

Nick's truck is parked a few spaces down from a small yellow car positioned at the end of a very long parking lot. Once I say goodbye to Marcus, Slater, Emily, Noah, and Jacob, ensuring them I'll be seconds behind them, I pace to Nick's truck.

He's so deep in thought when I reach his driver's side window, he doesn't notice me standing outside for several seconds. His eyes are cloudy, and the veins in his fists are working overtime. When I tap on the window, he gives me an uneasy smirk before opening the door. Sparks of attraction ignite between us the instant I slip into the passenger seat. It makes the heat in the cabin so stifling, my palms slick with sweat.

"Jen—"

"Shh," I interrupt, the tension firing between us too strong for words. "I just need a few minutes."

I crawl over the vinyl seat before straddling his lap. I then kiss him before any of the thoughts I see in his eyes can be expressed. He sucks in a quick breath when my lips skim across his jaw, and down his neck until I playfully tug at his nipple poking out of his shirt.

He yanks his shirt off how every man does, via the scruff of its collar, exposing his panty-wetting body to my more than avid eyes. Once it's dumped on the floor, he works on my shirt. Warm air whips around me when he removes it as eagerly as he did his own. He then lowers his mouth to trap my pert nipple between his teeth. Even with still wearing my bra, his teeth grazing my hardened bud arches my back and has me calling out.

"Again." I hate begging, but I can set aside my annoyance when it comes to this man.

After pulling down my bra cup, he drags his tongue down the heated flesh of my breast, then circles it around the puckered pink skin. My hands shoot out to secure a grip on something when he sucks my nipple into his mouth, coating the sharp bud with warm, tempting saliva. He peers up at me when my purrs double. I love the way he treats my breasts as if they're just as important as the more needy regions of my body.

While watching me through lowered lids, he rocks his hips up, grinding his thick cock against the seam of my panties. He goes slower than we usually go, but it doesn't dampen the intensity in the slightest. It's as fire sparking now as it's always been.

When I shudder, Nick smiles a wolfish grin. He loves how quickly he has me floating on a cloud of ecstasy. Eager to wipe the egotistical glint from his eyes, I shuffle back until I'm once again on my side of the bench seat. He almost voices a protest. He would have if my change in position didn't quickly follow the unbuttoning of his jeans.

The hiss of his zipper lowering adds to the tension teeming between us, then the removal of his cock utterly detonates it. He's thick and heavy in my hand, twitching as purposefully as the pulse between my legs. Air whizzes between his teeth when I glide my tongue over the glistening bead at the crest of his cock.

After moaning about his delicious taste, I lower my moistened lips down his wide shaft. The corners of my mouth burn from their painful stretch, but his taste and smell more than makes up for the discomfort. I love sucking his cock—*almost as much as I love him.*

The more bobs my head does, the more Nick's crown glistens with his arousal, and the foggier his windows become. It's almost dusk, so the condensation on the windows glistening in the sunset adds an enticing orange glow to our reunion. It's as beautiful as the smirk Nick hits me with when I peer up at him at the same time my tongue laps up the sweet taste of his pleasure from his knob.

"Here I am trying to be a gentleman, and you throw out my attempts of decency by sucking my dick like a naughty little nymph." His words quiver at the end when I increase the strength of my sucks. I hollow my cheeks so profoundly, his cock pops out of my mouth with a crack when he snaps my panties off my body. He pushes me back until my head is squashed against the passenger door of his truck and my pussy is mere inches from his face. "Now it's my turn to show how being bad is ten times more fun than being good."

We spend the next hour reacquainting. We don't talk, not with words, anyway. We moan, growl, and let our bodies speak on our behalf. It's a beautiful hour filled with devotion and sexual chemistry. It's like it was before I left for college, except this time around, Nick is more attentive and gentle. He's savoring every moment, as if we might not have many left.

After finishing the buttons on my shirt, I peer over at him. He yanks up the zipper on his jeans before aggressively tugging his shirt over his head. He seems angry, or perhaps upset? I don't really know his emotions well enough to decipher between the two just yet.

"What's wrong?" I decide the straight up approach is better than tiptoeing around what's bothering him.

He takes in several deep breaths while staring out at the brilliant blue sky. When his eyes turn to mine, my breathing shallows. He's definitely angry; there's no denying it now. I try to hide my smile when he growls, "Sex parties and orgies. Really?"

I shouldn't bother. The giggle rumbling up my chest gives away my ruse. I may be weird, but I think it's endearing that he's jealous about my banter with Slater.

Unappreciative of my laughter, Nick huffs, "It's not fucking funny."

Grinning, I nod. It's more than laughable. Slater is like a brother to me, so just the thought leaves me with only two options: laugh or be sick. I went for the one that would create less mess.

"I was joking," I say once the veins pulsating in Nick's neck turn dangerous. "Besides my classes, I've barely left my apartment the past two months."

When his eyes drift from the steering wheel to me, my heart rate accelerates. He's assessing my face, storing every detail in his memory bank. I run my fingers through my hair, trying to get the frazzled pieces to calm down. If he's snapping a mental picture, I want it to be a good one.

Any kinks in my hair are smoothed out by Nick's fingers when we spend the next hour enjoying round two.

After checking my face in my rearview mirror, I clamber out of my car. My lipstick is no longer existent, and my hair is a rumpled mess, but the most visible sign I've been participating in vigorous sexual activities is in my eyes. They're glossed over and beaming with lust.

Praying my parents are too old to comprehend why my eyes would have this appearance, I take the stairs two at a time before rushing through the front door. My heart stops beating when I see my mom sitting at my dad's desk.

"Hi, Mom." I dash for the stairwell. My mom isn't as old as my dad, so I'm reasonably sure she'd understand what has caused the spark of lust in my eyes.

"Can I please speak with you?" Her stern tone indicates her question is not a request. It's a demand.

I freeze at the bottom of the stairs to suck in a deep breath. "Okay. I'll be right down after I take a shower."

"Now!" Her low, angry tone rumbles out of the office.

Crap!

My shoulders slump as I pad into my dad's office. My mom's narrowed gaze scans my face the instant I step inside. Heat flushes my cheeks when her gaze slits even more after landing on my eyes. She gestures for me to sit in the wooden chair across from her before reclaiming my father's chair. My brows scrunch when she lifts her chin at someone behind me. The room closes in on me when I crank my neck to see Maria closing the double doors of my father's office.

This isn't good—not at all.

I swallow the lump in my throat before returning my eyes to my mom. This is more intense than the time Emily and I got caught skipping school to go to the beach.

"Did Nick give you that gleam in your eye?"

When I shake my head, my mom's top lip forms into a snarl. She's detected my deceit without a word spilling from my lips.

Hating the disappointment in her eyes, I change my head shake to a nod.

A mask slips over her face, the one she usually uses on her clients. "Did you ask him why he was in my office yesterday?"

I shake my head once more, mortifying my mother.

"Are you not the least bit curious as to why he needs a lawyer?"

I shake my head again. Nick's band secured a record deal six weeks ago, so I assumed he was having the contract looked at, but by my mom's stiff posture and the stern look hampering her usually docile face, I now realize my assumption was wrong.

Oh no.

CHAPTER NINETEEN

NICK

When gravel crunching under tires sounds through my ears, I stop staring at a tattered business card. Jenni's little blue car is rolling down the driveway of my dad's property. I was waiting for this to happen. The instant I nervously fumbled out of her parents' law firm yesterday afternoon, I knew this moment was about to occur.

I had no clue my lawyer was Jenni's mom. The name on the business card I'm clutching reads *Taylor Lee*. Jenni's last name is Murphy, so when she called my lawyer her mom, I was not only shocked, I shit bricks.

All last night and this morning, I was panicked out of my mind that Jenni would question me as to why I needed a lawyer. My panic wasn't needed. She didn't mention it today. Not once. That was when gratitude for lawyer-client confidentiality smacked into me.

I had planned to tell Jenni what was happening once we were alone, but when she climbed into my truck, my desire to have her outweighed my moral compass. Although I'm confident she will support me through this, just in case I didn't know her as well as I thought, I took my time memorizing every detail of her face and body.

By the time I finished my avid assessment, it was time for Jenni to go home. Her mom had given her a strict curfew, which was odd considering she's an adult living away from home. Jenni and I agreed to meet at Bronte's Café the next morning at ten AM, where I had planned to confess my sins, but it appears as if my honesty has come too late.

She has changed her clothes, and her hair is wet like she's just gotten out of the shower, but her face is marked with concern, and her eyes are brimming with tears. She doesn't know the entirety of my fuck up, but she knows I'm keeping secrets from her.

After scooting over, I motion for her to join me on the swinging chair bolted to the porch. She hesitates for a second before she makes her way toward me. Her backside has scarcely landed in her seat when she asks, "Why were you at my mom's law office yesterday?" Her voice is soft but riddled with nerves.

I rake my eyes over her face, absorbing and categorizing every perfect detail to make sure I have it right before I begin to speak. "I needed a lawyer for a paternity case."

Her brows scrunch as her pupils widen, but she surprises me by remaining relatively calm. "You have a child?" Her tone relays her confusion.

When I shake my head, she exhales a quick breath. It's sharply redrawn when I confess, "A girl is claiming I fathered her unborn child."

She watches me, but not a word escapes her lips. I'm having a hard time gauging her reaction. I can't tell if she's angry or upset. She just sits quietly, motionless and staring at me.

After a beat, she asks, "How far along is she?"

My increased heart rate slicks my palms with sweat. I don't want to answer this, because the instant I do, I know she'll be gone.

The longer I delay in answering her question, the more tears fill her eyes. Seconds from bursting, I stammer out, "Four months."

A sole tear drips down her pale face as she clamps her hand over her mouth to stifle her choked sob. Panic scorches my veins like a wildfire. All the terrible things I imagined last night are happening. The hurt, the anger, it's all being relayed by her beautiful eyes.

"It's not my baby. I swear to you, it isn't mine. I don't have unprotected sex." My words are rickety, but nothing can conceal their confidence. There's no chance in hell Megan's baby is mine. I have rules to ensure shit like this doesn't happen. Jenni is the only girl I've ever broken the rules for.

Jenni's lips quiver when she asks, "When did you sleep with her?" She's panting so hard, her chest rises and falls with every gasp she sucks in. She's genuinely devastated.

In a last-ditch attempt to keep her tied to me, I grab ahold of her hand. Pain hits my chest when she angrily yanks it away from me. "When did you sleep with her?!" This question isn't as calm as her first two.

Even knowing I'm digging my own grave, I answer, "The night I went to your aunt's salon."

She slaps me hard across the face. My cheek stings, but it's nothing compared to the hurt reflecting in her tormented eyes. She appears mortified that she slapped me, but I don't know why. I deserved it. I chased her relentlessly for months, then bedded her and another girl in less than twenty-four hours.

I'm a pig.

When she jumps to her feet to run to her car, the tears streaming down her face cause her to stumble on the gravel driveway. I rush for her, wanting to help her back to her feet. She recoils at my touch.

"Leave me alone!" she screams while jerking her bloody hand out of my grasp.

Her hands aren't the only wounded parts of her. Her knees are bleeding from gravel embedded in her soft, delicate skin. She's not feeling it, though. She's hurting too much to feel something as meager as pain.

Her sad eyes stare into mine as she demands, "Stay away from me, Nick."

The heaviness on my chest intensifies when she slides into the driver's seat of her car. It takes her several attempts to get her seatbelt to latch into place, but once it's fixed, her car goes darting out of the driveway, leaving me in a cloud of dust.

When a screen door creaking open shrieks through my ears, I turn back to face my house. My dad is standing in the doorway, his eyes holding the same anger and embarrassment Jenni's held when she asked me to leave her alone.

Shaking his head, he reenters our house, slamming the door behind him.

Call me a sucker for punishment, but the next day, I arrive at Jacob's house for the band's monthly BBQ. Jenni's car is parked in the same spot it was last time, but she doesn't turn to face me when she senses my presence. She just enters the house, leaving me under the suspicious watch of both Slater and Jacob.

When lunch is served, she waits for me to be seated first before picking a seat as far away from me as possible. Because she sits on the same side of the table as me, I don't even get the opportunity to glance at her.

It takes Slater a few minutes to realize she's avoiding me on her own accord, but when he does, he kicks me in the shins so hard, I'll be limping for a week. When the girls take the dishes into the kitchen to be washed, I follow them. I don't just want a chance to get Jenni alone this time, though. I genuinely want to help.

Jenni freezes when I enter the kitchen on Emily's heels. Her clumsy movements have the dishes clanging together so fiercely, they chip. After stuffing the broken plate into the cupboard, she storms out of the kitchen. I nearly go after her, but Nicole shoves a stack of wet plates into my hands, stopping me.

By the time I've finished drying up, Jenni is nowhere to be seen. My steps to check if her car is still here halt mid-stride when Jacob steps into my path.

"She left," he informs me, his tone clipped. "This is the *exact* reason Slater was trying to keep her away from you." His voice reveals his disappointment in me.

Join the club, Jakeyboy. I've got a list of haters as long as my arm right now, and my name is right at the top.

Since the only reason I come to these gatherings has left, I leave as well.

"Wow, The Player returns," Tina croons upon spotting me entering the Dungeon.

I shoot her a quick smirk before continuing my trip to Isaac's office. I haven't been at the Dungeon in over two months. The handful of times I came here without Jenni just felt weird. Every time I was dancing with a girl, I imagined she was Jenni. When I realized a doppelgänger would never come close to the real thing, my fantasies crashed and burned. Jenni and I never had an agreement to stay exclusive, but the Dungeon held too many memories of her. I couldn't bring myself to use it as my playground anymore.

When I enter Isaac's office, his dark eyes lift to mine. He's talking on his cell phone. After gesturing for me to enter, he spins his office chair around, then lowers his voice. I don't give a shit about his shady business dealings, so I don't know why he's acting sneaky.

"Alright, bye, Dee." Spinning back around, Isaac assesses my sour expression. "Are the test results in yet?" His tone is as low and demanding as always.

I shake my head. I've been waiting for the paternity test results for nearly a week. We had to wait for Megan to reach sixteen weeks before an amniocentesis could be performed. Despite Megan's best efforts, I haven't had any contact with her since she bombarded me two months ago. Her pursuit to engage with me has been relentless, but until the results are in, I refuse to associate with her.

I scrub my tired eyes. "Hopefully this week."

Hearing a worry I didn't mean to express, Isaac asks, "Are you worried?"

I shake my head again. I'm confident Megan's unborn baby isn't mine, but the results no longer matter. I'm reasonably sure Jenni will never speak to me again either way.

―――

The next morning, I'm awoken by my phone vibrating on my bedside table. Scampering, I slide my finger across the screen then press it to my ear. "Jenni?"

"Ah. . . Good morning, Mr. Holt, it's Emma, Taylor Lee's receptionist." She swallows, as embarrassed by my mistake as me. "I'm calling to advise you that the amnio results are in."

I sit up in my bed. "Okay. Good. Can you tell me the results over the phone?"

"No, sorry, I can't. Ms. Lee likes doing them in house. I can schedule you an appointment for—"

"Today?" I interrupt.

Papers being shuffled sound down the line. "She did have a cancellation at three o'clock; how does that sound?"

The hammering of my heart is audible in my reply, "Perfect."

―――

When I walk into Taylor's office, her usually charming personality has been replaced with an angrier, colder version. After wiping the sweat from my palms on my jeans, I sit in the chair opposite her. My knee bobs up and down, my body's way of ridding itself of the nerves fluttering in my stomach.

When Emma exits, closing the door behind her, I lock my eyes with Taylor. My heart races more with every second she delays freeing me from the noose wrapped around my neck.

Believing I've squirmed enough, she discloses, "You're not going to be a father anytime soon."

I let out the biggest sigh. I may even throw a fist pump in the air and slap my thigh a few times as well. "I fucking knew it," I murmur under my breath. "I never have unprotected sex."

Taylor slides an envelope stuffed to the brim with paperwork across the desk. "Here's the full doctor's report and your bill." Still pissed, she nudges her chin to the door. "You can show yourself out."

She could be breathing fire right now, and I wouldn't care. After the news she just delivered, I could kiss her! *Or better yet, I could kiss her daughter.*

After hightailing it to my truck, I drive to Jenni's house, eager to share my news with her. I take the stairs two at a time before banging on her front door. Not long later, an elderly Italian-looking lady answers the door.

"Hi, I'm here to see Jenni." I peer past her shoulder, seeking Jenni. I didn't pay much attention the first time I picked her up, but her house is fucking huge.

My eyes snap back to the lady guarding the door when she says, "Jenni is gone."

"Gone where?" She isn't scheduled to fly home until tomorrow morning, so she must mean somewhere local.

I'm proven wrong when she responds, "Back to school, she left yesterday afternoon."

I stare at the woman, utterly confused. When she closes the door, I head back to my truck. During my travels, I yank my cell phone out of my ripped jeans and dial Jenni's number. I'm shocked when my call is sent straight to her voicemail. No matter the time or the day, she always answers my calls.

"Hey, Jenni, it's Nick. I didn't think you were leaving until Tuesday morning?" I wiggle my tongue around my mouth to loosen up my next set of words. "I'm not the father. I just found out, and I wanted you to be the first to know."

CHAPTER TWENTY

JENNI

I can't believe I stupidly fell in love with a player. When Nick arrived at Jacob's house, I knew I would never enjoy the festivities. Just looking at him hurt. I had wondered the past few months if he was being exclusive. I prayed he was, but it was stupid of me to do. He didn't get the reputation he has by not sleeping around.

When I arrived home from Jacob's, I checked if there was any availability to catch an earlier flight. Thankfully, if I could get to the airport in an hour, I'd be back in New York in under four. Needing as much distance between Nick and me as possible, I jumped at the chance. If possible, I would have flown to Australia.

My dad was disappointed when I said I had to go back to NY earlier than expected. I made out that I had to study for an important test I'd forgotten about. He said he understood, but I could see his disappointment. He drove me to the airport on the promise he'd pass on my apologies to my mom for not saying goodbye.

After my abrupt departure yesterday, I fielded calls from Emily and Nicole, wanting to know why I left without saying goodbye. I lied, blaming horrific PMS cramps for my disappearing act. Nicole bought my lie, but Emily was more reserved. She knew something was off with me but didn't want to push. I even got a text from Slater Sunday afternoon asking if I was okay. I gave him the same excuse I had given the girls. He replied saying I was disgusting and that I was to never share that type of information with him again. That was the first time I had smiled since Saturday afternoon.

Nick also called me several times Monday morning. When I listened to the voicemail he left on my phone, I couldn't miss the excitement in his voice when he said he wasn't the baby's dad. I was glad he was relieved, but it didn't lessen my hurt in the slightest.

When he continued calling my phone every hour on the hour for the next two days, I googled how to block a number. The very first number I blocked was Nick's.

It was time for me to remove the blinders and start looking at the entire picture again. This snapshot doesn't have any room for players.

———

Today is a public holiday, so the university is deserted. It's a cloudy day, and for the most part, it's been drizzling with rain. It's the perfect weather to match my sullen mood. I've spent a majority of my morning snuggled on the couch, reading a book. I gave up when I realized I was reading the same chapter repeatedly. Now I'm watching TV.

When my cell phone rings, I expect it to be another call from Emily checking in to see how my cramps are going. My nose screws up when I see it's from an unrecognized number. Since the area code is local, I answer it. "Hello."

"It's been years, yet your voice still makes my heart race," croons a male I don't instantly recognize. It's only when he asks if I'm "ready to beg yet," do I realize who's calling me. I haven't seen or heard from Christian in over four years. I'm surprised he even has my number.

After laughing at my shock, he explains when he was in town last month visiting his family, my mom let it slip that I was studying in

New York. When he told her he was coming here to film a movie, she gave him my number.

"I was hoping you'd want to catch up?" He doesn't attempt to hide the sexual undertone in his voice.

I can't help but laugh. If he could see me right now, he wouldn't be so eager to "catch up." Half of my living room is covered in snotty tissues. I'm wearing a pair of yoga pants that have a hole in them from the time I snagged my leg on a steel fence when I went for a jog. My white shirt has last night's dinner spilled down the front, and I haven't brushed either my hair or my teeth.

"Thank you for making me smile, but I think I'll pass."

Christian sighs. "Come on, Jen, have a cup of coffee with an old friend while he's in town."

"I'm really not in the mood to go out." Hopping off the couch, I gather the mountain of tissues sitting on the coffee table. Even if I have no plans to go out, I don't have to live like a slob.

I freeze when Christian mutters, "Then I guess it's lucky I came to you." His comment coincides with three loud taps hitting the front door of my apartment.

I glare at my door, certain there's no way he could get past the security in the lobby. My dad rented this apartment because of its impeccable security services. Unless you're a tenant, or you've been placed on an approved list, you can't even access the elevators in the lobby.

"Answer your door, Jenni, or I'll have the security guy come and open it for me," Christian says down the phone. I also hear his voice rumbling through my front door.

Panicked out of my mind, my wide gaze flicks down to my outfit. I cringe. My apartment isn't the only slobbish thing around these parts. I look like I'm homeless. I consider running to my room and getting changed, then I realize my current state will be the perfect way to repel Christian. He's a player, meaning he and Nick can go row up the same creek without a paddle as far as I'm concerned.

I swing open my door before I can change my mind. Christian's plump lips curve into a large grin as his dazzling eyes stray to mine. He gives me a flirty wink before lowering his heavy-lidded gaze down my body. Taking advantage of his distraction, I scan his body, nearly stomping my feet. Of course, he's wearing an impeccably tailored suit. His long blond hair has been cut into a more mature style, and he has a slight bit of stubble on his jaw, making him appear more mature than his twenty-two years. His body has changed a lot the past four years as well. The skinny boy I was used to seeing has been replaced with a man. *A very well-built man.*

I snap out of my trance when Christian's eyes lift and lock with mine. "Still as dazzling as ever." He leans in to press a kiss on my cheek. His minty breath reminds me that I didn't brush my teeth this morning.

Curving my hand over my mouth to save face, I murmur, "I'll be back in a minute."

After shutting my front door, I dash into my bathroom. The shuffling of my feet along the floorboards echoes in the silence that has underscored our reunion.

In a record amount of time, I brush my teeth and hair and change into more suitable attire for guests. It isn't that I want to impress Christian; I just don't want to look like a slob. By the time I make it back to my living room, Christian has cleared away my used tissues and stacked my magazines and books into a neat pile on the coffee table.

"A book I was reading was really sad; one of the characters died. I've always been a bit of a crybaby," I inform him, covering up my tears with a lie.

He spins around to face me, removing his suit jacket on the way. "You've always been a big softie."

When my eyes zoom in on his impressive six pack visible under his nearly see-through white business shirt, I silently beg him to put his jacket back on. I'm not strong enough for this.

Spotting my scan of his body, he chuckles before moving to stand in front of me. "You've always been a blusher as well."

The back of his hand rubs my heated cheeks. It's a kind gesture, but it also reminds me that I attract the wrong type of man.

"Yeah, I have been — just like you've always been a player."

I pull away from his embrace and amble to the kitchen. He wants to have coffee, so we're going to have coffee. *And only coffee.*

Chuckling, Christian shadows me into the kitchen. I switch on the kettle and collect the mugs from the cabinet while he takes a seat at one of the two chairs I have around my shabby chic dining table.

I add coffee and sugar to our mugs while asking, "How did you get past my security?"

When he doesn't answer me, I spin around to face him. Grinning, he shrugs. I really wish he'd stop friggin' smiling. His smile is the main reason he became the school's biggest player. He didn't have to compete with the quarterback or the basketball captain. He just smiled, and the girls came running.

Although peeved at his unexpected arrival, the next two hours go smoothly. Christian and I spend the entire time talking. He tells me how he was studying at another university in New York before he caught the acting bug. For the past year, he's been filming a movie due to be released in a couple of weeks. He seems to have matured a lot over the years, but I can still see the player sparkle in his eyes.

"So what are you doing all the way in New York?" He sinks into his sofa chair before draping his arm so it touches my shoulder.

I reposition myself so he can no longer touch me. "I'm studying fashion design."

My lips curve into their first smile of the day. I've always loved fashion. I don't believe you need to find one style and stick to it. Why can't you love jeans, dresses, and skirts all the same? I love dressing to match how I feel for the day. That's why today's outfit was so lacking in personality.

"Like costumes?" Christian tugs on a piece of my hair that's fallen from my messy bun.

"No, like clothes you find in stores."

Jumping up off the sofa, I walk into the kitchen to place our empty mugs in the sink. I take my time washing them up. I need a moment to calm down. I swear I have a scent that attracts players. Just a look or a touch and I'm putty in their hands.

When I pace back into the living room, I spot Christian standing next to my small fireplace. He's looking at the collection of photos I have there. "Emily hasn't changed," he says, noticing I've re-entered the room. "Who's the guy?"

I move to stand next to him. He's referring to a photo I took of Emily and Noah at Bronte's Peak last year. They look so incredibly happy as they stare into each other's eyes.

"That's her boyfriend, Noah." I remove the frame from his grasp to place it in its rightful place on the mantel. During the process, my gaze flicks to a picture of Nick on my left. He's unaware I snapped his photo the same day as Emily and Noah's. He's staring out at the ocean with his brows scrunched and a smirk etched on his face. I love that photo of him because it captures his real personality. He can seem a little standoffish, and he often sits by himself whenever he attends any gatherings. I used to think that was because he enjoyed his own company, but I guess that's not really true. He just doesn't enjoy male company.

"Who's the blond?" Christian asks when he notices me staring at Nick's photo.

My chest deflates as my lungs lose the ability to breathe. "He's just a friend." I crank my neck to Christian. "What do you want, Christian?"

My voice is sterner than I originally planned, but with confusion fueling it, I'm not surprised. Why would he turn up now—days after I was deceived by a man just like him?

His hazel eyes flick between mine. I can see sexual hunger in them, but there's something else I can't comprehend. "When I found

out you were in New York, I had to come and visit my favorite girl."
He grips my hand in his, hoping it will hide the lie I see in his eyes.

It doesn't.

"Well, you've seen me now, so it's time for you to leave."

Removing my hand from his, I pace to my front door. My quota
for dealing with players this week has reached its absolute limit. I'm
not up for any more antics.

Christian snags his jacket off the sofa chair before shadowing me
to the front door. "I'll see you around."

I shake my head. I'm done with players.

He grins before pressing a peck on my cheek. "I *will* see you
around, because I live in this building."

My eyes snap to his. His are gleaming with mischief, but I know
he's telling the truth. They're not just beaming with lust; they're
wholesome as well.

He winks before sauntering out of my apartment. I stand still,
frozen in place with my mouth gaped open like a fish out of water.
When I snap out of my shock, I close my door. Just before it shuts
completely, I see Christian standing near the elevator bank, waiting
for the car to arrive to my floor.

Noticing my inconspicuous gawk, he cockily winks. "I'm in the
penthouse if you change your mind."

CHAPTER TWENTY-ONE

NICK

Eight fucking weeks. That's how long it's been since I've heard from Jenni. I tried her number every goddamn day the first four weeks. I kept getting the same message about her phone no longer being in service. I got so desperate to talk to her, I begged Jacob to give me her new number. After laughing at my kneeling position, he informed me her number hadn't changed.

That's when I realized she had blocked my number.

I'll admit my ego took a pretty big hit. Still, I went straight to a payphone to call her. When she greeted me with excitement, I thought she'd gotten over her anger. She sounded happy—I'd even go as far as saying pleased to hear from me.

It was only when she realized who she was talking to did her tone go from pleasant to pissed off in under five seconds. She told me to quit calling her before she hung up on me. I called her another three times immediately following that. She never answered any of my calls. I was so fucking pissed at her, I went to the Dungeon to pick up the first cute blonde girl with light blue eyes I could find. One way or another, I was going to get Jenni out of my head.

My plan was working. . . until I was sneaking the unnamed

blonde into my bedroom later that night. She was recreating memories I didn't want recreated. I liked them just the way they were.

After making up an excuse for her to leave, I drove her home. I'd never been eager to scrub a girl's perfume off my skin before, but I was that night. I scrubbed my skin so hard it nearly bled.

My desperation reached a new level two weeks ago when Rise Up was recording in the studio. While Noah was in the soundproof booth laying down some lyrics, I noticed his cell phone sitting on the bench across from me. I pretended I was getting some more sheet music, but really, I just grabbed his phone to sneakily borrow. It didn't take a genius to realize his lock code was Emily's birthday.

After logging into his Facebook app, I typed Jenni's name into the screen. Her profile picture hadn't changed since the day she blocked me. I sighed in relief when I realized her relationship status hadn't been updated either. It still showed she was single.

My eyes darted around the studio to make sure no one was paying any attention to me before scrolling down Jenni's Facebook wall. She was tagged in a few photos that revealed how her weekends were being spent. She was out clubbing and dancing nearly every Friday and Saturday night. There were also a few comments that popped up from the same guy.

"Christian Doherty," I mumbled to myself.

When Slater came barreling into the room, he startled me so much, I dropped Noah's phone on the ground. Slater's suspicious eyes flicked down at the illuminated screen before they darted back to me. Shifting his head to the side, his brow cocked. It was clear he had busted me.

Acting casual, I snatched Noah's phone off the floor then strolled into the recording booth, ensuring I signed out of his Facebook account on the way there.

"Emily just called," I lied, interrupting Noah mid-song.

He pulled off his headphones before accepting his phone I was holding out for him. The confusion on his face doubled when he returned Emily's call and got her voicemail.

While he left a message, Slater questioned, "Emily was calling, eh?" He stood in the doorway of the studio with his arms crossed in front of his chest.

"Yep." I sat down and picked up my guitar I was tuning before I hacked into Noah's phone.

"At two in the afternoon?" Slater's brow arched higher, calling bullshit even more than his mocking tone.

My eyes darted up to his. With a smirk, I shrugged. "Maybe one of her classes got canceled?" I strummed my guitar, hoping to avoid further interrogation from Slater.

Thank fuck it worked. "Yeah, maybe."

Fortunately for me, Emily didn't mention anything to Noah about not calling him earlier that day. I couldn't help the sly smirk that morphed onto my face when I realized my sneakiness had gone undetected.

I wasn't so lucky a few weeks later. . .

The sound engineers and Mickey have left for the day, leaving just the band and me in the studio. We've been putting in long hours the past few weeks, striving to get enough songs to fill an album. I tried to convince the execs to put "Player" back into the line-up, but they keep refusing. They argue that no girl likes a player. I can attest that that notion is full of shit. All girls like a player. . . *except perhaps Jenni.*

"Look at this." Marcus's smile beams as he heads for Slater. "I thought *we* were the ones set for fame."

After taking in the magazine article Marcus is showing him, Slater hands it to Noah. He scans the open pages before his lips etch into a large grin. He notices my curious gaze and passes the magazine to me. When my eyes absorb the two-page spread, I don't initially see what they're going on about. It's only when I hand the well-known magazine back to Noah do I see a small photo of Jenni in the top left-hand corner of the page.

I snatch it back, my eyes widening.

Holy hell, she looks hot as fuck.

She's wearing a sparkling mini dress made from nothing but shiny beads. Her hair is pinned to the side, exposing her delicate neck, and her lips are bright red in color. The contrast between her lips and skin makes her blue eyes even lighter than normal.

My rapidly stiffening dick softens when I notice she has her arm wrapped around a blond guy wearing a black suit. My jaw tightens when I read the small caption next to the photo: "Christian Doherty attending the premiere of his new movie *Chasing Kate* in New York with his date."

My eyes dart over the pages, seeking more photos of Jenni. I do notice Christian in a handful of photos that are part of the article about the opening night of his movie, but Jenni doesn't appear in any others except the first one I saw her in.

"Who is this Christian guy?" I question anyone listening.

Marcus and Noah shrug, as unsure as me, but Slater isn't as quick to deny knowledge of Christian's existence. He just smirks before spinning on his heels and walking out of the room.

I leap up from the floor and follow after him. "Do you know who he is?" I follow him outside so he can have a smoke.

"What's it to you?" He flicks a match head to light the cigarette dangling out of his mouth.

I play it cool. "I'm just curious, that's all."

My calm tone hides the fact my heart is racing a million miles an hour. When Slater's amused gaze lowers to my balled fists, I unclench them, then cross my arms in front of my chest.

"She's my friend, so I want to make sure she isn't getting herself into any trouble."

In reality, I want to know what the fuck this guy means to Jenni, and if she's sleeping with him. Even though I can't comprehend why the thought is annoying the shit out of me, it is. Very much so.

"He's her friend too," Slater replies.

I release the breath I'm holding in, grateful Christian and Jenni are just friends.

My relief doesn't last long.

"Although, from what I've heard from Marcus, he was more than a friend a few years ago." Slater's arrogant smirk says way more than his words ever could.

My fists clench again, but because they're hidden by my crossed arms, Slater doesn't notice them. I mask my anger with a weary smirk before pivoting on my heels and reentering the studio. This time, I don't hide the fact I'm borrowing Noah's phone. I just snatch it up, my mind focused on one thing and one thing only—seeking Jenni's contact details.

Noah eyeballs me but doesn't say anything when I unlock his phone and go straight into his contact details.

Bingo—now I've got you.

As soon as the band wraps up our recording session, I bolt to the airport. Seeing Jenni's arm wrapped around another guy has been playing havoc with my ego the past two days, and with her still refusing to answer my calls, I've decided drastic action needs to be taken. Hitting decline on a phone call is easy. Telling someone to leave in person is a shit ton harder. She'll have no choice but to talk to me.

My plan goes off without a hitch until the security guard at Jenni's apartment refuses my entrance because I'm not on her "approved list of visitors."

I barely make it halfway across the lobby before they stop me. "You need to be on the list," one of the officers grumbles as he removes me from the building.

I shrug out of his hold. "I should be on the list. You need to check again."

He gives me a look, one that reveals he has no intentions of checking for my name for the fifth time in under a minute.

"What about Christian? Do you have a Christian on her list?"

He shoves me onto the sidewalk. "Good evening, Mr. Holt."

After closing the thick glass door of Jenni's apartment building, he stands behind it. His wide shoulders reinforce his pose. I sneakily flip him the bird before pulling my cell out of my pocket. I dial Jenni's home number I stole from Noah's phone earlier this week. It rings and rings and rings, leaving me no other option. I'll have to wait for her to walk by.

I'm sure it won't be too long.

By the time two hours has ticked by, it's well past midnight. While scrubbing my tired eyes, I push off the wall and amble down the street. I'll grab a few hours of shut-eye before returning bright and early tomorrow morning to recommence my watch. I'm fucking exhausted, the long hours I've been putting in at the studio visible on my face.

Just as I round the corner, a black Escalade pulls up to the curb at the front of Jenni's building. Since it's a lot bigger and bulkier than Jenni's usual ride, I continue my brisk strides. I freeze halfway down the path when a familiar giggle sounds through my ears. I'd recognize that laugh anywhere.

When I whip back around, I witness Jenni being assisted out of the Escalade by the man she was photographed with. She's as beautiful today as she was in their photo. Her hair is pinned away from her face, and she's smiling about her awkward slide out of the car. After yanking down the hem of her mini dress, she heads for the entrance of her building. This is the opportunity I've been waiting for, but I'm so stunned at seeing her again, I can't force my feet to move.

Just before she enters her apartment building, her head shifts my way. Even with two dozen people between us, she appears to be looking right at me. I stand straighter, looking out of place in my ripped jeans and polo shirt. Rejection maims my heart when she shakes her head a few seconds later before she dashes through the front door of her building. Her dismissal impacts my already faltering ego more than I'd care to admit.

"What the fuck did you think she was going to do, Nick? Run into your arms?" I mumble to myself as I continue walking down the street.

When I turn the corner, I hear someone calling my name, but it doesn't impede my fast steps down the desolate alleyway. I need a stiff drink and a hot shower, because they may be the only things capable of lightening the heaviness on my chest.

My brisk pace comes to a standstill when a female voice I immediately recognize calls out, "Nick?"

When I spin around, I see Jenni standing at the end of the alley. Her pupils are wide, her brows pinched with confusion. She's even more ravishing up close.

She steps closer to me, her blue eyes shining with moisture. "I knew it was you."

CHAPTER TWENTY-TWO

JENNI

Do you know that weird feeling you get when someone is watching you? Well, I experienced that same sensation when Christian assisted me out of his town car five minutes ago. Christian's movie has rocketed his stardom to a new level, but it wasn't the same creeped out feeling I get from the paparazzi who are always following him. It was so odd, I tugged on the hem of my dress to ensure my unladylike maneuver out of his car wasn't to blame for my twisting stomach.

As we made our way to our apartment building, the flurry of camera flashes that track Christian's every move was still there, but there was something much denser demanding my focus. Incapable of ignoring my intuition for a second longer, my eyes darted around my location. My heart beeped in my neck when I thought I spotted Nick standing on the sidewalk that curves around my building.

Believing I was hallucinating, I shook the visual from my head before continuing my escape from the paparazzi. The further I moved away from the front door, the stronger my wish to go outside became. Something was beckoning me outside.

Christian peered at me with concern when I told him I'd be right back, but before he could voice a single worry, I hightailed it out of my building and headed in the direction I thought I had seen Nick. With my body's awareness guiding my steps, I trekked through the populated sidewalks until I took a detour down one of the side streets near my building. It was a risky move, but my risk paid dividends. Nick's long legs were marching him down the darkened alleyway.

"Nick?" I yelled. I didn't chase after him because I still wasn't convinced it was him. I hadn't seen him for months, so trusting my body's awareness of him was a foolish thing to do.

As a sticky breeze swept across my nape, goosebumps prickled my arms. The wind wasn't the cause of their brisk arrival; it was my body begging for me not to give up. And that's how we reached this point. My body is overruling both my head and my heart, and there isn't a single thing either of them can do about it.

I stop fighting the inevitable by kicking off my high heels. After gathering them in my hands, I jog down the scary unlit street. The padding of my feet is barely heard over my raging heart.

"Nick!" I call out again, louder this time.

I stop when he stops, then the entire world stops when he spins around to face me. *It is him.*

"I knew it was you." I stare at him, confused as to why he would turn up after all this time. "What are you doing here—in New York?" I'm suddenly aware he may not be here for me.

My panic fades when he answers, "I wanted to talk to you."

I'm about to reply that he could have just picked up the phone, but I realize that wouldn't have done him any good. I stopped answering his calls a long time ago.

Stepping forward, he reaches out to rub my earlobe. It takes all my strength not to sigh over his touch. That's nothing compared to the battle I face when he murmurs, "I've missed you, Jen."

My heart rate kicks up a gear, but the crushing blow I felt months ago keeps me from getting too excited.

"Can we talk?"

My head screams obscenities at my heart, but my body nods

before either of them can be heard. Just as he grips my hand within his, a raindrop hits my right cheek. I peer up at the sky, which is blackened with large, dark storm clouds.

When my eyes shoot back to Nick, he smiles before using his thumb to rub away the large blob of moisture running down my face. I can tell by the sparkling glint in his eyes that his brain is playing the same memory mine is currently running. One of the last dates we had before I left for college was at Bronte's Peak. A massive storm rolled in before we had finished climbing the trillion stairs on the cliff's edge. By the time we made it back to Nick's truck, we were saturated from head to toe and laughing like hyenas. There's nothing overly funny about being caught in a storm, but that day still rates as one of the most fun dates I've ever had. It was the first time Nick truly let his guard down. I finally got to see the person he hides behind a handsome face and a panty-wetting body.

That was the day I fell madly, deeply in love with him.

My focus returns to the present when Nick smiles a knee-weakening grin. "Do you want to get wet or do a runner?"

The loud crack of thunder above my head should answer his question on my behalf, but just in case it doesn't, I squeal, "Run!"

I hate storms in general, so the idea of being outside during one absolutely petrifies me. As the heavens open up to drench the humid night, I sprint as quickly as my mini dress allows. When Nick follows closely behind me, the huge smile stretched across his face slows my steps.

When he catches up to me—and before I have a chance to protest—he throws me over his shoulder like he did at the Dungeon months ago. I squeal loudly before ensuring my panties are hidden from anyone who may be walking in the pouring rain.

By the time we make it inside my apartment building, we're saturated and grinning broadly. He lowers me to my feet to accept the towels the doorman is holding out for us. My curious eyes float between Nick and the doorman. I doubt they've met before, but they have a weird vibe bouncing between them. Sure it's because Nick and I look like drowned rats, I accept a towel from George before using it to dry my hair. Nick follows suit, but he dries his body instead of his head.

The battle between my head and heart starts all over again when my eyes drink in the way his ripped jeans and blue polo shirt are clinging to his fit frame. Add the exciting visual of his practically naked body to the ringlets of blond hair edging his handsome face, and you've got a perfect panty-messing disaster.

Not wanting to be busted ogling him like a freak, I shift my eyes to the side. On the way, I catch sight of the time on the large clock hanging in the foyer. It's nearly one AM. Allowing my heart to win this round with hope that by tomorrow my head will convince my heart this isn't a good idea, I shift on my feet to face Nick. "Did you want to come up?"

When he nods, my heart flips crazily in my chest. I hotfoot it to the elevator, needing to distract myself again. After handing our soaked towels to George, Nick enters the elevator cart. I push my desired floor before moving to the far back corner. Even though he's barely in my eyesight, I can see Nick's smile reflecting in the stainless steel panels on the elevator doors. I swear I've never seen him smile so much.

"What hotel are you staying at?" I keep my tone friendly, praying it will hide the effect his closeness is having on my body.

My knees curve inwards when he replies, "I was hoping I could stay with you."

My eyes rocket to his. When he grins a full-toothed smile, I force my attention to the elevator dashboard. I need to concentrate on anything other than his captivatingly handsome face before months of hard work come undone. I don't date players; I'm not even friends with them, so they sure as hell don't get invited for sleepovers.

When he leans closer to me, his yummy aftershave destroys my defenses. Hating that I'm reneging so quickly, I snap, "You're sleeping on the couch."

The elevator doors pop open at the same time his boisterous

chuckle rumbles through my core. Ignoring the shake of my thighs, I make a beeline for my apartment. I flick on the lights, illuminating my small but adequate one-bedroom abode before pivoting to face Nick. "I'm going to change my clothes."

Not waiting for him to reply, I charge into my room. I take my time showering and getting changed, needing a few minutes to center myself. I'm still dazed, certain I'm dreaming.

Once I'm dressed in comfy pants and a fitted shirt, I pace out of my bathroom. When I spot Nick standing in my living room, I nearly bolt back in for a cold shower. He's wearing nothing but a pair of light blue cotton boxer shorts and a smug grin. His physique has changed a lot since the last time I saw him naked. By change, I mean he's added a nice amount of muscles to his athletic build. His washboard abs now have six precise bumps in the middle of them, and the width of his biceps has nearly doubled.

I stalk him from my post by the bathroom door. He moseys around my living room, taking in every detail of the space in true Nick form. It's only once he picks up the photo I have of him on the mantel do I span the distance between us. "I forgot to take that down."

I snatch the frame out of his grasp before bouncing my wide gaze around my apartment, seeking somewhere to store his photo. When I spot his cocky grin, I throw the frame into the unlit fireplace, wiping the smirk right off his face. When his hurt eyes lock with mine, I nearly crumple into a heap on the ground. No matter how much he hurt me, I hate seeing him upset.

"The shower is free," I say, desperately needing some space between us.

His lips twitch, but they don't utter a sound as he makes his way to the bathroom. Once he's out of sight, I snatch his photo out of the fireplace and use my hands to rub off the ash covering it. After placing it in my desk drawer for safe keeping, I head to the kitchen to wash the ash off my hands. On my way, I spot Nick's saturated jeans and shirt lying over one of my dining room chairs. I place them in a dry-cleaning bag before calling the concierge desk to collect them.

When someone knocks on my door a short time later, I open it. I'm expecting it to be someone from the concierge desk to collect Nick's clothing, so you can imagine my shock when Christian strolls inside.

Shit! In my excitement at seeing Nick again, I forgot I left Christian hanging after our date tonight.

"Did you shower without me?" He leans in to plant a kiss on my lips.

I pull away from his embrace before closing the door. "I got caught in the rain."

When I turn back around, my heart slithers into my gut. Christian and Nick are standing across from each other in an intense stare-off. With Nick's hair wringing wet from his recent shower, and his body only covered by a pair of boxer shorts, the situation Christian has walked in on appears more scandalous than it is.

Christian stops shooting daggers at Nick to swing his eyes to me. "Busy?"

I shake my head at the same time Nick replies, "Yes."

As Christian returns to glaring at Nick, he stands taller and straightens his shoulders. Nick smirks an arrogant grin before folding his arms over his chest. He then props his shoulder on the doorframe of my room, acting as if he's always belonged here.

"I wasn't asking you; I was asking Jenni." Christian's tone isn't the only thing heated in this room. I'm seconds from fainting under the tension.

Nick makes matters worse by running his eyes over my body. His prolonged glance quickens my pulse, but not as much as it does Christian's when he says, "She'll tell you the same thing."

I narrow my eyes at him before placing myself between the two bulls ready to charge at one another. I take a few moments to weigh my options before settling my wide gaze onto a pair of equally confused eyes.

"I'll call you tomorrow."

Christian's brows furl as he gives me his *are you serious?* face. When I nod, he turns on his heels and paces to the door. My eyes snap to Nick when I hear him snickering under his breath. His arrogance is at an all-time high, and the look of victory is across his face.

I take care of his arrogance by saying, "He's only here because he has nowhere to stay."

Christian laughs a menacing chuckle. "You're always helping the needy." He leans in to kiss me goodbye, his lips lingering longer than they did earlier. "I had fun on our date tonight." He emphasizes the word "date."

I offer him a friendly smile. I know part of his statement is to rile Nick, but most of it was genuine. We did have a lot of fun tonight. "Me too."

Happy with my reply, Christian awards me a frisky wink before he struts to the waiting elevator. He enters without looking back, confident there's nothing here he wants to see.

Once the elevator doors close, I shut my front door then turn around. My breath hitches when I'm confronted with Nick's livid face. "Are you two—"

"Don't you dare say another word," I interrupt, my voice low and dangerous. "You have no right whatsoever to question me."

My steps to the linen closet are heavy. After grabbing Nick a pillow and a blanket, I dump them on the sofa, mumble a goodnight, then dash into my room as quickly as my quivering legs will take me, ensuring I close my door behind me. Part of me feels like tonight was fate. I had thoroughly enjoyed my date with Christian, and I had every intention of following him to his penthouse when we arrived home.

I would have if I hadn't spotted Nick.

Christian has been nothing more than a friend the past three months, but that doesn't mean he didn't nag me relentlessly to go out with him. I always denied his requests, though. I didn't want another player in my life. As the weeks went on, our friendship grew. We went out a handful of times with mutual friends, and not once did he overstep the boundaries of our friendship. I saw a different side of him, and I liked what I saw.

Last weekend was the first time I agreed to go out with him alone. He needed a plus one for his movie premiere, and I needed to get out of the slump I had been in the prior three months. Christian acted like a gentleman the whole night. When he kissed me good-night at my door after dropping me home, I realized I was painting him with the same brush as Nick.

I was giving him this weekend to prove he had changed. His gracious departure tonight makes me believe he has. I felt terrible asking him to leave, but just spending the last half an hour with Nick makes me realize, even with him ripping it out and stomping on it, my heart still belongs to him.

He destroyed me, yet I still love him.

I'm an idiot.

I don't know how long I've been sniffling in my bed when I feel someone sliding under my sheets. Nick's familiar scent keeps my panic at bay. It does nothing to weaken my erratic heart rate, though. Remaining quiet, he rolls me over until I'm facing him. His thumbs make quick work of the tears staining my cheeks before he pulls me in close to his chest. His warm breaths tickle my ear when he whispers to me that everything will be okay and that I have nothing to worry about.

After the tumultuous few months we've had, his words should roll like water off a duck's back, but for some reason, they soothe me more than agitate me. He seems genuinely remorseful that I'm upset.

Over time, my devastation fades, and my breathing evens out before I eventually settle into a peaceful sleep.

The next morning, I wake up to a cold and empty bed.

CHAPTER TWENTY-THREE

NICK

When Christian asked Jenni if she had showered without him, it felt like my heart was ripped straight out of my fucking chest. I had traveled to New York wanting to see if Jenni was sleeping with Christian, and he confirmed my suspicions without me needing to ask a single question.

After Christian left, and Jenni stormed into her bedroom, I considered leaving right then and there. It was only when my eyes landed on my cotton boxer shorts was my plan foiled. No matter how frustrated I was, I couldn't walk around New York City half-naked.

Just as I located my clothing in a dry-cleaning bag by the door, the silence in Jenni's apartment amplified someone's quiet sniffling. When I moved toward the noise, it became apparent Jenni was crying. It took me days to get the image of her crying at my dad's house out of my head, so I couldn't walk away knowing she was upset.

Her body stiffened when I slipped into her bed, but she didn't voice a protest. My heart stopped beating when I saw the tears sliding down her cheeks. They were glistening in the moonlight, frustrating me even more than the thought of her with Christian.

Having her in my arms for that short period of time made me want her even more. I wanted to protect her and keep her safe. I didn't want her to hurt anymore, and that was when I realized the one person she needed protecting from the most was me. She was carefree and happy in the photos I saw of her on Facebook, but the instant I was back in the picture, she was crying herself to sleep. She deserves better than I could ever offer her, so I made the decision to let her go in the hope she'd find happiness.

She whimpered when I slipped out of her bed, making my plan to walk away even harder. While taking in her strawberry blonde locks fanned across her pillow instead of my chest, I leaned down to press a kiss on her lips before reluctantly leaving her room.

Once I was dressed in my still-drenched clothes, I made my way to the airport where I planned to go home and forget about the girl who makes me wish I could break every one of my rules for her.

That night was a little over two months ago.

For the past nine weeks, I've tried hard to return to my regular schedule. The band continues to work in the studio Monday to Friday; we perform at Mavericks every Friday night, and I go on the prowl at dance clubs every weekend. To an outsider, my life appears normal. There's just one small factor they've failed to see: I can't get a little blonde firecracker out of my fucking head.

I'm spending my Saturday night at a dance club in Hopeton called A+. It's become my regular haunt since I can no longer go to the Dungeon without thinking about Jenni. A+ is located in the basement of an old warehouse and has an underground dance vibe. The only lighting is the fluorescent bands partygoers wear around their bodies and the occasional flash of a strobe light choreographed with the music blaring from the speakers. When a song ends, the dance floor plunges into darkness until the next song starts.

I've just finished a beer in the bar in the foyer of the club. I'm about to go back to the dance floor when the hairs on my arms stand to attention. My eyes float across hundreds of partygoers as my date drags me back to the dance floor. Just as we're about to break through the large black double doors, I spot the reason for my body's odd response. Jenni is entering the club from the far end.

She's wearing a tight, one-shoulder blue dress and black stilettos. Her hair has been cut since the last time I saw her, so it's hanging loosely just above her shoulders. The shorter style makes her locks appear curlier than they usually are. She looks sexy and sweet at the same time.

When she cranks her neck to her right and smiles her knockout smile, my dick twitches. My fucking god. I forgot how perfect her smile is.

"Come on," whines my date when her attempts to drag me onto the dance floor are thwarted by my concrete-like feet.

I shrug out of her grasp so I can continue watching Jenni from afar. She must feel my intense gaze, because not even two seconds later, her eyes skim across the bar, like she's seeking someone. When she looks straight at me and smiles, my heart leaps. Its crazy beat turns catastrophic when she motions for me to join her.

I turn to my date, eager to dismiss her. My eagerness has me stumbling upon my fatal error. Christian is in the process of weaving through the packed crowd on my left. He's heading straight for Jenni, making me realize her smile wasn't for me. It was for him.

Now I'm certain my heart is being ripped out of my chest.

Once Christian barges through the dense crowd, he wraps his arms around Jenni's waist to twirl her around the room. Even over the deafening hum of the packed bar, I can hear her giggles. You'd think witnessing their connection firsthand would give me enough incentive to finally let her go—*for real this time*—but I fucking can't. My body yearns for her. I crave her like a drug addict craves crack, like a surfer craves his next wave, and like an adrenaline junkie craves his next thrill.

She's my thrill, my addiction, the one thing I can't control.

She's my rule breaker, and the main source of my confusion.

She's my girl.

I dismiss my dance partner so I can continue to stalk Jenni from afar. The whole gang is at the club tonight. I spotted Emily and Noah moving toward the dance floor earlier. *So much for Noah's stance on not dancing.* Slater and Marcus are at the bar with Nicole and Jenni, and Christian returned to his friends not long after he spun Jenni around the room. His quick departure gave me a little bit of hope that they aren't a couple.

"Another one." I tap the rim of my empty scotch glass, signaling to the bartender that I'm empty.

He has just refilled my glass when Jenni and Slater make their way to the doors that lead to the dance floor. Just before she disappears into the abyss, her brisk strides stop. Lifting her chin, she slings her head to the right before it drifts to the left. She appears to be looking for someone.

Seconds from being busted, I return my eyes front and center. I need her on the dance floor for my recently made-up ruse to work.

When she fails to find who she is seeking, she steps through the swinging doors. I down my nip of scotch in one hit then quickly follow after her. Because of the bright color of her dress, she illuminates under the strobing lights, making it easy for me to continue watching her in the pitch black room.

I wait impatiently for the perfect opportunity to make my move.

It takes another twenty minutes before the chance arrives. Slater has become distracted by a pretty brunette with a nose full of freckles. While he makes his way to her, I make a beeline for Jenni. When I reach her, I spin her around, yank her back until her body is flush with mine, then burrow my nose in her hair. Her unsure giggle is barely heard over the loud thump of the music roaring from the speakers.

Needing her even closer to me, I splay my hand across her stomach then draw her back even deeper. I feel her pulse raring through her body when I swing our hips in sync to the music. Her movements are more robotic than usual, but it doesn't take long for her to loosen up. We're not even halfway through our first song before her dance moves become fluid again.

The only time she stiffens is when I lick a bead of sweat rolling down her neck. She freezes as a scattering of goosebumps skate across her nape. The vein in her neck thrums when she cranks her head back to peer at me. Her eyes strain in the dark space as she battles to recognize my features. It's too dark for her to see anything.

Her breathing speeds up when I glide my hand up her stomach, past the generous swell of her breasts, and over her delicate neck before I rub her earlobe. My dick hardens when her soft moan vibrates through our practically conjoined bodies. It's ten times better than the scream I expected.

When she spins around to face me, I keep her body as close to mine as possible. She stares at me, confused and upset. Before she can voice her confusion, I lower my mouth over hers and give her a slow, teasing kiss. My dick hardens even more. She tastes like heaven and hell rolled into one. Her mouth is super sweet from the fancy cocktails she's been drinking, but salty from a handful of tears rolling down her cheeks.

I lap up her tears with my tongue before kissing her so passionately, nothing but my mouth is on her mind. When I pull back, a grin curls on my lips. The sadness on her face has completely vanished, although some of her confusion has intensified.

Confident I know how to make her smile, I dip her. She squeals with so much happiness, months of torment disappears in an instant. When I flip her back up, her knockout smile is carved on her beautiful face. This time, when I move our hips in rhythm to the beat, her previous apprehensions are nowhere to be seen.

Feeling the sexual tension in the air as rampantly as me, she spins around to grind her curvy backside against my crotch. I gather her hair to one side of her neck so I can kiss, suck, and nibble on her sweaty skin. Not a word is spoken between us as we dance as one for the next hour. If it weren't for Slater's deep rumbling voice interrupting us, I have no doubt we'd never leave this dance floor.

"Jen!" he calls out again when she fails to answer his first call.

Jenni's shoulders deflate as she lets out a soft sigh. "Over here." She has to project her voice over the music.

While pacing our way, Slater asks, "Are you ready to head out? Everyone is ready to leave."

Jenni's eyes lock with mine, wordlessly questioning if she should stay. When I remain quiet, her smile falters. I want her to stay with me, but every time she's near me, I can't think straight, much less form words.

Displeased by my hesitation, Jenni steps away from me. She doesn't even get two feet away before my hand darts out to seize her wrist, stopping her hasty retreat.

Her pulse darts past my fingers when I lean in to whisper in her ear, "Unblock my number."

I feel like all my Christmases have come at once when she replies, "I already have."

CHAPTER TWENTY-FOUR

JENNI

Nick smiles before awarding me another knee-wobbling, pussy-clenching kiss. He devours my mouth with long licks of his tongue and sweet movements of his lips. By the time he pulls away, I've lost the ability to walk and talk. While rubbing his thumb over my kiss-swollen lips, he stares into my eyes for several heart-thrashing seconds. Just when I think he's going to say something profound, his lust-crammed eyes flick to his right.

The narrowed eyes that return to me aren't the ones I was transfixed by only moments ago. He appears angry, somewhat frustrated. After a final peck, he disappears into a swarm of bodies on the overcrowded dance floor.

I'm so busy seeking him amongst the crowd, I'm scared within an inch of my life when Slater suddenly stops next to me. "You ready?"

When I pivot to face him, his eyes take their time assessing my face and neck. I don't know what he sees, but it must be amusing since he laughs before looping his arm around my back to guide me off the dance floor.

When I clamber into the back of Marcus's car, Emily stops sucking face with Noah to gawk at me.

"What?" I question, fidgeting.

With her eyes arrowed in on my inflamed cheeks, she mutters, "It was hot in there—but it wasn't *that* hot."

I avert my eyes to anything but her and spot Nick walking to his truck. He's peering down at his phone, deep in thought. Suddenly, he stops in the middle of the parking lot. The heat spreading across my cheeks descends to my neck when his eyes lift to me. He didn't look around; his eyes just locked straight in on me.

My sneaky wave goodbye awards me his panty-combusting grin. I still can't believe the events of tonight. Before tonight, I hadn't seen Nick since he vanished from my bed two months ago. When I woke up to an empty bed, I started to wonder if his comfort had been a dream. It was only when I rolled over and smelled his cologne on my pillow did I realize it wasn't.

I don't know what compelled me to do it, but the next morning, I unblocked his number from calling me. The first few days, I constantly checked my phone, hoping he had called or sent me a message. As the days went on, so did my stupidity. He was never going to call.

Like a desperate loser, I stalked his Facebook profile. Since we have so many mutual friends, I was able to view most of his posts and albums. Unfortunately, his account didn't give any indication of what he was doing or who he was doing. Nick is an extremely private person, so he rarely updates his social media accounts.

From a handful of photos he was tagged in, I knew he had returned to the club scene a few weeks ago, but I still had no clue I'd run into him tonight. When I was suddenly clutched on the dance floor, I assumed it was Christian. He asked me earlier to save him a dance. It was only when my body reacted differently did I realize it wasn't him. My body was responding sexually to the stranger's sensual dance moves. It had only ever responded that way to one person.

My suspicions were confirmed when my dance partner licked my neck. My body was once again right: Nick was in its vicinity.

When my eyes darted up to seek confirmation, I couldn't see any of his features through the poor strobe lighting. When his hand ran from my stomach to my earlobe, goosebumps followed his path.

I couldn't help the moan that parted my lips. I can't help but react to him. My body craves him. Even his simplest touch causes it to melt, and when his lips sealed over mine, my pussy throbbed. I can't explain my attraction to Nick. It's unexplainable. Even knowing he has the ability to destroy me doesn't stop me from wanting him.

When he dipped me, images of *Dirty Dancing* flashed before my eyes. It honestly made me the happiest I've been in six months. I felt beautiful, cherished, and wanted. When he swung his hips, wordlessly asking me to dance, I granted my body permission to have the one thing it craved most. *Him.*

I so enjoyed dancing with him that when Slater asked if I was ready to leave, I was hoping Nick would beg me to stay. No matter how many times you're rejected, each new case burns more than the first. Thankfully, I seemed to have misunderstood Nick's silence. He didn't want me to leave. He was just as confused as me.

I don't know where we go from here. I'm only back in town for the Christmas-New Year holiday period. I had every intention of spending as much time with Emily and Nicole as possible, but things feel different now. My feelings for Nick aren't new, but they're not as daunting as they were months ago.

My friendship with Christian has proved what I have with Nick is different than anything I've experienced before. My feelings for him are all-encompassing and somewhat scary. Christian and I have grown close the past few months. The morning after Nick left was pretty awkward, but over time, Christian was grateful Nick's unexpected arrival forced him to maintain his "player etiquette" of not sleeping with the same girl twice.

His blockbuster movie has propelled him into super stardom, and his player lifestyle grew right along with it. I don't know how many times I've witnessed him in compromising positions in our building elevator the past two months. He also uses my apartment to hide in until his "dates" get the hint to leave.

I've been tempted to warn the women of New York about Christian's player ways as Tina cautioned me about Nick all those months ago, but then I realized, neither Christian or Nick hide who they are. They're brutally honest—even when it stings to hear the truth.

I don't know what planet I was living on when I expected Nick to be faithful to me when we weren't even together. It hurts knowing that at the same time he was chasing me, he was also chasing other women, but its burn isn't as bad now as it was back then.

Lessons were learned, and adjustments were made, but one thing has remained the same: the love I have for him.

———

Halfway home, my phone dings with a text. Peering down, I notice it's a message from Nick. Since Emily's attention is still rapt on me, I drop my cell into my purse, deciding to read his message later—once I'm alone.

I shower and settle into bed before reading his message. I wish I didn't wait so long.

Nick:
I never wanted anyone.
I never needed anyone.
Until I met you.
Why have you always been my rule breaker?

With a smile big enough to compete with the moon, I reply:
Me: *Because rules are meant to be broken.*

CHAPTER TWENTY-FIVE

NICK

I spot Jenni the instant she enters Mavericks. She's smoking hot in a strapless red lace dress and sky-high stilettos. Her heels are so tall, I reckon if I stand next to her, she'll match my five-foot-eight height.

Yeah, I'm short. Kind of happens when you're conceived in a test tube, then delivered eight weeks early so your stem cells can save your brother's life. Obviously, I don't recall a single thing that happened during my first three years on this planet, but I'm certain I don't regret a moment. Isaac can be a little shady at times, but he's *always* been there for me. There's nothing I could ever want that he wouldn't give me. The shirt on his back. An apartment. A lucrative stake in his multiple business operations. If I want an in, he'll give it to me. I guess that's why I've always been a bit of a rascal, because I know no matter what happens, he'll be there to pick up the pieces.

You'd think this knowledge would have me going a little easier on him, but hey, aren't painful, teeth-grinding moments what little bros are about?

I'm drawn back to the present when I spot Jenni in the corner of my eye. Her wide gaze reveals tonight is her first time inside Mave-ricks. Because she's not over twenty-one, we had to get permission from the owner for her to attend Emily's surprise nineteenth birthday party tonight. She also had to fly home for the occasion —*thank fuck.*

I've been missing her like crazy. We've talked regularly the past month, but it can't compare to seeing her in person. The band was supposed to be performing one last hurrah before our album drops, but we all agreed that celebrating Emily's birthday was more important.

With the songs for our album written, we start laying down tracks next week. It's been a long and tedious six months, but the high caliber of the songs we've created will soon rocket us to the superstardom we've actively been seeking the past four years.

I stalk Jenni from the side of the room. She greets Nicole, who is placing Emily's birthday cake on a table in the middle of the room before she scans the hundred or more people crammed on the dance floor. We spent Christmas morning together before we had our first official "date" on New Year's Day. I surprised myself by acting like a gentleman the entire day. It nearly killed me, but I did it—barely! I know how good Jenni tastes, and I crave her more than my next meal, so keeping my hands, lips, and dick to myself was more than an effort. *Luckily, she's worth it.*

After ensuring I'm not being watched, I snag my phone out of my pocket and send a quick message.

Me: *As beautiful as ever.*

When Jenni pulls her phone out of her red clutch, a large smile stretches across her face. After reading my message, her head pops up, seeking me in the thrumming space. I can tell the exact moment she spots me because the most beaming smile shines out of her. It grows wider the longer she assesses my outfit. I've dressed for the occasion, switching out my ripped jeans and polo shirt for black trousers and a button-up dress shirt. I didn't just put in an effort for

Emily. I may also be trying to impress an up-and-coming fashion designer.

Before I can offer a formal welcome, Slater and Marcus enter Mavs and make a beeline for Jenni and Nicole—as they always do. I catch Jenni peering at me numerous times in the next ten minutes. I give her a playful wink every time our eyes meet and hold for longer than a second. I'm not going to lie; I want to strut like a peacock when her neck gets a pink hue after every wink.

Our flirty banter continues for the next thirty minutes. It only stops when Marcus and Nicole usher everyone to the entrance of Mavs, so we can surprise Emily as she walks in. The best thing about a bunch of people being crammed into the one space is not having enough room to move. I can touch Jenni and not get in trouble. I even get to sneakily hold her hand during the ten minutes it takes for Emily's family to be pushed aside by her friends so they can give her their well wishes.

After squeezing my hand, Jenni rushes toward her best friend. She wraps her up in a tight hug, their bond displayed for the world to see. I love seeing how close they are, but it also makes me jealous. If Jenni was to greet me the same way, I wouldn't be bombarded with the admiring glances she and Emily are getting.

Mine would be pronged with venom.

It doesn't take long for the party to wind down. Emily got absolutely smashed on three glasses of wine. When she left with Noah, a handful of her family and friends stayed at Mavs to continue the party without her.

I stayed as well. It's a prime opportunity for me to get some alone time with Jenni, especially considering Slater left not long after Noah and Emily. When Jenni rounds the corner from the hallway, I pull her into a dark corner of the room. When she squeals in fright, I have no choice but to muffle her screams with my mouth.

I was right about her killer high heels. Her body is aligned with mine. Her breasts are pushed up against my chest, her pussy the perfect height to nestle my hardening dick, and I don't even need to dip my head to ravish her mouth with my tongue.

She tastes like heaven and hell all rolled into one. Heaven, because she tastes so good. Hell, because that's where I'll end up when I claim her as my own.

She giggles when an annoying cough interrupts our heavy make out session. I heard it the first three times but was trying my best to ignore it. When the intruder coughs again, I reluctantly pull away from Jenni. My annoyance is sliced in half when I notice her neck and cheeks are a nice shade of pink. Her lips are swollen, and her eyes are beaming with lust.

After running my hand down her inflamed cheek, my eyes drift to the person killing my attempt to woo her. Jacob is standing next to us. His arms are crossed in front of his chest, his eyes shooting daggers at me. "Hey," he greets us, acting casual.

"Hi." I peer at him curiously. "Did you need something?"

He takes a large gulp of his beer. "Nah, I'm good."

When he props his shoulder on the wall next to Jenni's head, my confused gaze shifts to Jenni. She shrugs while battling to keep her smile at bay. I return my gaze to Jacob, hoping the width of my pupils will give him the hint to leave. When they don't work, I try straight-up honesty. "Do you mind? We're kinda busy."

"Nope, I don't mind." He smiles a full-toothed grin. "Slater asked me to keep an eye on you." His smile turns blinding. "I'm keeping an eye on you."

Jenni giggles as anger rains down on me. The one fucking time I can be with Jenni without Slater breathing down my neck, he asks Bigfoot to take over his command.

My attention diverts from Jacob to Jenni when she caresses my cheek in her hand. "Tomorrow?" She peers into my eyes, assuring I can hear the words she can't speak.

My eyes roam over her beautiful face, assessing every perfect feature before nodding. I've waited this long to claim her as mine, so what is another twenty-four hours?

After a quick peck to my cheek, Jenni slips under my arm, which is leaning against the wall. Jacob chuckles, happy he has forced us to part ways.

"You're an asshole." I backhand him in the chest before making my way to the bar to replenish my beer. Nearly everyone in this room has warned Jenni to stay away from me. I would have warned her too if she were my friend, but it's too late now. I want her more than anything, and I plan on making her mine. . . as soon as I can get her alone.

After finishing my beer, I head out the back entrance of Mavericks. Jenni left a few minutes ago. I couldn't help but smirk like a smug fuck when she came over to say goodbye. I may have even given Jacob the finger when she kissed me goodbye on the lips.

Jacob took my ribbing in stride. He even smirked. I'm trying not to get my hopes up, but maybe since he's finally come around when it comes to Jenni and me, the rest of our friends will too.

When I reach the edge of my truck, I'm startled within an inch of my life by a figure stepping in front of me. "Sorry." Jenni giggles, amused she scared the shit out of me.

After gathering my heart off the ground, I ask, "What are you doing here?"

My eyes drift around the parking lot, ensuring we're alone. Other than a few empty cars, we're the only two people here. Jenni fists my dress shirt in her hand as her needy eyes rise to mine. "I thought maybe you could give me a ride home?"

My heart beats double-time. "What happened to your ride?" I already know her answer, but I want her to spell it out for me.

She follows along nicely. "I asked her to leave."

My dick turns to stone when her tongue delves out to replenish her dry lips. I help ease their dryness by running my tongue along them. Because she's removed her high heels, she's no longer the same height as me.

I lift her to sit on the bed of my truck before nudging her knees apart so I can stand in between them. I don't want an ounce of air to squeeze between us while I ravage her tasty mouth. For the next several minutes, her sweet little moans are the only noises heard. They're fuckin' music to my ears, each one increasing the girth of my dick.

"No," Jenni whimpers a short time later when I pull back from our embrace. I could sample her mouth for years and never grow bored, but I swear I heard someone shuffling behind us.

I was right. There's a shadowed figure at the end of the parking lot. When they realize I've spotted them, they shuffle to a yellow car parked a few spots down from my truck. I wait for their door to close before shifting my eyes back to Jenni.

"You're killing me." She drops her bottom lip into a pout.

"*I'm* killing *you?*" Sarcasm highlights my tone. Our calls and text messages have been so heated the past month, I've been walking around with a hard-on 24/7.

When she nods, I place her hand on my rock-hard dick. Upon feeling how horny she's made me, her eyes missile to my crotch as heat creeps across her cheeks.

I arch my brow. "Who is killing who?"

I steal her chance to reply by sealing my mouth back over hers.

After spending a few hours at Bronte's Peak being reacquainted, I dropped Jenni home later that night. We spent the next night dancing at the Dungeon. It was like no time at all had passed. The only difference was that my gaze never left Jenni. There wasn't a girl in the entire place enticing enough to steal her spotlight. She was the most beautiful girl in the room—and perhaps the entire planet.

It was at that exact moment I realized my ultimate rule breaker had forced me to break another rule.

The one rule I swore I'd never break.

I'm falling in love.

CHAPTER TWENTY-SIX

JENNI

This morning, when I wake up in Nick's bed, I don't run like I usually do. Instead, I snuggle into his chest, feeling like the luckiest girl alive. This weekend has been the most phenomenal three days of my life. I aced a test, celebrated my best friend's nineteenth birthday, then spent every waking moment the past forty-eight hours with Nick. I'm exhausted but deliriously happy.

I can't hold back my smile when Nick curls his arm around my waist to tug me in tighter. The exhausting activities we undertook last night soon have me falling back to sleep.

When I wake for the second time, Nick's half of the bed is empty. While scrubbing my tired eyes, I shift them to the alarm clock on his bedside table. My pupils widen when I see it's a little after noon. Gingerly rising from the bed, I scan the room, seeking the dress I wore last night. My pulse quickens when Nick's bedroom door shrieks open. I yank up the sheets, praying I'm not about to have my second embarrassing run-in with his dad.

I start breathing again when Nick enters the room. "Morning." His voice is more gravelly than I've heard it before.

"Good morning," I respond while running my hands down my unruly hair. This is the first time he's seen me so disheveled.

Smiling, he hands me a large cup of coffee before pressing his lips to my temple. I swear I swoon like a virgin who's never been kissed. Loving my heated cheeks, his smile enlarges as he sits on a wooden chair next to his desk—a desk that looks as if it's never been used.

Faster than I can click my fingers, his smile is replaced with a set of hard lips. The reason for his swift change in composure comes to light when he asks, "Do you fly home today or tomorrow?"

"Today," I murmur with a sigh.

He jerks up his chin before taking a sip of his coffee. After his throat works hard to swallow, he asks, "Can I drive you to the airport?" His tone makes his question sound more like a plea than a demand.

I bite on my bottom lip to hide my excitement before nodding. "Okay."

He smirks behind the rim of his mug, and after another large gulp, he sets it down then rejoins me in bed.

Approximately two hours later, we're heading to the airport. Today, I'm not as excited about returning to New York as I have been previously. I'm actually dreading it. This weekend, Nick was gentle, kind, and sweet, while also making my libido reach peaks I didn't know existed. His talents in the bedroom are as impressive as his skills on the dance floor. They truly blow my mind.

Noticing my sullen expression, Nick leans over and grasps my hand within his. It's the simplest act, but it causes the biggest response from my heart. It swells so fast, my chest has to puff out to accommodate its new size. He continues holding my hand as we mosey through the terminal, only releasing it when we reach the line for security so he can check the time on his watch. I have a little over an hour before I'm due to board my flight.

"Come on." Nick races to the ticket counter, his strides so fast and efficient, I have to jog to keep up with him. "I need a ticket," he advises the pretty blonde lady behind the counter.

She smiles. "Excellent. Where are you flying to today?"

"Anywhere," Nick answers, handing her his driver's license.

My confused gaze shifts from the lady serving us to Nick. When he notices my shocked glance, he smiles his panty-combusting grin.

I stop pressing my thighs together when the airport staff member says, "I have a flight scheduled to leave in three hours to—"

"I'll take it," Nick interrupts before handing her his credit card.

After processing his ticket, she passes Nick his boarding pass. He's so grateful for her assistance, he awards her one of his infamous smirks. My tongue peeks between my teeth when her cheeks fluster from his attention, glad to see I'm not the only one who melts over his smile.

My giddiness grows the further we move down the queue to pass through security.

"What?" Nick questions when he spots my squirming.

I swivel to face him. "How many 'player' rules did you just break?"

His eyes rocket to mine. Noticing my cheeky smile, he grins back. "Around three or four, depending on if I catch my flight to. . ." he glances down at his ticket, "Texas or not."

"Texas, wow." A wolf-whistle sounds through my lips. "Can you get me a big shiny belt buckle?"

He chuckles while yanking off his running shoes and socks. He then stands behind the yellow line as required by the TSA officer. Today, he's returned to his favorite ripped jeans and a shirt, long-sleeve this time instead of a polo. The dark material makes his blue eyes appear lighter than normal. It's a striking combination.

Once we've cleared security, Nick grasps my hand within his

before striding to my assigned gate. There's no surprise the terminal is packed with tourists heading to New York. Since every seat is filled with a bottom, we lean against a wall. I prefer it this way. In a seat, I'd only see his profile. Standing directly in front of him means I get to see his whole face.

When he notices me drinking in his ruggedly handsome features, he runs his hand down my cheek. I lean into his touch, encouraging him to draw me in closer. He does exactly that by pulling me into his strong, firm chest. Not an ounce of air sits between us.

Can someone say swoon? I'm reasonably sure Nick Holt—*the world's biggest player*—is swooning me. He just paid a ridiculous amount of money so I can snuggle into his chest an hour before my flight. If he isn't swooning me, I'm not head over heels in love.

When the loudspeakers announce it's time for me to board my flight, Nick gives me one of the slowest, most tantalizing kisses I've ever experienced. My knees go weak; my pussy throbs, and my heart races all at the same time. It's a kiss I'll remember for eternity, one that wipes out every kiss I've had before it. It burns my eyes with tears, while dampening my panties with just as much moisture. It's pure perfection.

When he inches back from our embrace, he's so deep in thought, I expected him to say more than a simple, "Bye."

My efforts aren't any better. "Bye."

After a final peck, I mosey to my gate. An ache spreads across my chest when I hand my ticket to the gate agent. She scans it and hands it back before gesturing for me to go down the gangway. I do after a final wave to Nick.

My heart screams in protest with every step I take. Walking away from him is one of the hardest things I've ever done.

My steps stop mid-stride a short time later when Nick calls out, "Jen!"

I pivot around to face him so fast, my hair smacks me in the face. He's standing on the other side of a hard plastic wall erected to keep passengers away from the boarding area.

"No one else," he half-questions, half-informs.

I want to jump in the air in excitement. I want to run back to him and throw myself into his arms. Instead, I calmly reply, "No one else."

Nick's smile is so big, the lady standing next to me eyeballing our exchange, uses her ticket to fan herself. I'm close to following her lead when a commotion steals my attention. "Sir, you can't board without a ticket!"

When my eyes drift to the noise, I'm devoured by Nick. Hands, lips, and teeth crash into me at once. I drop my ticket and carry-on baggage so I can run my hands over his body with the same passion as his touch.

"Sir, I'll be forced to call security if you don't leave the boarding area immediately," advises the gate agent, her words breathless.

I whimper when he's yanked away from me by a brawny security officer. The agent's narrowed gaze floats between Nick and me. The longer she stares, the less harsh her glare becomes. After a small huff, she instructs the security officer to let Nick go. He hesitates until he catches her angry wrath.

The instant Nick is freed from his grip, he caresses my cheek in his hand. "I'll see you next week."

I'm so stunned by the events the past twenty-four hours, I can't form a response, so I simply nod. I watch Nick be escorted out of the area by the gate agent and a security officer. When he reaches the end of the long corridor, he spins around to face me. His heated gaze keeps me warm until I enter the plane, then it takes the entire flight back to New York to settle my racing heart.

Nick kept his word. The very next weekend he arrived at my

doorstep late Friday night. He was exhausted from his flight, but that was all forgotten when he noticed I was wearing nothing but the polo shirt I had stolen from his room the week before.

This time when he murmured, "No one else," I squealed and threw myself into his arms.

By the time Sunday morning comes around, I'm absolutely exhausted. Nick's stamina in the bedroom still astonishes me. I always thought guys needed time after each round to recuperate. Not Nick. I just have to look at him a certain way, and he's primed and ready for another round.

I don't know how late it was last night before we crashed, but my stomach wouldn't quit growling, so I reluctantly crawled out of bed to prepare us some breakfast. Nick mumbled something incoherent under his breath when I walked out of the room, but considering that was nearly thirty minutes ago, I'm assuming he must have fallen back asleep.

Just as I finish flipping the last batch of pancakes, I hear someone knocking on my front door. I glance down at my bare legs sticking out of Nick's shirt. I should probably put on pants, but not wanting to wake Nick, I don't bother.

I rush to the door when Christian yells, "Come on, Jenni."

As I throw open my door, I press my finger to my lips, wordlessly pleading for Christian to be quiet. He doesn't notice my request. His eyes are too busy zooming in on my legs to pay attention to my face.

"I remember them being wrapped around my—"

I slap him. "Shut up."

After ushering him inside my room, I pace to my bedroom door to close it. When I peer inside, a grin curls on my lips. Nick is sprawled on my bed, lying on his stomach, and my pink sheets are barely covering his delectable backside.

When I close the door, Christian arches his brow. "Blondie?"

I try to hold in my smile but miserably fail. I'm beyond happy.

"I should have known out of all the women in the world, you'd be the one to bring a player to his knees," Christian chuckles, following me into the kitchen.

When I enter the usually sweet-smelling space, smoke smacks me in the face. *Shit! The pancakes!*

I rush to the hotplate to remove the now burnt pancakes from the skillet. I use a tea towel to fan the smoke away, hoping it won't trigger the smoke alarm. Not just because I don't want to wake up Nick, but because the last time the fire department arrived at my apartment to remove my burnt microwave dinner, my dad was sent a hefty bill.

Once the smoke has settled, Christian's gaze shifts from the giant stack of pancakes I just prepared to me. "Are you *that* serious about him?"

Nodding, I turn to face him. *I'm way past serious.*

Christian's lips tug into a weary smile. "Lucky guy."

His tone doesn't convey the kindness of his words, but before I can respond, a deep voice from outside the kitchen says, "Yes, I am."

CHAPTER TWENTY-SEVEN

NICK

Christian's eyes rocket to me faster than a bullet fired from a gun, his face marred with worry. Rightfully so. I heard the possessiveness in his tone. That's why I nearly broke my neck stumbling out of bed. I was so eager to find out who was visiting Jenni so early on a Sunday morning, I threw my feet into my jeans without considering my weary muscles. I've never been stiffer in my life. I shouldn't be surprised. Jenni and I tried positions I didn't even know existed last night.

I was pissed when I spotted who she was talking to, even more so since Christian's eyes were locked on her delectable ass while she fanned the smoke detector, but before I demanded he get his eyes off her, he asked if she was serious about me. When she nodded, I felt like I had won the fucking jackpot. She didn't know I was in the room, so she had no reason to put on an act for me.

Although startled by my unexpected arrival, Jenni's cheeks flame with need instead of annoyance. "Good morning." Her eyes return to my face after taking their time absorbing my naked torso.

I give her a playful wink. "Morning."

With Christian's eyes locked on us, I give Jenni a slow and

possessive kiss, assuring he knows without a doubt that she's off the market. When I pull back from our embrace, I instruct Jenni to put on some pants. I'm not being an alpha male jerk; I just don't want Christian getting any more sneak peeks at a backside and stellar pair of legs that solely belong to me.

Jenni rolls her eyes before doing as instructed. The instant she's out of earshot, my eyes drift to Christian. I'm about to speak, but he beats me to the task, "I didn't touch her because I knew she deserved better than a player."

He stands taller, his eyes narrowing as he glares down at me. He has maybe two or three inches on me in height, but his build is similar to mine, although it's hard to say exactly how similar since he's wearing black jogging shorts and a sweat-soaked gym shirt.

"You didn't touch her because she wouldn't let you touch her." My tone is confident, as is my killer glare. I saw the way Jenni's cheeks flushed when I walked into the kitchen. Her body doesn't react to Christian like it does me, making me confident she'll never run into his arms like she did mine Friday night.

"If you fuck her over, I'll hunt you down." Christian's voice is only a whisper, but his threatening snarl can't be missed.

I smirk a smug grin. *What's another name on a very long list?*

I'm set to retaliate, but the patter of Jenni's bare feet becomes noticeable in the silence of our standoff. When she enters the kitchen, she places herself between us, her nervous eyes exposing her suspicions. "Is everything okay?"

Christian breaks our intense stare-off first. He turns toward Jenni and winks before pressing a kiss to the edge of her mouth. When Jenni's fretful eyes snap to mine, I smile at her. I'm not the least bit worried. She doesn't have an ounce of pinkness on her skin.

When Christian leaves, Jenni and I enjoy the chocolate chip pancakes she prepared for us in silence. It isn't uncomfortable or tense; it just enhances the sexual connection zapping between us. Every time she notices me watching her, she smiles, then her neck gets a pink hue. That makes me watch her even more intently.

My attentiveness gets rewarded in the most brilliant way. I'll never eat pancakes again without getting a hard on, because syrup has never tasted as good as it did until I licked it off Jenni's skin.

Our routine continues on the same path for the next couple of months. I travel to Jenni as often as my bank balance will allow, and she comes home any time she has more than a two-day break in her school schedule. Our relationship has been so good, it's almost surreal.

This morning, Jenni is flying home for spring break. I'm dying to see her. I plan to spend every waking moment I'm not in the studio with her.

My steps into the kitchen are extra springy, anticipation lightening them. When I head to the coffee pot to fill a mug with steaming brew, my dad peers up from his newspaper to eye me curiously. I flash him a quick smirk en route to the fridge to add a dash of milk to my coffee.

Scorching hot liquid dribbles down my hand when a pair of arms unexpectedly sling around my waist. I pivot around to face the person embracing me from behind, hopeful Jenni caught an earlier flight. A knot twists in my stomach when a pair of hazel eyes peer up at me. "What the fuck are you doing here?"

"Nicholas!" my dad scolds, shocked by my rude tone.

I glare at him, blinking and confused. Does he not know what is going on here? This isn't normal. Far from it.

My focus returns to Megan when she slaps my chest. "You're so funny."

I take a stumbling step backward. "Who let you in?"

Finally realizing the dangerous situation we're in, my dad stands from his seat.

When Megan fails to answer my first question, I ask another, "How did you get into my house?"

"You invited me here, silly." Her tone is extra chipper—somewhat manic.

When I take another step back, my eyes absorb the entire picture. It isn't pretty. Megan is wearing the shirt I left discarded on the bathroom floor last night after I took a shower.

No longer capable of holding back my anger, I grab ahold of her arm and drag her to my room. Upon entering, I notice a dress, handbag, and a pair of open-toed shoes resting on my desk. My chest thrusts up and down when I gather her items in my other hand before hotfooting it to the front of my house. My steps are hurried and shaky, my fury uncontrolled.

"You said you loved me; you told me you wanted to have a baby with me," Megan cries when I deposit her and her clothing on my paint-peeled front porch.

When she mentions the baby, my eyes dart down to her stomach, which is noticeably flat. That's not surprising. She should have given birth a month or two ago.

I wonder who watches her baby while she breaks into strangers' homes?

Upon noticing my glance at her stomach, Megan places her hand over a non-existent bump. "Don't worry, darling, Daddy is just joking." My fearful eyes rocket to hers faster than a nanosecond. She rolls her shoulders, happy she's gained my attention. "Do you think we will have a boy or a girl?"

I stare at her, more confused than ever. Her happiness doesn't wilt under my heated glare. If anything, it grows. Her smile enlarges as she bats her lashes excessively. My attention diverts from her wild, crazy eyes when a screen door creaking open breaks through the silence teeming between us.

Spotting my panicked face, my dad moves to stand next to me. "Is everything okay?" His question is for me, but his eyes are fixed on Megan.

"I think we'll have a little girl," Megan continues, not acknowledging that my dad has joined our conversation.

"You need to leave." My tone is both stern and worried. "If I ever see you here again, I'll call the police."

Megan's watering eyes bounce between mine. She appears genuinely surprised by my rejection. I don't know why? I could never be accused of tiptoeing around my feelings. When she remains standing, I jerk my chin to a yellow car parked in my driveway, demanding she leave with as many words as she's using to beg me to let her stay.

She takes a step closer to me. I shake my head and take a step back. *This is not up for negotiation.*

Defeat crosses her features as tears drip down her face. With slumped shoulders, she pivots on her heels and stalks to her car. The wild beat of my heart slows when her car bolts out of the gravel driveway a few seconds later. She barely brakes to clear the gate, her speed as manic as her craziness.

Once her taillights are blurs of red in the distance, my eyes drift to my dad. "She was in the kitchen when I woke up this morning. She introduced herself as your girlfriend," he explains.

"She's not my girlfriend." I scrub my hand over the stubble on my chin, hiding its brutal shaking. "She's fucking crazy."

When he nods, agreeing with me, I add on, "You need to lock up the house every night."

After slapping his shoulder to ensure him I'll make this right, I head inside to call Isaac. My run-in with Megan has rattled me enough, I need advice from someone who's handled this type of thing before.

CHAPTER TWENTY-EIGHT

JENNI

I came home for Spring Break with the intention of getting as much time with Nick as possible. For the first few days, that's exactly what I did. My days were spent with Emily while Nick was in the studio, then my nights were a blur of lust-filled fun and wickedly naughty adventures only a man with a stamina like Nick's could pull off. I was loving every minute of my vacation. . . until I got hit with the worst stomach bug you could possibly imagine.

I can't keep anything down. Even the smell of coffee, which I usually love, has me rushing to the bathroom. Nick was disappointed when I called to cancel our plans for tonight, but he said he understood. Since I can't hold down any nutrients, and I'm incredibly tired, I decided to have an early night. I've only been in bed for around an hour when I hear someone tapping on my door.

"Come in." My voice is groggy, strained by the number of times I was sick this afternoon.

Maria paces into the room with a bowl that smells distinctively like her famous chicken noodle soup. The aroma filling the air makes my stomach growl and my mouth water. It's tempting enough I'm willing to risk a night of hugging the toilet just for a spoonful.

The smirk stretched across my face from Maria's kindness expands to a full-blown smile when I spot the person tailing her.

He came.

"Hey, how are you feeling?" Nick kneels next to my bed, the concern in his eyes growing when they assess my pale face.

"I've been better," I respond, struggling not to breathe on him.

The last thing he needs is to become sick. Rise Up is putting the final touches on their album, then they have some press junkets scheduled to promote it. He doesn't have time to be unwell.

Nick runs the back of his hand down my cheek before pressing his lips to my forehead. "You don't feel hot, but you don't look too good."

I pout. My sunken cheeks and eyes were the main reason I canceled our date. I look like hell.

Noticing my drooping lip, Nick sucks it into his mouth. My heart screams blue murder when I pull away from him, but I really don't want him getting sick.

When I tell him that, he replies, "You'll be worth it."

The minty freshness of his breath when he presses his lips to mine settles my swirling stomach.

He kisses every inch of my face before kicking off his shoes and undoing his belt. "Scoot."

My pupils widen as my pulse quickens. Not just because of his impromptu strip but because we're in my parents' house. Maria may have placed the soup on my bedside table before leaving, but my dad is home. I said goodnight to him before I went to bed.

"My dad is home," I advise Nick, who is standing in front of me in nothing but a pair of cotton boxer shorts.

Even though my stomach is swirling, and I'm deliriously tired, my eyes can't help but drink in his delicious body. It's too perfect not to ogle. Not overly muscular, but not skinny either. A hint of a V muscle, slim hips, and tight, compact pecs. Pure perfection!

My eyes snap back to Nick's face when he asks, "I know; who do you think let me in?" He waggles his brows, his tone cheeky. "Now scoot."

Once I've wiggled to the far side of my bed, he pulls back the comforter then glides in. I giggle when he repositions the mountain of pillows on my bed. He even throws a handful of them onto the floor like missiles. When he's comfortable, he motions for me to join him. With a smile, I scamper across the bed so I can lay my head on his bare chest. His heart is beating as wildly as mine, his skin just as sticky.

I peer up at him when he asks, "Have you eaten anything today?" He sighs when I shake my head. "You have to eat, Jen, or you'll get even sicker."

Leaning over, he grabs the bowl of chicken noodle soup from my bedside table before nudging me with his shoulder, requesting I lift my head. When I do, he lowers a spoonful of Maria's famous chicken noodle soup into my mouth. I moan when the delicious flavors engulf my taste buds. Grinning at my positive response, Nick offers me another spoonful.

Our routine continues until I've eaten the entire bowl of chicken noodle soup. "Good girl," Nick praises.

I snuggle back into his chest. The rapid beating of his heart soothes my thumping head while his gentle rubs on my back make my swirling stomach less noticeable. I feel safe and protected in his arms. I'd even go as far as saying cherished.

And perhaps loved.

Just as the words I've wanted to say to Nick for months prepare to escape my lips, so does the chicken noodle soup. I dive over him before darting into the bathroom. I make it to the toilet with only a second to spare. My body doesn't stop heaving until every drop of the soup is expelled from my stomach. It's a brutally long five minutes.

Groaning, I rest my head on my forearm slumped over the toilet seat. I feel ten times worse when Nick wets a cloth in the vanity sink. I really don't want him to see me like this. Ignoring my silent protests for him to go, he wipes the vomit from my chin as his worried eyes dance over my ashen face.

Confident he's cleaned up the mess, he tosses the washcloth in the sink. "Do you feel better?"

I nod but continue to lean against my arm. I'm so tired, I don't have the energy to move. Noticing my exhausted state, Nick scoops me into his arms. He flushes the toilet and switches on the exhaust fan before placing me back in my bed.

This time, he throws off every pillow but two. Once he lies down, he rolls me over so he can spoon my back. As the soft curves of my body melt into his, my blinking lengthens and my breathing shallows.

Just before tiredness overcomes me, I whisper, "I love you, Nick."

CHAPTER TWENTY-NINE

NICK

Jenni's sleepy confession should freak me the fuck out, but for some reason unbeknownst to me, it doesn't. That falling I mentioned months ago isn't just falling anymore. I've *fallen*. That's why I rocked up to her house uninvited. I didn't expect her father to let me in—his wife isn't a fan of mine because of the whole paternity fiasco—but I was worried when Jenni canceled our date because she was sick. I hated the thought of her being ill and alone.

When I explained that to her dad, he considered my response for several long painful minutes before opening the door for me to enter. He probably wouldn't have been so accommodating if he knew how hard I got every time Jenni's lips circled the spoon.

Even pale and tired, she's as beautiful as ever, and taking care of her has those feelings I mentioned months ago catapulting to a new level, freeing me to express myself without fear of backlash. "I love you too, baby."

I press my lips to her temple before snuggling in closer. My ultimate rule breaker just made me break the very top rule on my list, yet I couldn't be happier.

What the fuck is happening to me?

I don't know what the time is when something pokes me in the back. I grunt before moving away from the sharp pointy object, only to be struck again a second later. When I sluggishly open my eyes, I almost jump out of my skin. Jenni's mother, Taylor, is standing over me. The sharp pointy object digging into my back is her finger.

"Can I have a word—in private?"

Nodding, I kiss Jenni's temple, then slip out of her bed, trying my hardest to cover my morning glory with my hands. I realize I'm failing when Taylor's eyes narrow after landing on my crotch. I don't know what she's expecting. It's god-knows-what-time in the morning, and I was just snuggled up to the most perfect ass in the world. A stiffy is bound to happen.

Taylor's eyes slit more before she motions for me to join her in the hallway. I grab my jeans, shirt, and shoes off the floor before walking out of Jenni's room on the heels of her mother. Taylor watches me get dressed in the clothes I was wearing the night before, her anger intensifying the more clothes I put on.

"She's sick," I explain, not wanting her to think we were doing anything sexual under her roof. I may be an ass, but I understand respect. Furthermore, Jenni is sick. She isn't up for vigorous activities.

Instead of my statement giving her comfort, Taylor's anger flares. Her face lines with redness as the veins in her neck bulge. "How much will it take?"

I bend down to tie my shoelaces. "How much will what take?"

My eyes float from my shoes to her when she answers, "For you to leave my daughter alone. How much money will it take for you to agree to never see her again?"

"I don't want your money," I inform her angrily and perhaps a little loudly, considering Maria opens her bedroom door. When she is subjected to Taylor's angry glare, she dashes back into her room.

"I love her," I say without any remorse.

Taylor rolls her eyes. "You don't even know the meaning of the word love."

A year ago, I would have agreed with her, but there's no doubt now. It took me a while to figure out why my heart would race every time Jenni entered the room, and how I couldn't even eat without thinking about her, but there's no confusion now.

After flashing a smirk at an irate Taylor, I head to my truck. I have a meeting at Destiny Records' head office scheduled for this morning, and her eagerness to pay me off makes me just as eager to get a head start on my meeting.

"I won't let you destroy her," Taylor hisses under her breath.

I nod before I continue walking. I have no intention of destroying Jenni, so her mom has nothing to worry about.

CHAPTER THIRTY

JENNI

I wake up feeling better than I was the night before. My bed still carries Nick's warmth, but I don't need to open my eyes to know he's gone. My body senses when he's nearby. It's not picking up anything right now. When I reluctantly open my eyes, my first thought is to snap them back shut. My mom is standing in my doorway. She looks angry.

"How long have you been sick?" she questions, her voice as stern as her lips.

Rolling over, I hide my face in the pillow. The last thing I want to deal with right now is another lecture. I begged Nick to keep quiet about our relationship because my mom can't stand him. Actually, she kind off hates him.

When my mom huffs, I mumble, "I have a bug."

I hear her heels click across the floor before she drops something on my bed. Curious, my head pops off my pillow. My brows scrunch when I spot a brown paper bag on my bed.

With my mom not giving me any hints, I scamper across the bed, grasp the bag and yank it open. My heart launches into my throat when I spot what is inside. "I'm not pregnant!" I inform my mom as my woozy brain struggles to calculate the last time I had my period.

The swirling of my stomach intensifies as my panic reaches a dangerous level.

Oh shit.

I use all three tests my mom bought. Every one of them returns the same result. I'm pregnant.

Holy.

Fucking.

Shit.

When I exit the bathroom, it only takes one look at the expression on my face for my mom to know the results. "How could you have been so stupid?" she yells, her blue eyes welling with tears. "I told you to stay away from him, and look what you go and do. He's going to destroy you, Jenni."

I shake my head. I love Nick, and he loves me. He won't be happy we're having a baby, but I'm sure over time, the idea will grow on him.

"You have to get rid of it."

"No." I glare at my mom, utterly mortified. I can't believe she'd suggest I do such a thing. "I can't kill a baby."

She returns my glare. "I won't let you do this! I won't let you ruin your life like mine was ruined when I had you."

Tears well in my eyes. I've always known I was a mistake, but hearing her admit it, makes it feel like she stabbed my heart with a dagger. "What's so wrong with your life? You live in a stupidly large house; you have more money than you could ever spend, you—"

"What about love? I don't have that."

I freeze and shift on my feet to face my mom. Nothing but hurt and pain is etched on her face.

"Daddy loves you," I say through the tears streaming down my cheeks. "And Nick loves me."

My mom grits her teeth. "He *will* leave you the instant you tell him about the baby."

"No, he won't." I shake my head so fiercely, tears fling off my cheeks.

"Yes, he will. He'll leave you, and you'll be left raising a baby that every single time you look at her face, you'll see his face reflecting back at you."

"Nick would never do that to me; he loves me." My tone is quickly switching from upset to angry.

"Your dad said he loved me too, and where did he go? He left! He left me! He left you! He left us!"

Her eyes widen as her hand clamps her mouth. I stand still, frozen in shock as everything she said replays on repeat in my head. *Your dad left. Your dad left me. Your dad left us.* My eyes burn from a sudden rush of moisture forming in them. Through quaking legs, I dart out of my room and run down the stairs, screaming my dad's name.

My mom follows closely behind me, pleading for me to stop. She assures me that she didn't mean what she said, and that she'll explain everything once we've calmed down, but it's too late, my dad is here now. He ran in from the garden so fast, he's still wearing muddy gloves. My screams must have really panicked him.

"Is it true?" I angrily brush a stupid tear off my cheek. "Am I not your daughter?"

My dad's face cracks as his eyes fill with tears. The grief on his face confirms what my mom just said. "You'll *always* be my daughter."

When he moves toward me, I angrily shake my head, halting his steps. "You lied to me for years," I whisper fiercely. "Both of you!"

My wild eyes bounce between the two people who are supposed to protect me from anyone trying to hurt me, yet they're the ones hurting me the most. After dashing back into my room, I angrily yank a suitcase down from my closet. I grab everything my hands can hold and shove them inside my bag.

I need to leave. I can't stay here. It hurts too much.

CHAPTER THIRTY-ONE

NICK

My eyes rise from my hands when Cormack gestures for the band to enter the boardroom. When we enter, he introduces us to a lady I swear I've met before. Her name is Delilah Winterbottom, and she'll be responsible for all public relation matters for the band. She's a little snappy at Noah at the start of our meeting, but the rest of the band remains fairly unscathed. Her fierce daggers and vicious snarls have my thoughts returning to the run-in I had with Jenni's mom this morning. I still can't believe she wanted to pay me off. Who does shit like that anymore? We're not in the 50s.

My focus returns to the meeting when Delilah informs Noah he can't publicly declare he's engaged because she wants the band to appear attainable to our fans. Noah is as shocked by her demand as I am. When he tells her he's not hiding Emily away, I sit on the edge of my chair, primed to back him up. It's taken me months to woo Jenni, so you can be assured now that I've fallen in love, there's no chance in hell I'll hide my relationship. I was hoping with Jenni's approval that we could tell the band this weekend that we're a couple.

"Noah." Cormack's gentle eyes urge him to calm down since he pretty much just told them to go fuck themselves. "We're not saying you need to break up with Emily. We just can't have the public knowing about your relationship."

"This is bullshit," I jump in, startling Cormack and Delilah.

Believing Noah is the only one in our group in a relationship, their attention was fixed on him.

They're fucking wrong.

"We don't make music so immature idiots can daydream about marrying us. We do it because we're fucking good at it." I stand from my chair and splay my hands on the table. "You don't get to pick who you love, so leave them alone."

The veins in my neck bulge with every word I speak. I'm sick of people believing they have the right to tell people who they can and cannot love. I've dealt with it for months, and I'm fucking over it.

"This is not negotiable. You either agree to our terms, or the record deal is off the table!" Delilah rises from her chair and storms out of the office.

Cormack tries to calm the rocky waters by advising us that this type of agreement is nothing new in the music industry, and that it's a publicist's job to let the public know only what they want them to know. I'm not fucking buying it. There are thousands of musicians in the world who are married, and they still sell millions of CDs every year.

"Fuck this shit! This is bullshit, Noah; you can't let them do this," I plead when he remains quiet, like he's considering their request.

Noah's dark eyes scan my face. I can tell the exact moment when realization dawns on him. He sinks into his chair as a blistering smile spreads across his face.

"Shut up, Noah, just shut the fuck up," I demand, pissed at his arrogant smirk.

When his smirk grows, I storm out, kicking one of the boardroom chairs on my way. I've finally fallen in love, and now my career wants me to hide it away like it's a dirty little secret. Fuck that. I'm not doing it.

Needing some air before I do something I'll regret, I push open the glass door at Destiny Records' head office with force. When the warm air fails to settle my anger, I yank my phone out of my pocket and dial Jenni's number. Her voice will calm me down. It always does.

Just as I'm about to hit the call button, Delilah breaks onto the sidewalk. When she notices me standing at the side, she saunters my way. My blood pumps even faster from the haughty expression on her face. She has a plastic smile, loving the rift she's made between the executives of our label and the band.

"Nicholas Holt." Her evil eyes float over my face before dropping to assess my body. With her lower lip caught between her teeth, she murmurs, "I can see a small family resemblance; pity you missed out on the gray eyes."

Winking at the growl rumbling up my chest, she hops into the back of a black town car that has just pulled to the curb. I watch her leave, confident my earlier assumption was right. I knew I had seen her before, and her comment on the gray eyes makes sense. She must know Isaac.

Once Delilah's town car disappears into the bustling street, I redial Jenni's cell phone number and lift my phone to my ear. When my call goes to her voicemail, I leave a message.

After a few deep breaths, I reenter Destiny Records. Not wanting to make a decision about Delilah's request without talking to Emily, Noah heads to Emily's university while the band and I make our way to the studio. We've got a lot of tracks we can finalize without him, and it will give me time to settle my anger before discussing similar subjects with Jenni. I want to make our relationship public. Not just to the band—to everyone.

I'm in the studio, recording a solo portion of our new song "Tastefully Despised," when Marcus informs me there's someone waiting for me outside.

I'd be lying if I said I wasn't praying it was Jenni.

As I exit the double glass doors of the studio, a pair of arms clamp around my neck before my mouth is attacked by painted lips.

CHAPTER THIRTY-TWO

JENNI

I drive to Hopeton with tears streaming down my face and a shattered heart, confident there's only one person capable of easing the pain shredding me to pieces. Nick will make everything better, then, once my tears have settled, we'll work out where we go from here.

As I said earlier, he'll be shocked to discover I'm pregnant, but I doubt he'll respond in the manner my mom is claiming.

When I pull onto the curb at the front of the studio Nick has been recording at the past twelve months, I spot him standing outside.

Now, I wish I hadn't.

CHAPTER THIRTY-THREE

NICK

I t takes me less than a fraction of a second to realize the tongue sliding along mine doesn't belong to Jenni. These lips taste *nothing* like hers. They don't have the same wicked sweetness her mouth has, and my body is recoiling from her touch instead of craving it.

I yank away while dragging my hand over my lips, aggressively removing the lipstick before locking my furious eyes with the person assaulting me in broad daylight. I'm at a loss on who the strawberry blonde is until she raises her chin.

Megan.

The fact her new hair color perfectly matches Jenni's freaks me the fuck out. I rush into the studio, locking the glass door behind me. Even with her fleeing down the street like her ass is on fire, I call the police. Her level of craziness has reached a point I'm no longer comfortable with. It's gone too far.

If I can't convince her that I'm not interested in her, maybe the authorities can.

CHAPTER THIRTY-FOUR

JENNI

I have nowhere else to go. Emily and Nicole are at school; my dad's parents died years ago, and I've never met my mom's parents, so a mere hour after leaving, I pull into my parents' driveway with my tail firmly tucked between my legs. I sit in my car for several minutes, trying to muster up the courage to walk up the front stairs. I can't bring myself to do it. My heart was shattered today in more ways than one. First, finding out my dad isn't my real dad, then witnessing Nick kiss another girl outside his recording studio. I don't know how much more heartache I can take.

I cowardly hide in my car for another thirty minutes before a tap on my passenger window startles me. When I hit the unlock button, my mom slips into the passenger seat. Even with tears flowing down my face, her angry glare doesn't slacken.

"You were right." I choke on my words, utterly confused by how much has changed in a few hours. I swear I could feel the love beaming out of Nick last night, but today, he kisses another girl in broad daylight. That's not something a man in love would do.

When I drag my hand over my wet cheeks, my mom watches me with concern, but she doesn't offer me any comfort. She keeps her cool, calm bitch façade firmly in place like she has my entire life. "You need to go back to New York. I'll arrange everything from here. We will get this taken care of." She speaks as if she's scheduling a doctor's appointment for her client instead of killing her own grandchild.

No longer having the strength to argue, I nod. I'm riddled with what I now know is morning sickness, and I'm overwhelmed by fatigue. I'm too exhausted to fight.

"Your flight leaves in an hour." She hands me a printed voucher for a prepaid flight. The time stamp reveals it was printed before I discovered Nick kissing another girl. "A taxi has been arranged to drive you to the airport."

After briefly running her eyes over my face, she steps out of my car, leaving me utterly dumbfounded and wholly heartbroken. Not long later, a taxi arrives to take me to the airport. I hop out of my car to collect the suitcase from the trunk. The cab driver kindly assists me in placing my overstuffed bag into the back seat of his idling taxi.

Just as I'm about to slide in next to it, my eyes stray to my family home. My heart beeps in my neck when I spot my dad's shadow standing at his office window. He's peering down at me, begging me not to go. I love him, but I'm too hurt from being lied to for years to speak to him right now. So instead, I slide into the taxi with my cheeks as messy as my heart feels.

CHAPTER THIRTY-FIVE

NICK

Ryan, a detective at Ravenshoe Police Station assists me in filing a restraining order against Megan. When the judge approves my request, Megan is no longer allowed within five hundred feet of me. I request that Jenni be included in my order, but Ryan informs me that she needs to request one of her own. With that in mind, the first place I go after leaving the police station is Jenni's house. I want her to file the order immediately, but I also want to check in and see how she's feeling.

After parking my truck at the front of her mansion-like house, I dash up the stairs two at a time before banging on her front door. It takes several hard knocks before her dad answers. He's a little disheveled, like he's hit the bottle early.

When he notices my amused smirk, he mumbles something incoherently before staggering into his office. I follow him inside, closing the front door behind me. When he slumps into his chair in his office, I take the stairs two at a time to Jenni's room.

I'm surprised when I find her room empty. After striding to her bathroom, I knock on the closed door. Several seconds pass in silence.

I'm about to knock again when a soft, accented voice says, "Jenni is gone."

Pivoting around, I see Maria standing in the doorway. I smile at her, but she doesn't smile back. That's odd. She was super friendly last night.

"Is she better?" Hope is evident in my voice.

When Maria shakes her head, my brows scrunch. As a sense of unease rolls through me, I sprint back down the stairs. I race through each room in Jenni's house, calling her name. I don't get a single reply.

Jenni is gone, and her mom is nowhere in sight.

"Where's Jenni?" I ask her dad, who's chugging down whiskey directly out of the bottle in his office.

His glazed eyes drop to his watch. "At the airport?"

My heart slithers into my gut. Jenni isn't scheduled to fly home until Wednesday, and the last time she left early, I didn't see or hear from her in months. My heart races as I sprint back to my truck. The heavy compression of my accelerator leaves a cloud of dust when I skid out of her driveway. While weaving through the heavy traffic that always clogs the streets surrounding Ravenshoe, I dial Jenni's cell phone on repeat.

She doesn't answer any of my calls.

I make the forty-minute trip to the airport in under twenty. I leave my truck parked in the drop-off only section and bolt to the entrance. A parking attendant screams at me to come back when I dart through the double glass doors, but I keep going. This is more urgent than any ticket he could possibly give me.

My eyes scan the departure board to check when the next flight to New York is leaving. The board informs it's currently preparing to depart. Not thinking about the repercussions, I vault over the security barrier that requires a boarding pass before sprinting to the assigned gate. An overweight TSA officer runs after me, but his chubby legs can't keep up.

It's lucky I live in a small town, otherwise I would have been tasered by now.

When I reach gate thirty-four, commotion stirs in my gut. Jenni's plane is taxiing away from the gate. I'm about to beg the gate staff to stop her flight, but my words fail when I'm suddenly tackled hard from the side. The weight of the security officer slamming me to the ground nearly crushes me to death. He is at least one hundred pounds heavier than me and wheezing with exhaustion.

After fixing cuffs to my wrist, another officer assists him in arresting me. I'm read my rights, ushered out of the airport terminal by five guards, and remanded in police custody.

CHAPTER THIRTY-SIX

JENNI

Call me a sucker for punishment, but I switch on my phone the instant I deplane in New York. I have missed several calls from Nick, but I'm surprised to notice I only have one voicemail message.

With my stomach in my throat, I dial my voicemail then push my cell to my ear. "Hey, baby, I hope you're feeling better. Give me a call if you're well enough to go out." Nick chuckles nervously. "Actually, just call me. I love you, Jen."

My heart soars during the last part of his message, then my stomach swirls as I recall the last time I saw him. After clamping my hand over my mouth, I bolt for the bathroom.

Miserable. That's the only word I can describe how I'm feeling right now. I left home two days ago, and I haven't heard from Nick that entire time. I'm beginning to wonder if he realized why I was sick Thursday night. When you put all the pieces of a puzzle together, it isn't hard to work out what's going on. I hate admitting this, but I think my mom was right. The instant Nick had an inkling I was pregnant, he ran.

When I arrived home, I couldn't stop crying. All I did Saturday was sleep and cry. By Sunday, I was angry. I wanted to yell at Nick and tell him to grow the hell up. I hadn't planned on having a baby so young either, but I can't run from my problems like he can.

By this morning, denial hit. *Baby? What baby? Nick? Nick who?* That's been my motto the entire day. I've gone about my day as if it's any other Monday. I had brunch at the corner café; I went grocery shopping, then for the past two hours I've been working on the design for Emily's wedding dress.

She gave me a few pointers during our chats last week, but I have free rein with the overall design. I'm so immersed in drawing up different styles I've completely forgotten about the drama of the weekend. . . until someone knocks on my front door.

After setting down a stick of charcoal, I jump up from my drawing desk and pace to the entranceway. My head is a little dizzy. I want to pretend it's because of my sudden movements, but that isn't true. Part of me is panicked my unexpected visitor is Nick. The other part is stupidly praying it is.

When I swing open the door, disappointment smacks into me. Christian is standing behind it, holding two paper bags brimming with groceries in his arms.

"I heard you were back in town early." Not waiting to be invited in, he plants a kiss on my cheek before heading into my kitchen. I close my door and follow after him. My already sluggish pace slows even more when he asks, "Curry chicken or sweet and sour?"

My stomach churns. I've been living off graham crackers and lemonade because they're the only things that stay down. When I remain quiet, Christian spins around to face me. "Have you already eaten?"

His eyes flick to the clock on the wall so fast, he misses me shaking my head. Noticing it's only 5 PM, he shifts his eyes back to me, then asks again. I choose curry chicken with the hope I can keep down the plain rice it's served with. Smiling, he begins prepping everything. While he cuts up an onion, I move back to my drawing board to pack away my pencils and sketches. I have three designs ready to show Emily. With her body type, she can wear any style of dress, but I want to give her a good selection. She's only getting married once, so I want her to have a dress she'll love.

When curry filters into the living room, I'm surprised my stomach doesn't protest about the smell. It actually grumbles. I follow the delicious aroma into the kitchen. Christian is moving around the small space with ease. It's nice experiencing all the different sides of him no one else gets to see. He's funny and a good cook; he cares deeply for his friends, and he'll always have your back if you need him.

He just also happens to be one of the world's biggest players. It's his duty to pleasure as many women as possible with his "gift." No, I'm not the one who thinks that. Christian has quoted that exact phrase to me many times before.

Feeling the heat of my watchful eye, Christian spins around to face me. My brows stitch together when he laughs. I shoot my eyes down to my clothing, seeking anything he could find funny. I'm wearing a button-up cotton dress and a pair of boots. All my buttons are fastened, and I don't have anything spilled down the front of me, so I have no clue what he finds so amusing.

When my confused eyes lift to Christian, he bridges the small distance between us. My nose screws up when he runs his thumb down it. "You have charcoal smeared on your face." He chuckles while wiping my cheek and lip with his thumb.

A ghost of a smile cracks onto my lips. I did get a little excited while sketching Noah standing next to Emily in a black suit. I wanted Emily to see the complete picture, and focusing on something other than my heartbreak gave me a nice escape from reality.

"There you go. Perfect."

He keeps his hand cupped over my cheek as his eyes appraise my face. My gaze darts between his, confused and feeling another sensation I can't explain. When he leans down to press his lips to mine, I freeze. I don't want this, but I don't *not* want it either. His tongue licks the seam of my mouth, requesting that I open up for him. I'm shocked when my body chooses its own reply to his boldness by parting my lips.

The instant my lips open, his tongue slides between them. Within seconds, his kiss shifts from innocent to needy. He rakes his fingers through my hair, securing my mouth firmly to his before doubling the strength of his tongue. The minty freshness of his breath eases my swirling stomach, but it slams me with a shit load of guilt. Images of Nick kissing me the past year play in my mind. The needy, the loving, the ones that made me forget everyone but him. *The ones that solidified my love for him.*

I yank back. I can't do this. Even though I'm hurting, two wrongs won't make a right.

Just as my lips break away from Christian, smashing glass booms through my apartment. Cool water splashes my overheated face as the flowers that usually sit on my entrance table collide with the wall near Christian's head. My breath snags halfway to my lungs when my eyes stray to the entranceway. Nick is standing just inside my door. His jaw is ticking, and his fists are clenched in tight balls. He looks prepared to charge at any moment.

I move off the barstool to place myself between Christian and Nick. My change in position frustrates Nick. His fists clench tighter as his hurt eyes scorch my soul.

"I'm sorry." I don't know why I'm apologizing. He hurt me first; I just returned the favor.

After shaking his head, Nick storms out of my apartment. He slams my front door so hard, the photo frames on my mantel topple over.

Flustered by my tears, Christian rubs them off my face with a sense of urgency. I yank away from his touch. "Please go."

"Jen. . ." He sounds as tormented as I feel.

"Leave, Christian!"

Hoping to give him the hint our night is over, I dump his half-cooked food into the waste bin next to the fridge before throwing the saucepans into the kitchen sink. I'm not even concerned when I break a glass. I should be happy Nick experienced the hurt I was slapped with three days ago, but I'm not. I feel terrible and spiteful. I'm also ashamed. The look on his face is going to haunt me for the rest of my life. . . way longer than his child's eyes will.

CHAPTER THIRTY-SEVEN

NICK

Don't ever fall in love. If you do, your heart will be ripped out of your chest and fucking stomped on. Trust me, the pain isn't worth it. I'd rather stay alone the rest of my life than feel what I felt when I saw Jenni kissing Christian. The first thing I did when I was granted bail was catch the next available flight to New York. Curry was filtering in the air when I entered Jenni's apartment. I was pleased she was well enough to eat real food again.

My happiness vanished when I rounded the corner. Christian's lips were attached to Jenni's.

I froze, confident she'd pull away. When she accepted his kiss, my heart broke.

Enraged, I grabbed the first thing I could get ahold of and sent it hurtling across the room. The vase shattered on impact when it hit the wall just to the side of Christian's head. Jenni was surprised to see me standing in her entrance way. Christian was more arrogant than anything. He smirked and winked, like he was pleased about my timing.

That's when my anger reached breaking point. I was going to kill him, and I was going to love every second of it. Just as I was about to charge for him, Jenni placed herself in front of him, like she was protecting him.

That hurt more than anything.

If she was going to protect anyone, it should have been me.

After my eyes floated over her beautiful face, making sure every detail was memorized correctly, I left her apartment. With the elevator taking too long to arrive at her floor, I ran down the stairwell. Incapable of holding back my anger for a second longer, I unleashed it halfway down the stairs, throwing punch after punch against the concrete wall. I didn't stop until my knuckles were bleeding and swollen and my hands were on the verge of never playing guitar again.

Still, their pain was nothing compared to the one ripping through my chest.

I raced through the foyer before taking a taxi to the closest bar. I didn't just plan on drowning my sorrows; I was going to find the first girl I could and use her to help me forget the little blonde firecracker who tore my heart in two.

Now, four weeks later, I'm being forced to spend the weekend with the girl who brought me to my knees. Because of my outburst in the band meeting, Noah continually questioned me about who I was in love with. His grilling got so intense, I wanted to scream at him to leave me the fuck alone.

After two weeks, he finally did.

My volatile moods of late convinced him to give up on his endeavor to unearth every tidbit of information on my love life rather quickly, but he hasn't budged on my request to skip the weekend getaway he and Emily have planned for the band this weekend. He said this is our last hurrah, a chance for us to have a bit of down time with those we care about the most before things get crazy. He wants the band's bond to be the strongest it can be before we're thrusted into the spotlight.

I more see it as a weekend that will crack my heart even more. It will shatter my soul while reminding me why I should have never fallen in love to begin with. I've given every pathetic excuse I can find to get out of this fucked-up situation, but Noah hasn't bought any of them. He's adamant I need to do this to prove to Slater and Marcus that I am as integral to the band as they are.

That's the only reason I'm here. I want to prove I'm as worthy of fame as every other member of Rise Up, then perhaps, at the same time, I'll show Jenni what she lost by fooling around on me.

Excluding earlier today, I haven't seen or heard from Jenni since I left her apartment last month. She only called today because she heard my band's song "Hollow" on the radio. Her voicemail said she was proud of me, and that she always knew Rise Up would achieve the success we were aiming for. I nearly crumbled and called her back when she failed to stifle a sob before disconnecting her call. I would have if anger wasn't still burning me alive.

The fire in my gut inflames when I spot Jenni's blue car pulling down the driveway Noah and I pulled into a few minutes ago. Happy to skip the awkward, *let's pretend we don't know each other* stint we've done the past year and a half, I snag a case of beer out of my truck before bolting up the wooden stairs of the cabin Noah rented for the weekend.

I've just finished putting the case of warm beer in the fridge when Jenni rounds the corner. Even though she's lost a few pounds from her already petite frame, she's still gorgeous. After apologizing for interrupting me, she darts to the kitchen sink. Her hands rattle when she snags a glass from the rack to fill it with water. I stare at her when she gulps down the entire glass in three big swallows.

My anger is pushed aside when concern takes its place. She's doesn't look too good. "Are you okay?"

She wipes droplets of water off her quivering lips before glancing over her shoulder at me. After giving me a sad smile, she nods.

"Alright." Hating the awkwardness teeming between us, I grab a bottle of warm beer out of the fridge and flee to the covered entertainment area near the infinity pool. Since the beer is hot, it tastes like shit, but since it's the only alcoholic drink I brought with me, it will have to do.

Not long later, Slater, Marcus, and Nicole arrive. I nearly fall out of my seat when Slater introduces me to a girl named Kylie. It isn't the fact he brought a date for our weekend getaway that has me stumbling; it's the fact he called her his girlfriend. This is the first girlfriend he has had since Nikki. Unsurprisingly, trust has been an issue for him.

"Nice to meet you." While accepting Kylie's handshake, I give her my trademark smirk that usually makes the girls all flustered. I'm pleased she doesn't even notice it. Her eyes are fixed on one man and one man only: Slater.

The same can't be said for Jenni. She's glaring at me, her stare murderous. She noticed the smile I gave Kylie, and she's not happy about it. Her nose is screwed up like a rabbit, and her arms are folded in front of her heaving chest.

Welcome to my life, kiddo. Heartbreak and jealousy. It's a cruel fucking world.

Jenni keeps her distance the rest of the afternoon. I don't mind, because the longer my beers chill, the more I enjoy them. By the time we sit around the table to eat Noah's half-burned burgers and hotdogs, I'm well on my way to being drunk. It does nothing to fill the hole in my chest, but it blurs the movie of Jenni and Christian kissing playing on repeat in my head.

I chug down my beer while trying to participate in the conversations around the table. For the most part, I have everyone fooled. Only I know how many times my eyes have flicked to Jenni. It's way more than I'm comfortable admitting.

It's not my fault. She's acting odd. She loves food, yet she's hardly eaten anything. When we went out, she usually downed a bottle of red, but tonight she's refused Kylie and Nicole's numerous offers for a glass of wine. She's paler than normal, and her eyes aren't shining as brightly as usual. She's acting so differently, anyone would swear it was her who had her heart broken—not me.

With my anger incapable of shutting down months of feelings, I pass Jenni my plate of fries. Any time we ate out, she devoured them before anything else.

"Thank you," she whispers while accepting my plate.

I can't help but smile when she demolishes the entire serving in under five minutes. Maybe she isn't acting odd? Perhaps she's just not a fan of Noah's poor BBQing skills?

A short time later, I stop talking to Marcus when I notice Jenni hightailing it to the cabin. She's as white as a ghost, and her hand is clamped over her mouth. After scrubbing my hand along my chin, I excuse myself from the table and make my way inside. I find Jenni in the main bathroom, her back bending harshly as the fries splash into the toilet bowl. I switch on the bathroom light and the exhaust fan before ambling to the sink to wet a washcloth for her.

"I'm fine, just leave me," she murmurs between heaves.

She may have ripped my heart out, but I can't walk away while she's sick. I'm not a monster. After planting my ass on the side of the tub, I rub her back in a circular motion. I don't pay any attention to the goosebumps rising on her skin. They could be from the cool air blowing in the open window, not my touch.

When she stops vomiting, I flush the toilet. "Is it still the same bug or a new one?"

Even though I'm trying to keep our conversation neutral, I can't harness the concern in my voice. She was sick like this last month, and if it's the same bug, she needs to see a doctor—urgently.

Jenni's eyes cloud with confusion as she stares at me. "You don't know." Her words are more for her ears than mine.

"Know what?" I use the washcloth to remove a chunk of vomit from her chin while trying to gauge what she thought I knew. I know she's been sick for over a month, but other than that, I'm in the dark. .
.

My inner monologue trails off as reality dawns.

Oh my God. Oh. My. Fucking. God.

I stumble backward until I crash into the bathroom sink. "You're pregnant?" The mad beat of my heart is heard in my words.

Jenni nods, forcing the moisture in her eyes to drip down her cheeks.

"Is it mine?"

Her eyes narrow as her lips thin. When she jumps up off the floor, she's overcome with dizziness, but it doesn't slow her down. She stumbles out of the bathroom, murmuring under her breath. I let out a groan before taking off after her. I find her in a room at the back of the cabin, stuffing clothes into a small overnight bag.

"Is it mine?" My voice is more vicious than I expected.

She stops packing to turn around and face me. Hurt and anger is marked all over her face. "Who else would it belong to?"

"Christian."

I dart my head to the side, dodging the shoe Jenni pegged at my head. When the first one misses its mark, she throws another one. It smacks me in the shoulder. Out of shoes, she throws word grenades instead. "You're an asshole!"

"I saw you kissing him, yet I'm the asshole."

Ignoring me, she moves throughout the room, grabbing her belongings and shoving them into her bag. I don't know what hurts more, the fact she kissed Christian, or that I may never see her again after she leaves this room.

Realizing it's the latter, I grab ahold of her wrist, halting her hasty movements. The pain in my chest turns lethal when her tear-stained face lifts to me.

"There wasn't supposed to be anyone else. It was supposed to be just you and me." My voice is an angry whisper.

"I know that," she declares shakily, "and I'm sorry. I never meant for any of this to happen."

Her beautifully tormented eyes stare into mine. They draw me back in by forcing my heart to overrule my head. Even after everything she did, I still love her.

I can't give her up.

She's my addiction—my rule breaker.

She's my everything.

CHAPTER THIRTY-EIGHT

JENNI

I stare at Nick, begging him to see the remorse in my eyes. I'm sorry I wasn't enough for him to stay faithful. I'm sorry for kissing Christian because I wanted him to take away my pain, where all it did was make me feel worthless. I'm sorry for all the rules he broke for me. But more than anything, I'm sorry for everything I do from here on out.

I've used every delay tactic I could to stop my mom fixing my "indiscretion," but I no longer have a choice. The decision is out of my hands......

The two weeks after Nick caught me kissing Christian was spent with my head in the toilet. I couldn't hold anything down. I wasn't just brokenhearted, I was incredibly unwell.

I've just finished showering after a two-hour long toilet-hugging session when I leave the bathroom to find Christian standing in my living room.

"How did you get into my house?" My question isn't asked nicely.

He knocked on my door every day the two weeks following our kiss. Not once have I let him in. I'm living the life of a hermit.

Excluding the occasional text messages to Emily, Slater, and Nicole, I've kept to myself.

When Christian fails to answer me, I point to my door. "Get out!"

"Jennifer Jade Murphy!" roars through my ears, scaring the living hell out of me.

I'm surprised, and perhaps a little scared, when my mom stands from her post at my dining table to saunter my way. "I asked him to come."

When my eyes drift to Christian, seeking confirmation on her statement, his dart to the floor. It's in this instant I finally understand why he arrived at my apartment mere minutes before Nick. He isn't my friend; he's working with my mother to undermine my relationship.

"Why are you here?" I'm so angry, steam is almost billowing from my ears.

My mom adjusts the collar on the dress I'm wearing. "How was I to know you weren't dead or passed out on the floor? You haven't answered anyone's calls." Happy I look presentable, she shifts her focus to Christian. "Thank you, Christian." She gives him his marching orders with three little words.

When Christian moves toward me, my mom places herself between us. Christian's eyes narrow at her before they shift to me. I can see remorse in his eyes. He feels bad for what he's done.

"Call me if you need me." He waits for me to nod before he reluctantly leaves my apartment.

The door has barely closed when my mom moves to stand in front of me. "Your appointment is on Wednesday." She saunters to her handbag hanging over one of my dining room chairs. "He's very discreet and has assured me our family name will not be mentioned." She digs a business card out of her purse before shoving it into my hand.

"I'm not getting an abortion," I say when I read the card she gave me. It's for an abortion doctor in New Jersey. When I try to hand the card back to her, she refuses to accept it.

"We've already discussed this, Jenni; you need to have this taken care of." When she states *"this,"* her eyes drop to my stomach for the quickest second.

They rocket back to my face when I say, *"I'm keeping my baby."*

Even with how much I'm hurting, I could never destroy the baby I created with Nick. I loved him, and I'll love our baby just as much.

"You're willing to give up everything to have his baby?"

When I nod, the anger on my mom's face doubles.

"Your studies, your apartment, your family." Her words get louder with each one she speaks. *"If you keep this baby, everything will be gone. Everthing!"* she warns. . .

When I failed to turn up to my appointment on Wednesday, my mom followed through on her threat. My attempt to pay for some groceries with my credit card was declined, and when I arrived home from school on Thursday, I had a notice on my door that my rent was overdue. I nearly fell over backwards when I read how much it cost to rent a one-bedroom apartment in New York City. I spent all night Thursday adding up my expenses and searching the classifieds for any jobs for students.

It did me no good.

Even if I left school and got two full-time jobs, I couldn't afford my apartment, let alone living expenses. I had no choice but to accept my mother's terms.

I'm snapped from my thoughts when Nick runs his hand down my cheek. He removes my tears before drawing me into his chest. My heart races a million miles an hour when he promises that everything will be okay, and that he'll take care of both me and our baby.

"It's too late," I murmur through a hiccup. "It's been taken care of."

Nick takes a step back, his jaw muscle quivering. "What?"

I take a moment to gauge his reaction to my confession. He's always been hard for me to read. He's very reserved and doesn't wear his emotions on his sleeve, so I'm having a hard time comprehending whether he's relieved or mad about my decision.

"My. . . umm. . . mom. . . has arranged everything," I mumble nervously, incapable of saying the word "abortion" out loud.

Nick's eyes open wide before they drop to my stomach. The cracks in my heart enlarge when I see the sheen in his eyes.

His eyes return to me when I disclose, "I have an appointment on Monday."

I nearly crumble into a heap when devastation crosses his features. I thought the look he gave me when he witnessed me kissing Christian was bad. This one is ten times worse.

"No, Jenni," he whispers roughly. "You can't do this." He takes a step closer to me, his eyes begging. "Don't do this—*please*."

"I don't have a choice."

"Yes, you do." He nods. "I'll take care of you; I'll take care of the baby."

His glossed-over eyes beg me to give him a chance to prove what he is saying is true. I want to believe him, but I can't. He lost my trust when he left my bed to run into the arms of another woman. I don't want to live my life like that, constantly wondering what he's doing or who he's doing it with. No matter how much I love him, insecurities and distrust would eventually eat me alive.

Furthermore, my mom only agreed to pay my overdue rent and school fees when I proved I had scheduled an appointment with the clinic. I was days away from being homeless and living on the streets. I can't bring a baby into that environment.

"I'm sorry, Nick, my decision has been made."

"Your decision or *hers*?" His voice is an angry snarl. When I delay my reply, his fists clench. "You can't let them do this to you; you can't let them do this to us," he yells furiously, startling me. "You're letting their money manipulate you!"

After a final glare that relays his disappointment, he storms out of my room as quickly as he entered it. Warm, salty tears stream down my face as I collapse onto my bed.

Seconds later, I hear shoes scuffling across the ground. Hopeful it's Nick, I lift my head from the mattress. It isn't who I am hoping, but it's better than no one.

"Does he know?" Emily's face is washed with concerned.

I nod. "He'll never forgive me."

When she wraps me up in a firm hug, I cry uncontrollably in the arms of my best friend.

CHAPTER THIRTY-NINE

NICK

When I storm out of the cabin, the first thing I spot is the baseball bat Slater carries in the saddle bags of his Harley. With my anger at a point it's never been, I secure it in my hands. When Taylor's attempt to buy me off failed, she clearly switched her focus to her daughter. I never took Jenni for being shallow. Although her parents are loaded, she didn't flash her wealth in anyone's face, so to say I'm shocked she'd kill a baby—*our baby*— to maintain her luxurious life is an understatement. A major one.

Eager to expel some of the anger tearing me in two, I rush toward Jenni's expensive pride and joy. The crack of the bat on her windshield gives me an intense amount of satisfaction. My swing is so strong, her windshield shatters into millions of tiny little fragments.

Satisfied it's beyond repair, I make my way to the driver's side door. Someone shouts, "What the fuck are you doing? Stop!" from behind my shoulder as I slam my bat into the side window.

Adrenaline pumps through my veins, making me feel invincible when it explodes upon impact with my bat. "They can't do this. I won't let them!"

I move around Jenni's car, seeking my next target. Noah's dark eyes track my every move, but he doesn't say anything. What could he possibly say? He's confused about what's happening, and I'm a major part of it.

Noah's worry grows when I snarl, "They can't force her to do it!" I swing the bat with enough force, the passenger side window of Jenni's BMW is destroyed with one hit. It breaks like my heart—shattered beyond repair. "They have no say in what she does! It's her fucking body!"

When I lift the bat to take a hit at the back rear window, I'm suddenly slammed from the side. Noah plows me into the grass, his hit so hard, the bat is dislodged from my hand.

Noah rolls off me, clutching his winded lungs. "What the fuck, Nick?"

I remain quiet, facing the pitch black night. Wetness glistens on my cheeks, and my chest aches like an elephant is sitting on it.

My neck cranks to the side when Noah asks, "Jenni?"

Just hearing her name breaks my heart even more. "I love her so much it hurts." I want her to be my wife and the mother of my children. I don't want her to kill our baby.

"She's going to kill our baby," I force out through the violent churns of my stomach.

"She's pregnant?"

Noah's dark eyes glisten with worry when I nod.

"Can you ask Emily to talk to her? She's the only person Jenni will listen to. I don't want her to kill our baby, but without your help, I won't be able to stop it. Please, Noah. I'll do anything you ask if you do this one thing for me," I plead, aware that if anyone has the ability to get through to Jenni it will be Emily.

Sensing we're being watched, Noah's attention shifts to the cabin. Emily is standing near a window on the second floor. She looks like she's been crying.

After taking in a shaky breath, Noah returns his eyes to mine. "I'll try."

He doesn't sound confident, but it's better than the hope I was clutching only moments ago.

CHAPTER FORTY

NICK

Miserable, hurt, and fucking heartbroken. That's how I've spent the last three weeks. Our band is doing a radio tour on the West Coast. It should be weeks of excitement and ecstasy. The album we worked so hard to create is finally completed, and this is our chance to show off years of hard work, but I can't find the joy in it. I can't stop thinking about Jenni and our baby. I begged and pleaded on her voicemail every day the past three weeks. I sent her countless text messages as well, but she never responded.

Tonight I'm drowning my sorrows at the hotel bar. There's a pretty blonde sitting on the barstool next to me. Her super short leather skirt sits high on her thighs, and her silky blouse is struggling to contain her generous breasts. That's not surprising considering her shirt looks two sizes too small.

"Another?" The blonde leans in so close to my side, her breaths tickle my unshaven jawline, and her erect nipples scrape my arm.

I shake my head before returning my gaze to the nearly empty glass of whiskey in my hand. I swirl the brown drizzle coating the bottom until it matches my swirling stomach. The aroma of expensive whiskey fills my nostrils when I down the leftover liquid in half a swallow.

When I lower my glass to the marble countertop to request another shot, I notice a hotel room key sitting on my coaster. My gaze drifts to the blonde cozying up to my side. She's panting so hard, she's purring. Although she's a couple of years older than me, she has big breasts and a rocking body that compliments her pretty face.

After rising from her barstool, she puts on her jacket. She gives me a wink that speaks way more than her words ever could before she saunters toward the exit. Just before she disappears from my view, she cranks her neck back to me. The rake of her teeth over her bottom lip signals she wants me to join her. Usually, I'd jump at the chance, but not anymore. No matter how drunk I get, no matter how much I try to forget her, my little firecracker won't get out of my head.

"No one else," I murmur to myself.

And there hasn't been. I haven't slept with anyone but Jenni since the day we became a couple. Don't get me wrong; I tried. I came pretty close after I saw her kissing Christian, but I just couldn't do it. She is *it* for me. I'm forever ruined.

With that in mind, I flick the blonde's room key to the ground. She watches it land a few feet from her hooker heels before her slit eyes lock with mine. She's stunned as hell that I've rejected her.

Over the game, I signal for the bartender to bring me another double of whiskey. As he refills my drink, Slater fills the barstool the blonde just vacated. "I never thought I'd see the day."

He requests a beer from the bartender before twisting his torso to face me. Even though we're in a busy inner city bar, buzzing with noise, the silence between us is resounding.

He cracks under the pressure first. "I can't believe I'm about to do this." He scrubs his hand down his face before murmuring, "Fight harder for her."

I chuckle a menacing laugh. "I have; I've done everything I can."

"No, you haven't; you've sat here moping around for fucking weeks," he interrupts angrily. "You think it's hard for you? Imagine what it's like for her; she has nothing left."

"She has nothing left? She ripped out my heart, leaving me with nothing but an empty shell. *I* have nothing left—me! I'm empty without her!" I bang my chest to amplify its hollowness.

"Then man up and do what needs to be done—"

"I fucking tried! I promised to take care of her, to take care of our baby, but she didn't want my help. She killed my baby, Slater. She killed it."

The tears burning my eyes nearly roll down my cheeks when Slater murmurs, "No, she didn't."

My eyes snap to his. I have a million questions streaming through my head, but not one of them will leave my mouth.

I don't need to talk when Slater says, "She couldn't go through with it. She canceled the appointment."

"She's still pregnant?"

When he nods, I throw a bundle of money on the bar then snag my jacket from the back of my chair. Slater's encouraging cheer is barely heard over the bustling crowd I'm barging through. I sprint as fast as my drunk legs will take me.

I'm halfway across the hotel foyer when the hairs on my arms suddenly stand to attention. I freeze so I can scan the lobby. *I know she's here; I can feel it.*

I'm filled with relief when I spot Jenni standing at the reception desk. She's in a heated argument with the hotel desk clerk. Not impressed with whatever the desk clerk told her, she bends down to collect an overnight bag resting at her feet before heading toward the exit. She barely makes it two steps away when she notices me gawking at her.

Her other hand shoots up to cover her gasp as her eyes well with tears. We stare at each other for the next several seconds, not the least bit concerned by the hotel guests mingling around us.

It feels surreal seeing her after all this time, even more so when she whispers, "No one else."

Nodding, I reply, "No one else."

When she pushes off her feet to race my way, I follow her lead. We crash into each other almost violently. Hands, lips, and tongues go in all directions—as does the hurt from the past two months.

CHAPTER FORTY-ONE

JENNI

Ten little fingers and ten little toes was all it took for me to know I couldn't destroy the baby I had created with Nick. I was already having doubts when he left the cabin with his eyes full of tears and enough anger to smash my car to smithereens. My BMW used to be my pride and joy, a gift of love my dad gave me on my eighteenth birthday. Now, it symbolized everything my mom was holding over my head to force me to get an abortion.

I haven't seen my mom since the day she arrived at my apartment two weeks ago. When I landed at the airport Friday morning to spend the weekend at the cabin with Emily and Noah to celebrate Rise Up's upcoming album launch, she sent Maria to pick me up in my car. I dropped Maria home before I went to pick Emily up from school. You know how the rest of my day went from there. I broke Nick's heart as much as he shattered mine, then he took his grief out of my car.

When Noah returned after taking Nick to a hotel, he stormed angrily toward me. I was beyond shocked when he accused me of being selfish and said that it takes two people to create a baby, so shouldn't it be *their* decision to destroy it? When Emily defended me, Noah stared at her in horror before he stormed into their bedroom, slamming the door behind him. Emily murmured a quick apology before she went rushing after him.

I had barely gotten over my shock when Slater entered the room with his girlfriend, Kylie. When he noticed the tears flooding my cheeks, he whispered something to Kylie before he joined me on the couch. When he pulled me to his chest, I sobbed so much, his shirt dampened with my tears.

"I tried to warn you, but you didn't listen," he whispered while running his hands down my hair, offering me comfort.

He held me until I ran out of tears, and I fell asleep.

The following afternoon, when I was brave enough to leave my room, I was shocked to discover the shattered glass on my car had been replaced. It looked as it did before Nick attacked it. I asked Marcus and Slater if they knew who had repaired it. They were both as clueless as me.

After I left the cabin, I drove to my Aunt Dee's salon. I spilled my guts to her, starting from the day she met Nick at the salon up until last night. No details were spared. Once I finished blubbering, she offered for me to stay with her for as long as I needed. She even suggested I finish my hairdressing apprenticeship at her salon. I initially laughed at her offer, until reality dawned. I could barely afford to feed a baby, let alone clothe one.

When I failed to show up to my appointment Monday morning, my mom followed through with her threat. My credit cards, phone, and car payments were canceled. She had my car repossessed the following Friday. Because my aunt is old school, I had to rely on her home phone to keep in contact with people. Emily regularly inquired as to what I was going to do about the baby. I wanted to give her an answer, but I couldn't because I myself didn't know the answer.

It was my aunt who convinced me not to make a final decision until I went and saw a doctor. When she scheduled an appointment with a local obstetrician, I begged Emily to come with me. She agreed without a second thought.

The day before my appointment, while Slater was giving me an update about the band's radio tour, I let it slip about seeing Nick kiss a girl at their recording studio months earlier. Slater breathed heavily down the phone and cursed numerous times before he told me what I saw wasn't as it appeared.

He explained that he was so desperate to discover who Nick was in love with, when Marcus told Nick someone was there to visit him, Slater spied on him. He saw a woman throw herself into Nick's arms, but he said Nick pulled away from her immediately before he rushed back inside like a scaredy cat.

"Even though he wasn't cheating that time doesn't mean you should trust him," Slater advised sternly yesterday afternoon.

His words were still ringing in my ears when I went to my appointment the following day. I was so conflicted about what to do. I loved Nick, but I was worried he wouldn't forgive me for what I had done, and then Slater's warning made me even more apprehensive.

Everything changed when I saw our baby on the monitor for the first time. People say instant love isn't real. I don't believe them anymore. One sideways glance, and my reason for existing changed in the blink of an eye. I knew right then and there that I wanted both Nick and our baby. I was just praying Nick could find it in his heart to forgive me. I had plenty of excuses—that day was the worst day of my life—but there was only one I would use: I made a mistake.

With the help of my Aunt's now maxed-out credit cards, I purchased a ticket for Los Angeles. I wanted to confront Nick in person, because I needed him to see the remorse in my eyes when I admitted my wrongs. When I arrived at the hotel Emily told me the band was staying at, the hotel desk clerk informed me no band by that name was staying at their hotel.

When I asked if she had a Nicholas Holt visiting, she rolled her eyes before checking the screen. "No. No Nicholas Holt, no Rise Up, no Noah Taylor. We do not have any of those names staying at our hotel."

Since my cell phone had been canceled, I asked if I could borrow her phone so I could call Emily to make sure I had written down the right hotel.

"There's a payphone out on the sidewalk," the clerk snarled before she answered the phone ringing on her desk.

After gathering my bag off the floor, I spun around. I was pissed at the clerk's rudeness and hormonal from the long day I'd had. My anger was forgotten in an instant when I spotted Nick across the lobby. He was staring at me, his gaze so white-hot, sweat dribbled down my nape. He was wearing his standard ripped jeans and a light blue polo shirt, and his jaw was covered with a few days' stubble, but he still made my heart race.

"No one else," I whispered, praying he still wanted me.

He replied without pause, "No one else."

We met in the middle of the foyer, our fire-sparking reunion rivaling the most romantic scene in a blockbuster movie.

"There's never been anyone but you," Nick murmured over my lips. "And there will never *ever* be anyone but you."

CHAPTER FORTY-TWO

JENNI

Nick and I stumble toward his room, all legs and arms. We kiss the entire ride from the foyer to the floor his room is on, then we kiss some more while haphazardly stumbling down the deserted hallway. We barely make it to his room before he drags his shirt over his head and tosses it on the floor. His jeans are next to go, closely followed by his boxer shorts.

My breath hitches when I catch sight of the delicious bumps in his stomach, then I lose the ability to breathe altogether when my eyes land on his perfect dick. Nick's body isn't stacked with muscles, but he has very impressive ones in *all* the right places.

In all the spots that make my heart race.

While Nick removes my clothes as eagerly as he did his, we stagger toward a set of queen beds like two drunks giddy on more than lust. He unclasps the hook on my skirt and guides down the zipper before we've reached the first bed. After surrendering my lips from his heart-stopping kiss, he lowers my skirt down my shaking thighs. Once it's puddled around my ankles, he wrangles my shirt over my head.

Just as his hands drop to my panties, his eyes lock with mine. A massive surge of blood pumps into my heart. Nothing but admiration is reflecting from his gorgeous heavy-hooded gaze. I could have never dreamed our relationship would be like this. Don't get me wrong; Nick has always been an attentive lover, but his eyes have never held the spark they have now.

I've never felt so consumed by a look before.

Intimidated by the fire in his eyes, I take two steps back. My knees curve inward when Nick smiles his panty-dropping smirk. It's his true smile, the one that reveals his insides are as attractive as his outsides.

With one big step, he bridges the gap between us. "You can't run, and you can't hide, because I'll always find you."

The hunger in his eyes grows rampant when they absorb the bra and panty combination I scoured through my suitcase to find specifically for him. The vibrant red color of the satin material matches the color of my cheeks from his avid stare.

"I've never had an interest in collecting panties." His darkened-with-lust eyes lift and lock with mine. "Until now."

My breathing switches from calm to ragged when he slides the meager scrap of material off my backside, down my thighs, and past my red-painted toenails. After standing from his crouched position, he carefully places them on the bedside table as if they're the most precious gift in the world.

The calluses on his fingertips from playing guitar for years graze my skin when he curls his arms around my back to unclasp my bra. My jaw drops when his nimble fingers have the three hooks undone faster than I can snap my fingers. My hanging jaw gains leverage when his jutted-out manhood digs into my thigh as he lays me in the middle of the bed we're standing next to.

I bite the inside of my cheek, battling not to squirm, when he presses a peppering of feather-like kisses from my ankle to my throbbing core. The scruff on his jaw scratches my skin with every gentle

bite before his tongue soothes both their burns. I freeze in anticipation when his lips skim past my aching-with-need pussy as he moves
his lips to my left leg to lavish it with the same attention he bestowed
on my right.

By the time he finishes adorning every inch of my skin with
butterfly kisses, I'm on the verge of begging him to consume me. I'm
saturated, panting, and the horniest I've ever been.

"Please, Nick," I croak out between breathless moans. "I—"

My begging stops when his tongue delivers a perfectly placed
lash on my throbbing clit. I fist the floral bedspread when he
consumes my pussy with so much devotion, my race to climax jumps
from a leisurely jog to a hundred-meter sprint. He licks, sucks, and
nibbles on my clit until my thighs squeeze his head and my lungs
scream for air.

I don't know if it's because we've been apart so long or the new
hormones thickening my veins, but my climax hits me so hard and
fast, my vision blurs. While shouting his name, I thrash against the
sheets. My ride on the intensive wave of orgasmic bliss is long and
utterly devastating, but I ride it all the way to the shore, loving every
minute of it.

The blood surging to the lower regions of my body switches to
my heart when he presses a gentle kiss on my non-existent belly. He
lathers my belly with kisses before he slips into the bed next to me to
gather me in the crook of his arm.

Shocked, I crank my elbow and peer into his eyes. "What are you
doing?"

His lips twitch like he's dying to speak, but he remains as quiet as
a church mouse. Conscious that this isn't how things generally are
between us, I flatten my tingling breasts on his smooth pecs before
sealing my mouth over his. The tenderness displayed in our kiss
enlarges my heart even more. It's gentle and sweet and has me close
to free-falling into orgasmic bliss for the second time in under five
minutes.

While keeping my lips attached to his, I slither my hand down the rigid bumps of his abdomen. He hisses when I grip his firm cock in my hand. While I work on his shaft with the perfect amount of speed and pressure, his husky breaths fan my nape. I pump his cock at the same pace his tongue explores my mouth. It's a coil-tightening adventure that has every fiber in my body paying careful attention to every stroke he makes.

Several womb-sparking minutes later, I intuit that he's close to the brink. His chest is rising and falling more rapidly, and the veins feeding his magnificent manhood are thick and throbbing. When I pull my hand away, Nick seizes my wrist before directing it back to his dick, wordlessly demanding I continue my plot to unravel him.

"I want you inside of me before you come." The last half of my sentence is said in a throaty moan from his cock twitching in my hand. After straddling his lap so his heavy member sits between the folds of my drenched pussy, I lift my eyes to Nick's. A stabbing pain hits my chest when I see a cloud of apprehension in his eyes.

"I want you," he assures me upon seeing the devastation on my face. "I just don't want to hurt the baby."

Euphoria scorches my veins. For someone who has quoted multiple times that he never wanted a relationship, much less kids, our baby is already at the forefront of his mind. I cup his cheeks in my hands and rest my sweaty forehead on his. "I promise you, the baby is safe and protected. Nothing you do will harm him or her."

His eyes burn into mine as he seeks any deceit. He won't find any, but just in case he's still unsure, I help him see sense through the madness. "Furthermore, we don't need to use protection. It's kind of pointless, don't you think?"

His pupils dilate to the size of saucers. He looks as if his greatest wish has just been granted. A giggle parts my lips when he unexpectedly flips me over. My laughter is nipped in the bud when he rubs his thick crown through the folds of my pussy to coat himself with the residue of my earlier climax.

Shaggy blond curls fall in front of his face when he asks, "Are you sure?"

I feel heat creep across my cheeks when I nod. It extends all the way to my chest when he slides the first two inches of his cock inside me.

"My rule breaker," he moans when he enters me bare for the very first time.

———————

Later that evening, I'm snuggled against Nick's bare chest. The hotel room his record company booked is nice but basic. There are two queen beds on one wall and a small kitchenette on the other. The bathroom is small but adequate, although the bright red tiles are a bit overkill.

I didn't pay much attention to the room when we entered. I was too busy getting my fill of Nick. I swear to God, my heart couldn't enlarge any more tonight if it tried. Nick made love to me. It was an exhilarating experience that made me fall in love with him even more than I thought possible. He was attentive and sweet, while also rocking my world like he has many times the past year and a half.

After snuggling deeper into his bare chest, I continue absorbing the room. My brows furrow not long later when I notice a wallet and a set of keys sitting on the other bedside table. My confused gaze shifts to Nick. "Are you sharing a room?"

When he laughs, I pop my head off his chest. A grin tugs on my lips. I can't help it; his smiles are infectious. "I completely forgot."

After jumping out of bed, he sends a text message. While the whoosh sounds through my ears, he gathers our clothing scattered around the room. I get dressed, sans panties, since Nick added them to his recently started collection.

A smile stretches across my face when he also puts on his jeans commando-style. Once I'm fully covered, he heads for the door and swings it open. My cheeks heat when Slater enters the room two seconds later. When he notices me sitting on the bed, his lengthy steps freeze mid-stride. I run my hand down my hair in vain, trying to tame my unruly locks. I'm horrified he's seeing me like this. We're close, but we're not *this* close.

With a smile assuring me it's alright, Slater collects his wallet and keys from the bedside table then heads for the door. On his way out, he stops at Nick's side. He whispers something to him, but he's so quiet, I can't make out what he says. It must not be good, though, because Nick's throat works hard to swallow before he nods.

When he finally exits the room, I flop onto the bed, mortified. Even if I wanted to act innocent, the smell of sex filtering through the air would foil my endeavor. Chuckling at my groan, Nick joins me on the bed. When I turn to face him, he runs his hand down my burning cheek.

"I thought I was the only one who made you all flustered."

I smile. "You are." I drop my lower lip into a pout. "These are my embarrassed cheeks."

The switch from embarrassed to cranky when Nick chuckles. "I'm sure he's witnessed worse."

I stiffen. If the stories I've heard are anything to go by, I have no doubt Slater has seen much worse. He did walk in on Nick having sex with his fiancée.

When Nick spots my soured expression, his pupils dilate. "You know, don't you?"

I nod while my gaze drifts to the ceiling. Finding out what he did to Slater was one of the main reasons I tried to stay away from him. I knew he was a player, but knowing he could do that to his friend made it so much worse.

"I was young and stupid."

I return my eyes to Nick. "Your age isn't an excuse, Nick. What you did to Slater was wrong."

"I know." His head bobs up and down as rapidly as his Adam's apple. "I've tried to make it up to him."

My anger dampens from the genuine remorse in his eyes. "Have you ever said you were sorry? Sometimes that's all a person needs to hear."

He looks ashamed before he shakes his head.

"Then maybe that's a good place to start."

CHAPTER FORTY-THREE

NICK

I had never considered what Slater went through when he walked in on me fucking Nikki. I've always believed I was doing him a favor, but after seeing Jenni kiss Christian, I have more understanding of the hell I put him through. Saying sorry doesn't seem like enough, but what Jenni said is true: it's a start.

"I'll talk to him."

Jenni smiles before rolling over to balance her chin on my chest. "I knew you weren't all bad."

Her hot breath fanning my chest causes my cock to stiffen. She giggles when I roll her over until I am on top of her. I keep my weight off her with my arms, ensuring I don't crush our baby.

"I'm only bad for you."

Her giggles are stuffed into her throat by my tongue when my mouth seals over hers. Unlike our earlier romp, this one is greedy. We kiss until we're sharing the same air and our skin is slicked with an equal amount of sweat and arousal. It's as if the new hormones rushing through Jenni's veins make her obsessed with my cock. She strokes me through my jeans the entire time, never once relinquishing the rock behind my zipper from her hold. I don't mind. I'm more than fucking grateful for her commitment. It's been weeks since her hands where on mine; I was almost jealous when they were clutching the bedsheets in a white-knuckled hold when she orgasmed earlier.

When I un-pop the button on my jeans and push them down my thighs, my cock springs free, and Jenni licks her lips. She doesn't need to tell me what's on her mind. Her ravenous glance answers all my questions. She wants my cock in her mouth, and I'm more than happy to oblige. I'm a cocky bastard who has no shyness when it comes to saying I have a spectacular cock, but even someone with an ego as big as mine knows there's no way my cock will reach her belly if it's in her mouth.

"Oh fuck," I groan when my cock is surrounded by the pillowly goodness known as Jenni's lips.

I'm not a good man. I've bedded more woman than I care to admit, and fucked with my bandmates' minds like they're my little minions, so I have no fucking clue what I ever did to deserve this. Her lips are wicked enough I'd take it all back in an instant if I could. This shouldn't feel good. I should be scared by how unhinged she makes me, petrified her lips inching down my cock have me wanting to give up more than my player lifestyle, but I'm not. I'm ecstatic, and in all honesty, I'm looking forward to the next chapter of our life.

After drawing her lips all the way over her teeth, Jenni sucks down hard. My cock pokes the back of her throat, making her gag. I shouldn't love the noise, but I do. After raising my hips off the bed, I dip my cock in and out of her mouth on repeat, loving that not even her arousal coating every inch of my shaft has stopped her eagerness. It adds to the wickedness, blasting my excitement to never-before-reached levels.

I grip her hair a little rougher when she swivels her tongue around my knob. "Do that again."

My balls pull in close to my body when she follows my command without a protest. Her tongue slips over the slit in my crown before she drags it down my shaft.

"Now suck on my balls."

She groans, revealing she's loving my dominant personality, before she once again follows my instructions. She glides her hand up and down my cock as she licks, sucks and grazes her teeth over my balls. When the tingle racing through my sack becomes too great to ignore, I hoist her up from the bed before splaying her thighs on each side of my hips. Air hisses between her teeth when she feels the steel rod lodged between us. I'm so fucking hard right now, my worry that I'll hurt her or our baby smacks back into me.

Before I can voice my concern, Jenni raises herself to her knees, nestles my cock between the slick folds of her vagina, then slams down.

"Fuck. Christ. Shit."

She rises and falls another four times before any worries about hurting her are pushed aside for dominance. Just like it's always been between us, I want to satisfy her. This isn't about me fucking to get my rocks off. It's about her and how I make her feel. I want to be the best fuck she's ever had, then maybe I can fool her into keeping me forever.

Going bareback for the second time was just as thrilling as the first. I fully plan on ditching condoms forever, so I better get a good health plan with how many kids Jenni will be popping out.

When I say that to her, she gags. "You can say that because you're not the one with your head in the toilet all day."

Her reply takes care of my confusion about her weight loss. She's lost a few pounds the last month. Her already slender frame has more bones protruding than usual.

"Have you been to the doctor? Maybe he can give you something to settle your stomach." I have no clue how this whole pregnancy thing works, but she can't afford to lose any more weight.

"Yes!" She dives off the bed, her leap as excited as her reply. "I completely forgot to show you."

She rushes to her suitcase like her thighs aren't still trembling, removes a photo, then returns to the bed we've been making love on the past three hours. Smiling a grin that demands another three hours, she hands me a black and white image. My head slants to the side when I stare down at it. I have no clue what I'm looking at. It appears to be blobs of static.

"What is it?"

Jenni ribs me with her elbow. "It's our baby."

She braces her chin on my shoulder before pointing out blobs of gray. "That's the head, body, and those little things sticking out there are the legs."

When I squint, I can nearly make out the things she is stating. "It must be a boy." I point to a long thing in the middle of the legs.

Laughing, she snatches the photo out of my hand. "That's the umbilical cord." Her brows join. "I think." She admiringly glances at the photo for a few more minutes before setting it down. "What do you think about us having a baby?"

"I'm scared," I reply truthfully.

A deep V forms between her brows. She's not angry; she's more concerned than anything.

"Not about having a baby. I'm scared I'll fuck everything up." I lock my eyes with her. "That I'll fuck *us* up."

The past few weeks I was struggling to get over the heartache of losing Jenni. It was only the last week did I realize I was also devastated about losing our baby. The idea of having children petrified me. . . until I met Jenni.

"I'm scared too." Her tone lowers to match her brows.

"What do you have to be scared about? You'll be a natural." I'm not lying. I have no doubt she'll be a wonderful mother; that's why my panic about becoming a father isn't as strong this time around.

"I'm scared our baby is going to grow up alone."

When my thumb rubs the little V between her brows, her scared eyes meet mine. "It won't grow up alone, because he or she will always have us."

This is all new to me, but I must have said something right because Jenni smiles her knockout grin. After resting her head on my shoulder, she spends the next twenty minutes sharing the story of how she found out her dad isn't her biological father.

My heart broke for her from the devastation in her tone. She's not upset Michael isn't her actual dad—she could have never asked for a better man to be her father—she's more upset that he hasn't attempted to reconcile with her the past month.

I draw her closer to my chest before promising, "He'll come around."

CHAPTER FORTY-FOUR

NICK

Jenni's dad never came around. Jenni hasn't heard from her parents in months. She toured with the band while we completed our radio commitments on the West Coast, then when we returned home, I begged her to move in with me at my dad's house—on my knees, I groveled and begged.

She was hesitant to begin with, but that only lingered for as long as it took my father to convince her that he'd appreciate the company. Just like everyone I've ever known, Dad took an immediate liking to her. At times, I think he likes her more than he likes me.

When I first went on the road with the band, my dad drove Jenni into town to get groceries or to take her to her doctor's appointments, but it was pretty apparent very early on that she needed a car if we were to continue living in the middle of Whoop Whoop. Her smile when I gifted her a little Matchbox car I purchased with my first royalty check was priceless. I thought she loved her BMW because of its expensive price tag. That wasn't the case at all. She loved the independence it gave her.

During my second stint on the road, I took Jenni's advice and apologized to Slater. It was one of the most awkward conversations

I've ever had. Did he accept my apology? Yeah, he did. Does that mean he likes me now? No, not yet. Things are still rough, but they're getting better every day.

A couple of days after my return, I discovered I was right about the thing I saw dangling between our baby's legs. We're having a boy. All I have to say about that is, thank fuck! I know what guys are like. If we were having a daughter, I would have bought a gun, just to ensure guys like me stay away from her.

Jenni's morning sickness eased as the weeks went on. Now she eats anything she gets her hands on. She's gained back those few pounds she lost at the start of her pregnancy and has even added on a few extra as well. She's afraid of her small weight gain, but I fucking love it. Her hips are a little bigger, and her tits have grown substantially. They're the perfect combination for her petite frame. It gives her an appealing hourglass figure.

I've just returned home after a short stint in Los Angeles. Two songs from our debut album are rocketing up the charts. We're being inundated with interview requests and have been performing live on morning news shows and radio gigs. I hate leaving Jenni every time we go on the road, but I'm fortunate she's home waiting for me when I'm not touring. Noah isn't as lucky. He's not handling our time on the road as well as the rest of the band.

Our weekends are spent doing gigs and building hype for our debut album, but the weekends are the only time Emily has off school, meaning she hasn't seen Noah for a few weeks. I was shocked this past weekend when Noah openly flirted with a girl in front of me. I nearly told him to pull his head out of his ass; then I realized, I have no clue what he's going through. I miss Jenni when we're apart for a day, so I know I'd never survive five weeks.

With royalty checks slowly flowing in, I've saved enough to put down a deposit on a house. The mortgage for our home isn't through a bank, though. It's being endorsed by my brother. The bank manager took one look at me in my ripped jeans and polo shirt and rejected my application on sight.

I'll be sure to remember him when I'm rolling in money.

When Isaac heard our loan had been rejected, he offered to fund it. I only agreed to his offer when he agreed to charge us the same interest the bank would charge. We sealed our agreement with a handshake a little over six weeks ago. That's why I'm walking into my old haunt. I've arrived at the Dungeon to collect the check Isaac had drawn for us. Once I hand it over to the real estate agent this afternoon, the deed for our very first home will be placed in mine and Jenni's names within the hour.

I'm not going to lie; I'm fucking stoked. I got my girl; we have a baby on the way, and we're about to move into our first home. This is the stuff dreams are made of.

When Tina spots me strutting through the double doors of the Dungeon, she squeals before running over to throw herself in my arms.

"Miss me?" I chuckle before returning her embrace.

She drops her arms from my neck and takes a step back. "You were here every day for years, then poof, I never see you again."

I laugh. That's not quite how I remember things, but I guess it'll do.

"Did you hear I'm going to be a dad?" Nothing but pride is audible in my tone.

Tina's smile sparkles out of her. "I did." She nudges me with her hip. "With beer girl."

My chuckle bounces around the interior of the Dungeon. I guess Jenni is going to be forever referred to as Beer Girl from here on out.

My chuckles stop echoing when a female voice on my left says, "Congratulations."

I pivot toward the greeter, eager to thank her for her good wishes. My smile is wiped off my face when I spot Megan standing at my side. Her hair has returned to its usual light brown coloring, but her floral dress is more concerning than attractive. It's cold today.

Her crazy eyes dart between mine when she takes a step closer to me. "I've been looking for you everywhere; where did you go?"

I swipe my hand through the air, warning her to stay away from me. When she fails to heed my command, I say, "You can't be within five hundred feet of me."

Hearing the concern in my voice, Tina bolts for Isaac's office.

"I've missed you," Megan murmurs through a sob.

I hate that she's upset, but I'm done dealing with her shit. "You need to leave me the fuck alone. This shit isn't funny."

Before she can reply, Isaac comes barreling out of his office. He signals for Travis to follow him just as Megan lunges for me. Travis grabs her around her waist, but it comes too late. Her nails run down my cheeks while she screams obscenities at the top of her lungs, "You said you loved me! You told me you wanted me to have your baby!"

She continues screaming until the exit doors of the Dungeon swallow her words. While turning to face Isaac, I run my hand down my cheek. It's stinging from her nails marking my skin. When I pull my hand away, blood trickles down my fingers.

"Who the fuck was that?" Isaac questions as his furious eyes absorb my wound.

I'm about to answer, but Tina beats me, "A psychopath."

I couldn't agree more.

CHAPTER FORTY-FIVE

MEGAN

*I watched him every day. I claimed him first. I don't care what the
doctors, judges, or police officers say. Nicholas Holt is mine, and I'm
never giving him up.*

I spotted Nick nearly two years ago when he strolled into a
nightclub with a flirty smile and a twinkle in his eyes. I had been
traveling for six hours straight and badly needed to use the bathroom.
That was all forgotten when our eyes collided. A bolt of electricity
coursed through my body, kickstarting both my heart and my obses-
sion. I was supposed to keep driving because I had another four
hours of driving to do, but I couldn't leave him. It was like I had
found the other half of my soul. I was drawn to him, magnetized, and
I finally understood what instant love meant.

When I moved to the end of the bar to watch him, his love for me
was beaming out of him. It was so bright, everyone around us could
see it. He was about to come over and talk to me when his friend
interrupted our intense connection. Not wanting to be rude, he

handed his friend a beer, and they went and talked in a booth at the side of the bar. I repositioned my stool so I could see him. It also assured our connection remained strong.

As the night went on, the floor space between us filled with dirty, sinning whores who wore scraps of material as clothing. Nick wasn't interested in them, though. He only had eyes for me. . . until I stupidly requested a glass of water from the bartender.

Aware I had lost my visual of Nick, the whores were quick to trick him to the dark side. I was so frantic, when I leaped off my barstool to search for him, I knocked over my glass of water. I looked for him everywhere before taking my hunt onto the dance floor. The instant I stepped on the mahogany floor, I was elbowed, poked, and prodded by filthy disgusting pigs. I felt like I had fallen through the gates of hell. It was more burning than the hot baths my mom used to run for me.

When my cell phone rang in my pocket, it was time for me to leave. I had no other choice.

"Wait for me," I whispered into the air, knowing Nick would hear me.

It took longer to return than I had hoped. Daddy was even sicker than the doctors let on. I thought about my love every day, and I was confident he would be waiting for me when I returned.

He was.

My heart leaped out of my chest when I spotted Nick sitting at the exact spot I first saw him. He was so excited to see me again, he bounded off his barstool to pull a set of keys out of his pocket. He had just removed them when the wicked witch behind the bar snatched them out of his grasp and placed them down the front of her shirt.

I was disgusted she'd do such a thing, but it also gave me the opportunity to talk to Nick. I made my way to him to offer him a ride. I was more than happy to take him anywhere he wanted us to go.

During our drive to an old rusty bar, I told Nick all about myself. He was so invigorated by what I was saying, he never once interrupted me. He sat quietly, absorbing every word that escaped my lips.

We made our way to the bar together, but since his job was crucial to him, he went on stage to prepare for his performance while I waited for him near the bar. His eyes were on me the entire show. When his band finished performing, he rushed back to me. His excitement was so overwhelming, he had to dash into the bathroom to freshen himself up first.

Once he was done, we spent the next several hours talking about everything and anything. Our plans for the future, where we should live, and what our children will look like. It was so much fun.

It's lucky I carry my daddy to bed every night, because Nick was so excited about seeing me again, he could barely hold his own weight when I helped him into my car later that night. Thankfully the motel clerk gave me a ground floor room, or I may not have gotten Nick inside. He didn't murmur a word when I removed his shoes, jeans, and shirt. Once I had him prepared for bed, I snuggled into his chest, and had the most peaceful sleep I've ever had.

I didn't realize Nick had to work the next day, or I would have set an alarm clock to wake him up, then he wouldn't have needed to rush out of our room as quickly as he did. I was disappointed our time was over, but when he nodded, saying he'd see me next week, I gave him a long, love-filled kiss.

I thought about Nick all week and was so excited to see him again. When I saw him strolling past the long line I was standing in to enter the club we met at, my heart raced. It plunged into my gut when I realized he was holding another girl's hand. She had obviously brainwashed him into thinking I wasn't coming back for him. A week is a very long time to be away from the person you love.

I was certain once Nick saw me again, the sparks between us would reignite, so I raced to the front of the line to plead with the bouncer to let me in. No matter how many times I told him Nick was waiting for me inside, he wouldn't let me in. Because I had left the line, I had to join it again at the end.

By the time I made it inside, Nick was walking back out. *That girl was still holding his hand.* I didn't know who she was, but I didn't like her. *I hated her.*

That night, I followed them to a lookout not too far from the nightclub. I felt ill from all the unimaginable things they did in his truck. I can't tell you what they did—it's too vulgar for me to repeat. But I can tell you I went home heartbroken and distraught.

A few weeks later I finally realized why my stomach wouldn't stop swirling. It wasn't because I was upset about losing the love of my life. It was because I was carrying his child. Nick had blessed me with God's greatest gift. It was his way of making sure I would be tied to him forever.

Nick was pleased when he saw me waiting for him outside of the rusty bar his band plays at, although he didn't take the news about our baby as well as I hoped. He was concerned he couldn't provide a good life for our baby. He didn't need to worry. I took care of every-thing before I returned to him, so I had enough money to look after us.

I waited and waited and waited for his call Saturday morning. It never came.

I was crying in my hotel room bed when my phone finally chimed Monday afternoon. It was Nick's lawyer calling me to schedule an appointment.

That appointment didn't go well. Nick's lawyer wanted to put a needle into my belly to prove my baby is Nick's. I sternly told her my baby wasn't anyone else's. I had never slept in another man's bed, so I knew it was Nick's baby. I tried to explain that to Nick, but every time I turned up to Mavericks, he was too busy working to talk to me.

I went to the doctor's as requested by his lawyer. The cold gel made me giggle when the doctor placed it on my belly. I was so excited to see the baby I had created with Nick, and when the doctor waved the gray wand over my belly, I stared eagerly at the screen. I saw a flicker, and from what I read in the maternity books, that was the baby's heart.

That was the only good thing that came from that appointment.

I left feeling dirty and violated. After the doctor ran his wand over my belly, he made me lie down on a bed, and he looked at me *down there*. That wasn't the worst thing, though. He also touched me *down there*.

Nick was so disappointed in me, he sent his lawyer to my hotel room with two men in white coats. The hotel they took me to was much nicer than the one I was staying at. The staff was super talkative, asking me a million questions about Nick and my dad, but I didn't like the prenatal vitamins they were giving me. They made me tired and woozy, but I couldn't complain. I had my own room; my meals were cooked for me every day, and I didn't have to use any of the money I had saved for Nick and our baby.

They were so desperate for customers at my hotel, they wouldn't let me leave when I asked. I had to be extra sneaky when I wanted to visit Nick, sneaking out in the darkness of night. Most of the time Nick was alone, except one night, he was kissing a whore on the back of his truck.

The hotel staff wasn't happy when they caught me sneaking back in. They started locking my bedroom door as well as the ones around the hotel. I was so sick and tired of talking about Nick and our baby all the time. That was all the hotel staff ever asked about. I soon realized if I kept the thoughts in my head quiet, they stopped asking the same questions over and over again.

Over time, the hotel staff let me go out during the day again. Then, as the weeks went on, I was allowed to go out on weekends. The very first place I went was Nick's house. I knew where he lived because I followed him there one night a few months ago.

My goodness—Nick looks so peaceful when he's sleeping. I didn't realize how long his eyelashes were until I watched him sleep for eight hours straight. *I really hope our baby inherits his eyelashes.* You should be warned, Nick is *not* a morning person. He was so angry when he woke up one morning, even with me cooking him a hearty breakfast, he rudely removed me from his house. It was only after I left in tears did I realize my mistake. He was upset about his dad seeing my bare legs peeking out of his shirt. Next time I'll be sure to wear pants.

I followed Nick again later that morning. He went straight to his whore—again! *I hate her!*

I didn't understand why he kept running back to her. It was only when I caught my reflection in the rearview mirror did I realize my error. Nick likes blondes. I could fix that.

First thing Monday morning, I had a hairdresser dye my hair. I made sure the silly whore perfectly matched it to the whore Nick kept running to. It's safe to say, Nick liked my hair. His kiss that morning was so passionate, he let me put my tongue in his mouth. It was only a quick visit because he had to get back to work. He's always so busy.

I was shocked when a police officer arrived at my hotel later that day to give me a piece of paper. The staff at the hotel were not happy about his visit, and it caused their questions about Nick and the baby to start up all over again.

My throat was so raw when I had to remove the pills they keep feeding me from my stomach. I probably shouldn't have hit the hotel staff member so hard with the steel chair, but no matter how many times I told him I wanted to check out, he never listened.

It took a few weeks for Nick to show up again. I didn't know where he had been, but seeing him again made my love for him grow even stronger. He was excitedly telling the wicked witch about our baby when I sneakily approached him. I was confused when she said Nick was having a baby with beer girl. I don't drink beer. I don't drink any alcohol.

I didn't mean to attack Nick. Truly, I didn't. I was just so hurt when he told me to leave him alone, I couldn't help but lash out.

I love him, and he loves me. It's just *her* keeping us apart.

I can fix that.

CHAPTER FORTY-SIX

JENNI

"Oh my god, Nick, what happened to your face?"
As I rush toward him, I take in three large scratches down his right cheek. Someone has clawed him so brutally, they've drawn blood. He doesn't need to speak for me to know who did this to him. He told me about Megan a few months ago. I won't lie; it hurt hearing the details, but as the story went on, it soon dawned on me that something wasn't quite right with Megan.

We all have a bit of stalker in us. Heck, I dabbled in it when I stalked Nick's Facebook page after his first trip to New York, but Megan's level of craziness has pushed this way beyond a standard stalker case.

She's out for blood—literally.

Grasping Nick's hand in mine, I walk him into the bathroom. Once I have him sitting on the edge of the tub, I gather the antiseptic liquid and cotton balls from the cupboard. I soak the cotton in the liquid before carefully dabbing them on his scratches. I blow air on his cheek like my dad did any time I skinned my knee, lessening the burn of the antiseptic.

Nick watches me with hooded eyes, but my thirty-three-week

pregnant belly keeps a decent gap between us. Once I have the scratches dressed, I toss the blood-stained cotton into the bin. "There you go. Good as new."

It's not, but it makes me feel better pretending it is. Megan attacked him so aggressively, her scratch marks are so deeply embedded in his skin, they'll take weeks to heal.

Nick's eyes lift from my swollen belly to me. "Thanks."

The air between us shifts.

"You're welcome."

My heart warms when he scrapes his unshaven jaw over my breasts. I giggle. He has become obsessed with my boobs the past four months. "You know they're going to disappear the instant I give birth."

He bites down on my nipple through my thin cotton maternity shirt, making me yelp. "Yep! That's why I have to appreciate them as much as I can now."

My knees become weak when he sucks my budded nipple in his mouth to soothe the sting with his tongue. When a moan seeps through my parted lips, my eyes snap to the open bathroom door. Nick's dad's house is small. I don't just mean compared to my parents' house. It's small as in *tiny* small. Its two bathrooms, two bedrooms, and a combined kitchen, dining, and living area would fit in my parents' kitchen. It's awkward enough staying quiet when we're in Nick's room, let alone the bathroom. I'd be mortified if his dad walked in on us.

Noticing my panicked expression, Nick's soft chuckles bounce around the bathroom. Any concerns I'm having vanish when his rough hand glides under my shirt so he can cup my engorged breast. He teases my nipple into a hard, erect peak in less than a second. His impressive skills moisten my panties as quickly as they erase my inhibitions.

When he nudges his head to the door, signaling for me to close it, I slam it shut.

Putty—once again I'm nothing but putty.

The next morning, excitement beams out of me as we drive to our new house. I can barely sit still knowing today is the day we move into our own home. We can finally put together the nursery items we have stored in the shed on Nick's dad's property, and we have more than one toilet.

When Nick spots me fidgeting in my seat, he smiles his panty-dropping smirk. I lean over and press a peck on his freshly shaven jaw. I don't mind the roughness of a few days' stubble, but if forced to pick between prickles or his ruggedly sharp jawline, I'll always pick the latter. I hate when his handsome face is covered with too much scruff.

After adjusting his rearview mirror, Nick curses under his breath. I eye him curiously when he signals a left turn. Our new house is on the right. Once he turns down the unknown street, his gaze shoots back to his rearview mirror. Suspicious about what has his attention, I crank my neck to peer out the back window of his truck. Other than a yellow car a few spots back from us, we're the only cars on the road.

My head nearly collides with the window when Nick takes a sudden right. When the yellow car follows us down the unmarked road, he yanks his truck off the asphalt.

"Stay in my truck."

He waits for me to nod before he bolts for the yellow car that has come to a stop in the middle of the road. I try to take in the features of the female driver, but dark tint and the fact she's wearing sunglasses and a hat make it virtually impossible.

I don't know what Nick says to her, but not long later, her car roars past me with so much speed, Nick's truck wobbles. After she skids around the corner without braking, I turn my frightful eyes back to Nick. He's raking his fingers through his hair while cursing obscenities into the street. When he spots me watching, he drags his hand down his face before heading back to his truck.

"It was Megan, wasn't it?"

He slides into his seat while nodding. Once he sucks in some nerve-calming breaths, he turns his eyes to me. "I think we should wait to move into our house until I've returned from the road."

I shake my head. "No, Nick, then she wins. You can't let her dictate our life. Besides, yesterday was the first time you've seen her in months. I'm sure once she realizes you've moved on, she'll move on as well."

"I don't trust her, Jen. I'm scared she'll hurt you." His eyes fill with turmoil as they roam over my face.

"I'll be fine," I reply, confident I'm not who she wants. "If anyone should be concerned about their safety, it's you, Nick."

I scoot across the bench seat until I'm straddling his lap. It's a tight squeeze between Nick, his steering wheel, and my belly, but I manage—barely. Being cautious not to touch his scratches, I run my hand down his cheek and across his jaw before weaving my fingers through his hair. My touch soothes him so much, he's open to negotiation.

"We can move in on one condition." I wait with bated breath for him to spell out his terms. "My dad stays with you when I'm on the road."

"And. . .?" I ask, sure there has to be more.

He smiles, happy I know him so well. "And. . ." He waits, building the suspense. "You agree to put music decals in Bub's room. If he's going to grow up to be just like his daddy, he needs a music-inspired room."

I swoon something crazy. I love that he calls our baby "Bub."

I press my lips to his before talking over his mouth. "Deal."

We kiss for a few minutes before Nick suggests we take our make-out session to our new house. Nodding, I return to my side of the seat. He takes several wrong turns to ensure no one is following us before he pulls into the estate our home is in.

Our new home is the cutest house on the street. The front porch is big enough we can get a porch swing like Nick's dad has. The kitchen was remodeled with stainless steel appliances I'm still learning how to use, and the four bedrooms, two bathrooms, large living area, and small backyard mean we have plenty of room to expand from a couple to a family. It's everything we could have wished for and so much more.

It's perfect for our little family.

After taking a few hours to christen our bedroom, Nick and I spend the rest of the afternoon setting up a nursery in the bright, sunny room at the front of our house. The theme for the nursery is lullabies. I thought it was fitting, considering our son's dad is a musician.

As per Nick's request, musical decals have been scattered across the light painted walls, and a border with blue guitars stretches over three walls. It's taken nearly all day, but the nursery is finally complete, and it's a perfect addition to our house.

I'm lying on the floor on my side, exhausted but also ecstatic it's finally done. It looks just as I envisioned. When Nick enters the room, he grins before joining me. My smile beams out of me when he hands me a blue teddy bear holding an electric guitar. I giggle loudly when he pushes a button on the guitar. The bear rocks and rolls, his hips swinging in beat to the music.

My laughter fades when the light above my head reflects something sparkling on the ribbon tied around the bear's neck. There's a diamond ring attached to the ribbon. My excited eyes dance between Nick's when he removes the bear from my grasp so he can remove the ring. Once it's clasped firmly in his hand, he scoots so close to me, our stomachs touch.

I lean into his embrace when he runs his hand down my heated cheek. My eagerness to snuggle wipes the small glint of hesitation from his eyes. It's quickly replaced with his trademark cockiness.

"You've always been my rule breaker." His voice is riddled with excited nerves. "I wanted to do this at a fancy restaurant or during a sunset at Bronte's Peak, but I don't think I could find a more perfect setting than right here."

When his eyes float around our son's nursery, I nod. I couldn't agree more.

"There's never been anyone but you. There will *never* be anyone but you. You've ruined me for eternity, and I have loved every fucking minute of it." He sounds genuinely surprised during his last sentence.

I eagerly nod before attempting to give him a long, steaming kiss. It turns into a peck when his chuckle vibrates my mouth. "I haven't asked you yet."

When my bottom lip drops into a pout, he nibbles on it. I try to act annoyed, but I can't. There are too many emotions thickening the air to do anything but demand my lungs take their next breath.

Believing he has teased me long enough, he stares lovingly into my eyes before speaking four little words I don't think he ever thought he'd speak. "Will you marry me?"

He inhales a quick, sharp breath when I reply, "No."

It's quickly withdrawn when I add on, "One else."

His lips curve into an illuminating smile. "No one else," he quotes while slipping a diamond engagement ring onto my finger.

The three round brilliant cut diamonds in the middle of a thick white gold band sparkle when I lift my hand to inspect them more diligently. The gems are large in size, but not extravagantly over the top.

"It symbolizes us." Nick points to the three diamonds. "You, me, and our son."

I swear, my heart stops beating. This isn't the first time he's shocked me in the romance department, but it's the first time he's made me speechless while doing it.

"I love you," I whisper while bridging the tiny gap between us. "And I cannot wait to spend eternity with you."

Two days later, Nick has gone back on the road with the band. Their debut album has been more successful than anyone thought possible. Two of their singles are in the top twenty, and "Surrender Me" looks like it's about to become a top ten hit.

Nick's dad, Harrison, has stayed with me as requested by Nick. It's lucky we get along so well. That's not hard considering I see a lot of Nick in him. He appears quiet, but when you watch him, you realize his silence doesn't equal ignorance. He's always scanning his surroundings, absorbing every detail—just like Nick.

I have an appointment this morning with my obstetrician, Dr. Morgan. I swear my stomach can't grow any larger. I'm bursting out of every maternity shirt I own, and don't get me started on my pants. While sitting in the waiting room, I scan all the different bumps on display. I'm fascinated by how differently women carry babies. Some are huge like me, where others have teeny tiny little bumps.

The lady sitting next to me has a completely flat stomach. She must be only a few weeks along. "How far are you?"

Smiling, she lowers her hand to her stomach. "A few months. I'm having a girl."

"Congratulations." I mask my shock with a smile. Her belly is so tiny, I didn't think she'd be far enough along to know her baby's gender.

I'm snapped out of my shock when a nurse calls my name.

"That's me." I spring out of my seat. "It was nice meeting you," I inform the lady sitting next to me before making my way toward the nurse.

I love attending my prenatal appointments with Dr. Morgan because he does an ultrasound at each one. Our baby has grown so much from the little bean I saw on the screen months ago. Now he looks like a real baby.

While walking out of my appointment, I take a photo of the ultrasound picture with my phone to send it to Nick. Since I'm not paying attention to where I'm going, I accidentally bump into someone standing on the sidewalk. Our collision causes the contents of her handbag to litter the concrete.

"Oh my god, I'm so sorry." I dart down as quickly as my pregnant belly will allow to collect her items.

Once I have her lipstick, packet of tissues, and sanitary napkins gathered, I stand and hand them to her. When my gaze meets her wide hazel eyes, I realize who I just bumped into. It's the lady I was talking to in the waiting room.

"I've been such a klutz since becoming pregnant." She snatches the items from my grasp before shoving them into her purse. Once she has them locked away, her eyes drop to the ultrasound picture in my hand. "Oh, how adorable."

We stand on the sidewalk talking all things pregnancy-related for the next twenty minutes. It's nice talking to someone in the same predicament as me. Emily is great, but she won't fully understand my griping about weeping nipples and leg cramps until she's pregnant.

It's only when I'm driving home do I realize we never exchanged names. I guess it will have to wait for the coffee date we have scheduled for next weekend.

CHAPTER FORTY-SEVEN

NICK

"**F**uck!" Noah throws his phone down so hard, it shatters into pieces when it hits the tiled floor.

I watch the scene unfold from the corner of the room, confident Slater and Marcus have everything under control. I don't know exactly what's going on, but I'm assuming Noah's call with Emily didn't go well. Things have been rough for them the past few months. I've overheard Emily's sniffles a handful of times when she's talking to Jenni the past two months, but believing it wasn't my place to intervene, I stayed out of it.

That all changes when Noah starts gulping down whiskey like it's water. He went down a similar path after his brother died, and I just sat by and watched it happen. I'm not doing that again. He has worked too hard to let it all be flushed down the toilet right when it's getting good.

We're only in LA because we're performing on MTV Live. Cormack believes this gig will be the final push we need for our song "Surrender Me" to hit the top ten on the billboard charts. It was a last minute spot that meant we had to cancel events with our loved ones, but we knew the sacrifice would be worth it.

Now I'm not so sure. Noah barely survived losing his brothers. I don't see him coping if things go downhill with Emily.

"You're not your fucking dad, Noah." I snatch the bottle from his hand, screw the lid back on, then place it back on the bar in the green room we're camped out in.

The grief in Noah's eyes cuts through me like a knife when he locks them with mine. "Emily fucking left me."

Fuck. It's worse than I thought.

Playing it cool, I assure him, "One step at a time. Perform the shit out of this song first, then tomorrow morning, we'll go sort this shit out—*together.*"

When Noah couldn't reach Emily because she was in class, he asked Jacob to drive her back to Ravenshoe—our hometown. She'll be there waiting for him, just like Jenni will be waiting for me. I'm 100% confident on this. Their relationship is so solid, I often watch them for hints on how I can improve mine with Jenni. I've got a lot to learn when it comes to romance, but I'm giving it my best shot.

When Noah arches his brow, surprised by my admission, I smirk. I've never considered him a friend, but I realized how wrong I was the past six months. He was the only one who had my back with everything happening with Jenni, and now I'll have his.

"I could sing to her? Make it just about her?"

Noah's dark eyes flick between his bandmates who are peering at him, wordlessly gauging their thoughts to his suggestion. Tonight is an important stepping stone for our band, but our journey won't be anywhere near as sweet without our other halves. Emily has supported us from the get-go, so she is as much a part of our band as I am.

When Marcus, Slater and I all agree to his suggestion with a unanimous vote, I call Jenni.

"Hi, baby," she greets groggily into the phone.

My eyes drop to my watch. It's only a little after seven PM, so she shouldn't be tired. "Are you okay?"

"Yeah, I think so."

My heart races. She doesn't sound good.

"I think I have a tummy bug."

I chuckle softly. "It's called a baby; I thought we figured that out already?"

Her giggle settles the erratic beat of my heart by replacing it with a much more viral response. I can't believe how much our relationship has grown the past six months. She's something I never knew I wanted but now crave more than anything.

Recalling I'm supposed to be helping Noah, not planning a hookup with my brand new fiancée, I inform Jenni about Noah's plans to perform an acoustic version of "Surrender Me." Our call ends with a promise that she'll do everything in her power to force Emily to watch Noah's performance.

———

Around an hour later, Jenni texts saying Emily went to bed before watching the show. The devastation on Noah's face when I told him Emily didn't watch his declaration of love was fucking gut-wrenching.

He hardly speaks a word during our six-hour flight home. He's deep in thought, entrenched by the darkness that nearly swallowed me whole six months ago. Once we exit the plane, he takes off on foot for the closest taxi. I had planned on offering him a ride, but he shot out of his seat so fast, I didn't get the chance.

When I enter the front door of our home twenty minutes later, Jenni greets me like she does every time I return home. She's as gorgeous as ever, although she does look tired.

"Did you sleep at all last night?" I run my hand down her face, needing any part of her body on mine. I've hardly seen her the past two weeks, and it fucking killed me.

"A little." She nudges her head to the kitchen where a sullen-faced Noah is hunkered down. "I'm worried about them."

I pull her to my chest and kiss her head. "They'll work it out. They're one of the strongest couples I know. Second only to us."

She smiles, agreeing with me before guiding me into the kitchen. When we enter, Noah's dark eyes float up at me. "How'd it go, Noah?"

His shoulders slump even further. "I haven't talked to her yet."

"Emily is still sleeping," Jenni informs me before curling her arms around my waist. "Are you hungry?"

I'm not, but I nod, aware she needs something to distract her from her thoughts while Emily sleeps.

For the next hour, Noah sits on the barstool, not speaking a word. Any time he looks my way, I give him a nod and a quick smirk, word-lessly assuring him it will be okay. Jenni prepares a full breakfast for us, but Noah doesn't eat a thing. I can imagine how much his stomach is swirling. Mine did the exact same thing only six months ago.

When Jenni finishes stacking the uneaten food in the fridge, she fills the seat next to me and rests her head on my shoulder.

"What are you drinking?" There is a glass of weird-looking tea in front of her.

"A herbal tea a friend made for me." She screws up her nose. "It's supposed to help the baby, but it tastes disgusting."

I laugh when she takes a delicate sip from the tea before gagging. If she hates it so much, why is she drinking it?

Full, tired, and badly jet-lagged, but aware I won't sleep until I see Noah through his latest crisis like I should have his first two, I decide to take a quick shower. I need to do something to wake me up before I crash.

———

I take the fastest shower I've ever. We have absolutely no hot water. It was the equivalent of jumping into the ocean in the middle of winter. After changing my clothes and unpacking my suitcase, I stroll into the kitchen. My eyes dart down to my feet when they're jabbed with something sharp. Confusion makes itself known with my gut when I take in shattered glass and a pink-colored liquid extending from one end of our kitchen to the other.

Before I can work out what it is, a tormented scream rips through my ears. I bolt toward the noise, not at all concerned by the glass cutting my feet. I recognize the scream, except this time, it's filled with pain instead of euphoria like usual.

Fear clutches my heart when I spot Jenni crouched on the ground, leaning against the refrigerator. She's cradling her stomach, and her beautiful face is constricted with pain. I freeze for a mere second, panicked out of my mind, before I rush for her.

"Jen, what's wrong? Is it bub?"

Her tear-filled eyes lift to me, but no words escape her lips. When another scream shreds through her body without warning, I gather her in my arms and race out of the kitchen, ensuring I keep her feet away from the glass.

After carefully setting her on the sofa, I run upstairs to grab my wallet and keys off our bedside table. By the time I make it back downstairs, she's on her hands and knees halfway down the hallway. My heart slithers into my gut when I spot a trail of blood running down the back of her nightie. With my mind in a dark and tormented place, I gather her in the crook of my arm before hotfooting it to the front door.

"Noah, hurry!" My roar echoes in the crisp morning air, alerting Noah and Emily, who are huddled together on our front lawn to my distress. Emily rushes to Jenni's side faster than I can snap my fingers.

"It's too early, Em," Jenni mumbles to Emily seconds before another ragged scream buckles both my heart and her knees. "He. . . can't. . . come. . . yet."

"It's okay, Jen, babies come early all the time. He'll be fine. You just need to breathe." Emily mimics the noises the Lamaze instructor taught us earlier this month while guiding Jenni into the passenger seat of my truck.

"My bag! I haven't packed my hospital bag," Jenni grunts between screams.

"Emily will pack your bag, then we'll bring it to the hospital for you," Noah offers, stepping forward.

I offer my thanks with a dip of my chin before tossing him my keys. After rounding the bed of my truck, I slide into the driver's seat, snag my spare key out of the sunglasses compartment, then fire up my old black beast. My mind is so shut down, I'm operating on auto-pilot.

I take off down the street like a maniac, my stomach rolling as effectively as my truck's tires. My eyes bounce between the road and Jenni as we race toward the hospital. She's relatively calm. . . until her long, ragged squeals change to a blood-curdling scream.

After weaving between a pair of delivery trucks, I turn to face her. Fear clutches every fiber in my body when I notice her hands are covered in bright red blood. "Hold on, baby."

I flatten my accelerator until it sits flat on the floor. My truck is old, but her engine is good, meaning we make it to the hospital at a record-setting pace. After mounting the curb outside the maternity depart-ment entrance, I rush around to the passenger side. Jenni is as white as a ghost, and the lower half of her nightie is saturated with blood.

Gathering her in my arms, I sprint inside the maternity ward.

"Nick." Her voice is so weak , I can barely hear her over the thump of the doctors and midwives' feet who are rushing toward us.

"It's okay, baby, you're going to be okay."

A dark gray-haired doctor shines a light in Jenni's sagging eyelids before lowering his wide eyes to her soaked nightie. "She's hemor-rhaging; call surgery immediately."

He motions for me to follow him. When we enter a small white room on our right, he gestures for me to place Jenni down on a bed in the middle of the space. When I do, he pushes on her stomach, making me note how low her belly is now sitting compared to two weeks ago.

The doctor's blue eyes lift to mine. "How far is she?"

"Thirty-five weeks." I pace to the end of the bed so I'm not in the way of the handful of nurses completing observations on Jenni.

A few minutes later the head doctor says, "She's fully dilated; cancel the OR. It will take too long; we need to do an extraction."

While the nurses rush in all directions, I whisper into Jenni's ear. "It's okay, baby; you're okay." I run my hand down her pale cheeks, ignoring the fear clutching my heart from her lack of response.

"What's her name?" asks the doctor while two midwives lift Jenni's legs into stirrups.

I swallow the bile burning my throat before answering, "Jenni."

He nods before his eyes drift back to Jenni. "Jenni, I don't know if you can hear me, but I need you to push if you can. We're going to help you, but if you can push, it will help us greatly, okay?"

A midwife places her hand on Jenni's belly. When she nods, the doctor instructs Jenni to push. At the same time, a machine next to her bed starts vibrating.

My eyes jackknife back to Jenni when she whimpers from the midwife pushing hard on her stomach. She's here, but she's barely conscious.

"Push, Jenni, push as hard as you can," instructs the doctor.

When I see the bright red blood covering his white gloves, the room starts to spin. The warped floor pulling out from beneath my feet hits me with a severe bout of dizziness. I become unsteady, seconds from fainting. As the noises surrounding me fade, I fall forward at a pace too fast for my woozy head to stop.

Then all I see is blackness.

I'm awoken by tiny cries. It takes me a few seconds of scanning the room before it dawns on me where I am. I vault out of the reclining chair I'm slumped in. My movements are so quick, my head smashes a stainless steel light lowered from the ceiling. I nearly faint for the second time when I hear Jenni's beautiful giggles. This time my woozy head is from relief instead of fear.

"Welcome back." The doctor who assisted Jenni earlier stands from the stool he's sitting on to switch off the light. After raising it back to the ceiling, his eyes shift my way. They're brimming with amusement. I don't mind. He can laugh at me all he likes. He brought Jenni back to me.

When I make my way to Jenni, who is sitting up in bed next to me, my eyes bulge out of my head. Her tummy has significantly reduced in size. With my heart in my throat, my eyes go wild, seeking the person responsible for the noise that woke me. My chest rises and falls in an unsteady rhythm when I spot a teeny tiny little baby in the corner of the room being fussed over by two doctors and a nurse.

Excitement at seeing my son for the first time is replaced with remorse when I realize I missed his birth. "I'm so sorry," I apologize, my eyes straying back to Jenni.

She smiles. "It's fine."

As I stare at her, ensuring she can see how proud I am of her, I notice her cheeks are still lacking their normal pink hue. She looks exhausted and a little scared. Before I can assure her everything will be okay, a nurse paces toward us with our son wrapped in a blue blanket.

How could I have said I'd never fall in love? Just one look at his adorable face curtained by strawberry blond hair, and I'm just as smitten with him as I was the first time I saw his mother.

CHAPTER FORTY-EIGHT

JENNI

Nick's bandmates will never let him live down the fact he fainted during the birth of our son. I can't say I'm any better. I have no recollection of the birth either. The obstetrician had to extract Jasper as I was hemorrhaging so badly, I was close to passing out. I nearly needed a blood transfusion, but managed to avoid one since the birth was so quick. The instant the placenta was delivered, I stopped bleeding.

I'm exhausted and in absolute agony downstairs. Nick can shove his hope to never use protection again because I'm *never* going through labor ever again.

Alright, maybe I might. . .

It's only looking down at our son that makes me reconsider. I can see so much of Nick in his adorable little face, but he has my hair color. He is the cutest little baby I've ever seen.

Not long after being handed our precious little angel, Noah and Emily arrive at the hospital with my overnight bag. Emily's excitement beams out of her as her eyes roam over Jasper. Nick and I discussed baby names for weeks before we finally settled on one. We had very different ideas on the type of names we liked. I got so desperate, I read out every name from a baby book. It was only when I got to the J's did Nick finally speak. . . . . .

"What was that?" He peered up from the television screen to me.

Unsure which name caught his attention, I asked, "Jason or Jasso?"

He cocked his brow, his expression unamused. After scooting across the carpet, he removed the baby book from my hand. "This one." He pointed to a name in the book.

I removed his finger to read the name. "Jasper?"

He nodded while smiling. "It's strong and masculine while also unique. Just like our boy will be."

I tested out the name a few times in my head. I didn't love it, but I didn't hate it either. Since it was the first name that sparked a reaction out of Nick, and my patience was running thin, I gave up on the baby name search for that day.

It was only when Nick arrived home from a stint in Los Angeles the following week with a tiny blue romper with "Jasper" written across the front did I fall in love with the name.

It might have been more due to the fact Nick purchased the romper himself that made me love it. . . . . .

But now, when I look down at our son, I think his name suits him. I just hope he doesn't follow in his dad's footsteps of a player lifestyle since he's branded with his middle name.

A few hours after Emily and Noah leave, Jasper and I are transferred to the maternity suite on level three of the hospital. An hour after I've settled Jasper down for the night, Emily returns to visit me alone. Believing her fight with Noah centered around her inability to both study and support him, we researched ways she can complete her studies without physically living on campus.

It took a few hours, but we discovered a perfect solution. I was so relieved. Noah and Emily are the perfect couple, but their fight proves even the strongest relationships have bumps. My relationship with Nick has been a crazy-ass ride, but the past six months have more than made up for the massive bumps we endured at the start.

It just keeps getting better and better.

The next morning, Nick appears apprehensive when he enters my hospital room. It took the nurses kicking him out at 3 AM before he agreed to go home to rest, so he's clearly exhausted, but the groove between his brows isn't the one he gets when he's tired. This is his worried face.

After placing a kiss on my temple, he makes his way to Jasper, who is sleeping peacefully in his crib. My heart melts when he carefully lifts Jasper into his arms before snuggling him into his chest.

"Are you okay?" I ask when he spins around to face me. "The guys aren't giving you too many hassles, are they?"

His lips tug high. "I'll never live that down, will I?"

I shake my head. I plan on reminding him of his fainting episode every time he pisses me off. Considering we have a good seventy-plus years left to live, that gives me a lot of leverage.

When I hold out my arms, wordlessly begging for some more baby cuddles, Nick walks over to my bed to hand me Jasper. His glistening eyes take their time scanning my face before he mumbles, "They want us to go on tour."

I stop tucking Jasper's hands into his blanket to peer up at Nick. My jaw falls open as excitement overwhelms me. This is precisely what the band has been aiming for the past five years. Their dreams are about to come true.

My excitement is short-lived when Nick adds on, "Next week."

My heart plummets into my stomach so fast, the breakfast I consumed earlier threatens to resurface. "What?" I question, certain I heard him wrong.

When he locks his eyes with mine, I realize my error.

They're brimming with conflict. I gingerly hop out of bed to place a sleeping Jasper back in his crib. I want to sit down and talk about this like adults, but a horrifying two days lead me to speak before I've stopped to consider what I'm saying. "I just had a baby. . . I just gave birth. . . I don't even know what I'm doing."

My tone is riddled with nerves. I've had a hard time the past twenty-four hours recovering from the birth; I don't want to walk through the maze of motherhood alone.

"You'll figure it out in no time."

Nick meant for his words to be assuring, but I don't hear them that way. "I don't want to figure it out alone, Nick." My crackling voice exposes how close I am to crying. I'm seconds from cracking.

When he paces toward me, tears stream down my face. He's as devastated as me. His brows are hanging low, his lips turned down. I cry even harder when his delicious scent engulfs me when he pulls me to his chest.

"Why does it have to be so soon?" I sob.

This is everything the band has been working for, but I've just given birth to our son, and now he's going to leave. A tour isn't just a few days on the road. It's months at a time.

After clearing my tears with his thumbs, Nick raises my eyes to his. "I'll work something out." His eyes hold just as much promise as his words. "It will be okay. I promise you."

Our necks crank to the side in sync when my hospital door suddenly swings open. Emily steps back, mortified she has interrupted our private conversation. "Sorry." She darts back into the hallway before I can tell her it's fine.

After taking a few more minutes to settle my tears, I ask Nick to go get Emily. He does, albeit hesitantly. When Emily enters, her eyes well with tears. "I didn't even think when Noah was telling me about the tour last night; I'm so sorry," she apologizes, like it's her fault Rise Up has been scheduled to go on tour.

"It's not your fault; I'm just scared." I bite on the inside of my cheek, striving not to let tears form again. "Motherhood is kinda scary."

She giggles. "You're a natural—"

I've barely acknowledged her praise when Nick comes barreling into the room, scaring the living daylights out of us. "Noah is a fucking genius!"

He plants a long, hard peck on my smiling lips. Although I have no clue what is going on, I can't help but smile. He walked out of our room with his shoulders slumped and his eyes hollow. He entered like a kid waking up Christmas morning.

After pulling me back by my shoulders, his twinkling eyes drop to mine. "You and Jasper can come on the road with us."

I choke on my spit. "What? I can't take a baby on tour."

"Why not?" Nick's massively dilated eyes stray to Noah, who has just entered my room. "They just sleep, eat and poop. Jasper can do that anywhere."

With burrowed brows, I shift my eyes to Noah. "This was your idea?"

He smiles a blinding grin before nodding.

I wipe the smile right off his face by asking, "So a baby screaming at two in the morning won't bother you?"

He takes his time seriously considering my question before he shrugs. "You won't be in my room, so that's okay."

Emily slaps her hand over her mouth to stifle her giggles. She's not laughing because she thinks Noah's idea is ridiculous; she's giggling in excitement.

My eyes float back to Nick when he says, "So?"

He's so excited, there's no way I can deny his request. I don't want to be away from him any more than he wants to be away from us—so with that in mind, I murmur, "Okay."

Nick jumps in the air so high, he startles Jasper enough to whimper. He's about to go and soothe him, but I stop him when I spot Emily creeping across the room. She carefully lifts Jasper out of his crib before cradling him to her chest like Nick did only minutes ago. Within seconds, his crying stops, and he falls back to sleep.

"Who's the natural?"

Emily smiles as her glowing eyes drift to Noah. The love bouncing between them while she holds our son with pride presents the perfect opportunity for us to ask if they'd do us the honor of becoming Jasper's godparents.

Emily cries happy tears. Noah's reply isn't as joyful. He stares at Nick and me, his face mortified. The reason for his odd response comes to light when he confesses to never attending church. After assuring him being a godfather means giving Jasper guidance and leadership in his life, not religion, he agrees to fulfill the role. He knows as well as I do that the little bump his relationship experienced this weekend was only a minor glitch, and that he and Emily are the perfect couple to be godparents to our children.

Later that night, Nick scares the living daylights out of Jasper and me again. He hollers so loud, I swear half the babies in the maternity ward wake up crying.

My screams of jubilation take care of the second half when he informs me Rise Up's song "Surrender Me" has reached number one on the Billboard charts. If that isn't already something to get excited about, their album is the number one album in the country.

Poor little Jasper will need to get his hearing checked with how loud we squeal.

As the days go on, I gain a better understanding of motherhood. I'm lucky Jasper is a very carefree baby. He literally does just sleep, eat, and poop. I've just finished nursing Jasper and have handed him to

Nick to settle when my obstetrician, Dr. Morgan, enters my room. His rosy cheeks are still prominent, even though it's winter.

After glancing down at Nick and Jasper, he smiles before pivoting to close the door. When he spins back around, my breath hitches. His usually docile face is lined with concern. My eyes dart to Nick, wondering if he too has noticed the change in Dr. Morgan's persona. He has. The goofy grin he regularly wears while holding Jasper has vanished, replaced with a frown.

Standing from his chair, he moves closer to my bed just as Dr. Morgan says, "I requested to talk to you both before the authorities are called in."

My eyes widen as they dart between Nick and Dr. Morgan. *Why would the authorities need to be brought in?*

Dr. Morgan answers my silent question by asking, "Have either of you heard of a drug called Misoprostol?"

Nick and I shake our heads.

"What is misop. . ." Nick attempts to question.

"Misoprostol," Dr. Morgan fills in, "is an abortion drug usually found on the black market in Brazil." My panic surges right alongside my confusion. "If you search hard enough, small amounts of it can be found stateside."

When his stern yet worried gaze shifts to me, my pulse spikes. He hasn't directly said he believes I've taken Misoprostol, but his eyes are holding a lot of suspicion.

"I would never. . . I didn't," I stumble nervously, trying to inform him I'd never intentionally harm Jasper.

While my eyes burn from a sudden rush of moisture, Dr. Morgan pulls over a hard plastic chair and sits close to my bedside. I angrily brush away the tears dripping down my face before he secures my hands in his. "The doctor at your delivery ordered a blood workup in case you needed a blood transfusion. We found a high dosage of Misoprostol in your bloodwork." He squeezes my hands, which are gripping his so firmly, my nails are digging into his skin. "Now I know at the start, you were considering going down this path—"

"I would never, I never took anything," I interrupt, my words barely heard over the sob tearing from my throat. "I wouldn't do anything to hurt him."

I lift my gaze to Jasper, who is cradled in Nick's arms. Nick is watching the exchange between Dr. Morgan and me with his brows stitched together tightly. He looks like he wants to jump in, but with his eyes flicking like he's recalling a memory, he's a little preoccupied.

Faster than I can snap my fingers, the confusion on his face evaporates. The temperature in the room turns scorching when he lowers his eyes to mine. Nothing but sheer terror is reflecting in his beautifully tormented eyes. "Who made you that herbal tea?" His words come out in a hurry.

"A lady I met at Dr. Morgan's office," I answer as Dr. Morgan's head bounces between Nick and me.

"What was her name?"

"Katrice, her name is Katrice," I respond, wondering why it would matter.

When I say the name Katrice, Nick sighs, and the anger burning in his eyes lessens.

His relief doesn't last long. "I don't have a patient called Katrice." Dr. Morgan sounds as confused as I feel.

I stop taking in his flushed cheeks when Nick asks me, "What does Katrice look like?"

I screw up my nose. "Umm. . . light brown hair that sits just above her shoulders and hazel eyes. Oh, and she has a chipped front tooth."

Nick curses harshly before rushing to place Jasper back in his crib. He presses a hurried kiss to my sweaty forehead before requesting to speak to Dr. Morgan outside. When Dr. Morgan agrees, Nick tells me he'll be back in about an hour, and that everything is fine before darting out of my room, leaving me utterly dumbfounded.

CHAPTER FORTY-NINE

NICK

"Is there a way to test a liquid to find out if it was spiked?" I question Dr. Morgan when he joins me in the corridor outside of Jenni's hospital room.

I have no doubt Jenni would never intentionally harm Jasper. It just took me a little while to realize what was happening. The morning I asked Jenni about the funny tea she was drinking was the day she gave birth. She said the tea was from a friend, and it was to help the baby. I didn't consider at the time that she was the first out of her friends to have children, meaning she wouldn't have been given the tea from Emily or Nicole.

When she said the tea was gifted by a friend she met at Dr. Morgan's office, I was relieved. . . until Dr. Morgan disclosed he had no patient by that name at his clinic. The instant Jenni said Katrice had a cracked front tooth, I knew she was Megan. If you can ignore the crazy in her eyes, Megan's cracked tooth is the only flaw in her looks.

My thoughts return to the present when Dr. Morgan says, "I'm sure if you have a sample, I could arrange for someone to test it." He stares at me, years of life experience making him infer there is more to my query than I'm letting on. "Why, what's going on Nick?"

"I think Jenni may have taken the drug unwillingly."

His brows pull together as a mask of confusion slips over his face. I give him a brief rundown of everything that has happened with Megan, including the paternity case, her crazy stalking, and how I was concerned she may be dangerous.

He's shocked but keeps his head in game mode. "I'll arrange for a security officer to be placed outside of Jenni and Jasper's room, but I strongly suggest you contact the authorities."

While he calls hospital security, I call Ryan, a detective from Ravenshoe Police Station. He requests I meet him at the house I share with Jenni so he can collect a sample of the tea stored in our refrigerator.

"I'll have it rushed through my contacts. If there are any illegal drugs in it, we'll know by tonight."

After thanking him with a smile and a handshake, I head to the Dungeon. As I enter the parking lot, I scan my surroundings, seeking the little yellow car Megan used to tail me last month. My shoulders slump when I fail to locate her car. From the intel Isaac's security team gathered on her, she's usually here waiting from me from 4 PM every day.

After throwing off my seatbelt, I bolt inside the club. There are a handful of people milling around. It's only late in the afternoon, so most partygoers won't arrive for a few more hours. I kick a barstool when I fail to locate Megan anywhere.

It's barely bounced two times when a deep voice at my side remarks, "You know how to fucking pick them."

Isaac is standing at the entrance of his office. His arms are folded in front of his chest, and his glare is lethal. He knows whom I'm seeking without me even needing to ask. That's not unusual. Isaac knows everything.

"Do you know where she is?" The blood surging through my

veins chops up my words, revealing how hard I'm working to reel in my anger. I've never been so enraged.

"I'm taking care of it."

When he pivots on his heels and enters his office, I follow after him. "What do you mean, you're taking care of it?"

He sits in his large leather chair before gesturing for me to fill the one across from him. I shake my head. I can't sit down. I'm too worked up with adrenaline to sit. When his eyes narrow, wordlessly demanding I follow his command, I plop into the chair. My foot taps up and down relentlessly as my body struggles to calm the tension surging through it.

It does little good when Isaac asks, "Why the fuck didn't you read the documents your lawyer gave you?"

My brows scrunch. "What are you talking about?" I'm confused as to why we need to discuss this now. I've got much more pressing matters to take care of.

Glaring at me, Isaac throws an envelope into my chest. It's the same one Jenni's mom gave me the day I found out I wasn't the father of Megan's baby.

"She told me everything I needed to know."

"No, she fucking didn't!"

Isaac moves around his desk to snatch back the envelope. Remaining quiet, he pulls out the chunky document inside. He flips through the first two pages, which is an itemized invoice. When I saw the total of my lawyer's bill, I understood why Jenni's parents are so wealthy. It was phenomenally high. Lucky for me, Isaac settled the account.

When Isaac finds the page he's looking for, he shoves the document back into my chest. "Read it."

After rolling my eyes, I do as instructed. The more I read, the more my heart slithers into my gut. "She was never pregnant?" I half-question, half-inform.

"She's a fucking virgin!"

My eyes dart up from the document to Isaac, certain I heard him wrong.

I didn't.

"When the gynecologist's scan didn't find a fetus, he did a little more research. Her hymen was still intact." He glares at me angrily. "You went and got yourself a fucking psycho." His voice bellows around the room as a vein in his neck looks seconds from bursting. "She's been in and out of the psychiatric ward for the past year. She did a runner a few months ago after knocking the orderly out cold."

As my panic soars, I vault out of my chair to pace back and forth. "I fucking knew she wasn't quite right."

After several minutes of cursing my stupidity, my gaze drifts back to Isaac. His ass is propped on the edge of his desk, and there's a weird look on his face. I'm about to question his odd expression when his cell phone rings. With his eyes arrested on me, he walks around his desk to answer it. During his conversation with a member of his security team, he gathers some documents from his drawer, then hands them to me.

Bile races up my throat when I scan the documents. There are several photos of Jenni entering Dr. Morgan's office, walking out of our local grocery store, and getting her sugar fix at a local bakery. Her eyes have been gouged out in every photo, and someone has drawn trails of blood down her legs.

The next lot of photos are of a scene you'd expect to see in a crime show. Duct tape, rope, and several medical instruments—including a scalpel and a pair of forceps—are spread across a stainless steel table. My stomach heaves as images of what Megan was planning to do with this equipment filter through my mind.

With my hand clamped over my mouth, I rush to the waste bin in the corner of the room. I lose my stomach contents inside, the last photo in the file too much for me to bear. It shows a step by step process on how to perform an illegal caesarean. The images are so graphic, all I can see is Jasper being cut out of Jenni.

Once my stomach settles, I lift my fearful eyes to Isaac. He has finalized his call and is watching me intently.

"How are you taking care of this?" I ask him, wanting to ensure there's no chance Megan will ever have the opportunity to hurt Jenni or Jasper again.

Isaac's nostrils flare as his pupils dilate. "You don't want to know. You just worry about your family, and I'll take care of everything."

Ignoring my shocked gasp, he shuffles through some papers on his desk, never once looking back at me. This is the first time I've been truly curious as to what he does for a living, and it makes me wonder if Nicole was right all those years ago. Is he a mobster like people claim? Or is nothing below him when it comes to keeping his family safe?

CHAPTER FIFTY

MEGAN

"No, no, no, no!"

I pound my fists on the television screen. I was just watching my regular entertainment program, waiting for pictures of my love to be shown, when it switched to a live press conference being held in Los Angeles. My heart leaped when the lead singer of my love's band stepped up to a wooden podium at the front of the press conference. When he announced their band was doing a six-week tour along the East Coast, I rushed to grab my phone and credit card, eager to buy tickets to every show. I was beaming with excitement as I dialed the number displayed on the screen.

That excitement vanished when Noah shared news that their lead guitarist Nick and his fiancée Jenni had given birth to a baby boy, Jasper Nicholas Holt, Saturday morning. I rushed toward the screen to seek any untruth in Noah's dark eyes. He stared straight down the camera, gleaming with happiness.

When a picture of Nick and his whore flashes up on the screen, I grip the TV and yank it hard. After several harsh pulls, I yank it off the wall mount and send it hurtling across the room. While throwing anything I can find, I scream and yell obscenities. I'm equally angry and confused. I took care of her and her bastard child. She should be dead! They're both supposed to be dead!

It nearly killed me sitting across from her at the coffee dates we had the past two weeks. I had to pretend to be friends with the whore solely responsible for Nick and me being apart. I was so confident once she was out of the picture, Nick would rush back into my arms, I took drastic action to make sure that occurred.

I initially considered keeping her baby since it was half of Nick, but I could never get his whore alone to put my plans into action. She was cautious any time I tried to schedule a coffee date at her house, and the times I attempted to follow her, she always lost me in traffic.

That's when I devised another tactic. I traveled to New York to purchase a drug I had researched on the internet. Several minority groups in the city use it for illegal abortions since they can't afford the ludicrous hospital bills. My plan was perfect. When Nick's whore consumed the Misoprostol I purchased for her, she'd hemorrhage so bad, both she and her baby would be taken care of, leaving Nick free to be with me.

She was apprehensive when I handed her the water jug full of the raspberry leaf tea I had laced with the drug. I explained that the tea would help her body prepare for the birth. When she remained cautious, I showed her several articles on my phone to back up my claims.

I had to be extra careful to ensure she didn't see the pictures I had of Nick stored as my screensaver. He was sleeping peacefully when I snapped them. I really miss watching him sleep. It's been months since I've snuck into his bedroom.

I tried to follow him to his new house when I saw him loading moving boxes into his truck, but he spotted me, and boy was he angry. He yelled and cursed more than my daddy used to when my mother put glass shards in his soup.

Since I no longer know where Nick lives, I waited for him every day at the Dungeon, but he never showed up. When I looked up his information in the directory, it said there was no one by that name in the area. I didn't give up, though. I searched and searched and searched for him for weeks. Not once did he turn up. I was beginning to worry I'd never find him again.

Now I have nothing to fear. I know where he is. He's at the hospital. I'm so excited about seeing him again, I want to go to him right now, but I can't. I need to gather supplies first.

I search for my purse and keys under the overturned mattress, in the toppled bedside tables, and next to the broken painting before I locate them under a broken picture frame. With an extra spring in my step, I head to my car in the parking lot of my motel. I'm just about to turn on the ignition when someone grabs me roughly from behind.

It feels like an elephant sits on my chest when an extremely large arm pins me to my seat. I try to scream, to announce that I'm being attacked, but the white cloth covering my mouth muffles my screams for help.

Within seconds, I feel woozy, and my vision blurs. As my eyes burn with tears and my throat dries, my blinking lengthens.

Then all I see is blackness.

EPILOGUE

JENNI

Two years later...

"I'm buying a gun." I giggle at the horrified expression crossing Nick's face. Earlier this morning, I gave birth to a baby girl—a girl Dr. Morgan assured us was a boy.

"It must have been the umbilical cord this time around," I jest, looking down at our blonde-haired beauty cradled in my arms.

Harper Jade Holt came screaming into the world three weeks early. She surprised us all when I went into labor just as Rise Up was due to go on stage to perform. Nick was panicked out of his mind, but I assured him he had plenty of time to wrap up his performance before we had to go to the hospital.

My labor was much different this time around since I hadn't unknowingly digested an illegal drug. The day before I was due to be discharged from the hospital after having Jasper, Ryan, a detective from Ravenshoe PD, informed me that my tea was indeed spiked with a significant amount of misoprostol. Nick was unable to maintain Ryan's eye contact when he informed us a warrant had been issued for Megan, and the instant she was located, she would be arrested.

He must have had an inkling that day wasn't going to occur any time soon. It's been a little over two years since I was drugged, but the person responsible for mine and Jasper's near deaths has not yet been brought to justice. No one has seen or heard from Megan since the day I gave birth to Jasper.

I hate that she's still out there, free to hurt another unsuspecting victim, but I'm confident justice will eventually prevail. If the authorities don't get her, I'm certain karma will. You can't exhibit her level of craziness and not expect it to catch up to you. Megan will face the consequences of her actions one day, but until then, I'll continue assuring Nick he isn't to blame for the craziness she brought into our lives.

He feels so incredibly guilty that his "player lifestyle" nearly cost him everything that he's worked relentlessly the past two years striving to fix his errors. Although I hate that he feels remorse—*he didn't even sleep with Megan, so how is he to blame for her drama?*—his endeavors to make things right haven't just made him a better husband and father; they've also made him a better friend.

For a man who was last to arrive and first to leave at every function the band held in the years leading to us getting together, he's grown incredibly close with his bandmates the past two years. Things are still rocky between Slater and him, but compared to four years ago, there has been a remarkable improvement.

I'm drawn from my thoughts when Noah ribs Nick from across the room. "At least you didn't faint this time around."

Smiling, Nick nods. He's tickled pink he made it through Harper's birth without kissing the pavement. He shouldn't be so cocky. It was a close call. Thankfully, this time around, a lack of blood kept him upright—for the most part.

Laughter breaks across the room when my dad jests, "Give him time. It's still early."

Nick and I were blindly walking through the puzzle of being first-time parents when Noah was involved in a horrific car accident. When Emily called to request that I contact my parents on Jacob's behalf, I was hesitant. I hadn't heard from my parents in months. After Emily explained what happened between Jacob and a member of the paparazzi, I promised to do everything in my power to help him.

I've never been more nervous than I was the day I called my dad's office. Even though he sounded pleased to hear from me, I was short and abrupt with him. I was still hurt by everything that had happened. My anger somewhat subsided when he agreed to represent Jacob free of charge.

Once Jacob was granted bail, my dad arrived at the house I share with Nick. Tears streamed freely down my face, and his familiar scent engulfed me when he wrapped me up in a firm hug. Being a new parent was daunting enough, let alone the chaotic mess thrown at Nick and me during Jasper's first two months. I was barely holding it together that day two years ago, and my dad knew that just from the quickest glance in my eyes.

When Nick entered the room cradling a newborn Jasper in his arms, absolute confusion morphed onto my dad's face. He was utterly gobsmacked. That's when I realized no one had told him about his grandson.

"Your mom said you didn't want to see me, and that you left because you were angry at me," he said when I explained everything that had happened the past six months.

After settling his shock, my dad disclosed that he and my mom separated not long after I found out he wasn't my biological father. Because the truth was exposed, my mom didn't have any reason to continue the lie she'd perpetuated for nineteen years. My heart broke for my dad. I could see how much he still loved her, but my mom's loss was my gain.

I am so ecstatic to have him back in our lives. Now, instead of being the world's best dad, he's also the world's best grandad—along with Harrison. Although Nick might have something to say about that if he keeps hounding him to "make an honest woman" out of me.

Nick and I still haven't gotten married. With the band having one of the longest-selling number one albums of all time, life got too hectic. We've spent more time on the road the last two years than we have at home. It's been a crazy, wonderful ride—one I'd sign up for time and time again.

My eyes stray to my hospital room door when it creaks. Isaac enters the room, looking confident even though he's holding a giant pink teddy bear. Things have been a little strained between Nick and Isaac the past couple of years. I've tried numerous times to talk to Nick about it, but he shuts down my attempts every time by assuring me that nothing is wrong, and that it's just the type of relationship they have. Isaac is stern, and at times a little scary, but he's a fantastic uncle. He treats Jasper as if he is his own son, and I'm sure he'll love Harper just as much.

Now that Isaac has arrived, everyone who has an important part in our life is in the one room. Emily and Noah are in one corner wrestling Jasper off their daughter, Maddison. Jasper loves Maddie so much, any time she's near him, he suffocates her with kisses. Slater, Marcus, Hawke, and Nicole are chatting at their left; and Harrison, Aunt Dee, and my dad are deep in conversation near Harper's crib, no doubt sharing grandparenting tips. Even Lola and Jacob are here.

My hospital room is full of people I admire and respect, but the most important person here is without a doubt Nick—my ultimate rule breaker. I'll forever be grateful for the day I let my heart overrule my head. He not only completes me, he is my other half. I could not imagine my life without him in it.

When Nick notices my intense gaze, his glistening eyes stop absorbing every adorable feature of Harper's face to look at me. After a wink that shows he's spotted my blushing cheeks, he smiles his trademark smirk.

Putty, I'm once again putty, and I wouldn't have it any other way.

The End!

The next book in the Perception series is Slater's.
You can find it here: Redeeming Slater

Join my Facebook page:
www.facebook.com/authorshandi

Join my READER's group:
https://www.facebook.com/groups/1740600836169853/

Join my newsletter to remain informed:
http://eepurl.com/cyEzNv

My Amazon Page:
https://www.amazon.com/Shandi-Boyes/e/B01D8C13WU

If you enjoyed this book - please leave a review.

ALSO BY SHANDI BOYES

Perception Series - New Adult Rock Star Romance

Saving Noah

Fighting Jacob

Taming Nick

Redeeming Slater

Wrapped up with Rise Up

Enigma Series - Steamy Contemporary Romance

Enigma of Life - (Isaac)

Unraveling an Enigma - (Isaac)

Enigma: The Mystery Unmasked - (Isaac)

Enigma: The Final Chapter - (Isaac)

Beneath the Secrets - (Hugo - Part 1)

Beneath the Sheets - (Hugo Conclusion)

Spy Thy Neighbor (Hunter - standalone)

The Opposite Effect - (Brax & Clara)

I Married a Mob Boss - (Rico - Nikolai's Brother)

Second Shot (Hawke's Story)

The Way We Are (Ryan Pt 1)

The Way We Were (Ryan Pt 2)

Sugar and Spice (Cormack)

Bound Series - Steamy Romance & BDSM

Chains (Marcus and Cleo)

Links (Marcus and Cleo)

Bound (Marcus and Cleo)

Restrained (Marcus and Cleo)

Psycho (Dexter)

Russian Mob Chronicles

Nikolai: A Mafia Prince Romance

Nikolai: Taking Back What's Mine

Nikolai: What's Left of Me

Nikolai: Mine to Protect

Asher: My Russian Revenge

Infinite Time Trilogy

Lady In Waiting (Regan)

Man in Queue (Regan)

Couple on Hold (Regan)

Standalones

Just Playin' (Presley and Willow)

COMING SOON:

Skitzo

Colby

Made in the USA
Monee, IL
03 November 2021